D0700802

Corvus

CALGARY PUBLIC LIBRARY

MAR 2016

Other books by Harold Johnson

The Cast Stone (Thistledown Press, 2011)

Charlie Muskrat (Thistledown Press, 2008)

Back Track (Thistledown Press, 2005)

Billy Tinker (Thistledown Press, 2001)

Corvus

HAROLD JOHNSON

thistledown press

©Harold Johnson, 2015
All rights reserved

No part of this publication may be reproduced or transmitted in any form or by any means, graphic, electronic or mechanical, including photocopying, recording, or any information storage and retrieval system, without permission in writing from the publisher or a licence from The Canadian Copyright Licensing Agency (Access Copyright). For an Access Copyright licence, visit www.accesscopyright.ca or call toll free to 1-800-893-5777.

Thistledown Press Ltd.
410 2nd Avenue North
Saskatoon, Saskatchewan, S7K 2C3
www.thistledownpress.com

Library and Archives Canada Cataloguing in Publication
Johnson, Harold, 1957-, author
Corvus / Harold Johnson.
Issued in print and electronic formats.
ISBN 978-1-77187-051-1 (paperback).—ISBN 978-1-77187-092-4 (html).—
ISBN 978-1-77187-093-1 (pdf)
I. Title.
PS8569.O328C67 2015 C813'.6 C2015-905169-X
C2015-905170-3

Cover and book design by Jackie Forrie
Author photo by William Hamilton
Printed and bound in Canada

Thistledown Press gratefully acknowledges the financial assistance of the Canada Council for the Arts, the Saskatchewan Arts Board, and the Government of Canada for its publishing program.

To my wife Joan.
To my children Michael, Harmony, Ray, Anangons, Memegwans, Sabrina, and Tasha.
To my grandchildren, Elizabeth, Hayden, Nevaeh, Geneva, Ethan, Gus, and Patrick.
To my mother for teaching me stories.
To my father for teaching me to read and write, especially to write.
To Leo for the inspiration.
You are all part of who I am, and therefore part of what I create, hence, you are all part of this novel and I dedicate it to you all.

The emptiness of the land swallows the raven's call, absorbs it into the white frozen earth. The bird sends out another, a repeat of the first, a throaty plea of loneliness, out to the forest, to the boreal, to the spindly black spruce and naked tamarack. Again there is no reply. He is the only raven here, and here is nowhere. He throws himself up from the ground, beats hard at the frozen air, black wings over white snow, and seeks the grey sky. Purposefully, deliberately, he flies a straight line, a rhythm of wings and wind, due east toward the pale light of daybreak.

This forest was once forever upon the earth, but time and warming pushed surviving humans, the world's greatest invasive species, into it. They came seeking the shade and the cool and bulldozed the trees for their cities. They came for the water, the lakes and rivers and places to bathe and splash and laugh and forget the draught and sand and dust of further south. They came, they thought, as pioneers; at least that's what they told themselves, and forgot, or never mentioned; that they were refugees.

Raven banks left where the forest stops, where the earth is torn and the concrete begins. He appears perhaps undecided, whether to return or stay; wavers on outstretched wings, a hint of blue on the black now that there is more light to catch and reflect. He stays, then spirals down from the grey sky and folds his wings before his talons touch the concrete.

1

When God quit attacking poor people who lived in trailer parks with tornadoes and began to pay attention to mansions, those who could afford it took to the sky. At forty thousand feet there are no storms. The Kenilworth, Illinois twister boosted sales in the sky cities, but most people agree that the flattening of Gladwyne, Pennsylvania marked the beginning of the exodus.

George Taylor needed three more good years and he would have the down payment for his own condo above the clouds. Others argued it wasn't worth it, that the chance of being killed by a storm was probably less than the risk of living at the end of a tether. But it wasn't just the storms. George wasn't all that afraid of those. It was terrestrial people that bothered him. Not that they were terrestrial, earth wanderers; it was that there were so damn many of them and more came from the south every day.

To George, the sky represented a last chance for freedom and maybe, maybe, it was a bit about prestige, about the symbolism of living above everyone else. A tenancy in Bel Arial would be a real mark of success.

Of course there were drawbacks, such as the weight restrictions, but he had never been heavy, had always taken care of himself, exercised regularly, and watched his diet. There were those who said that it was all about image, about only beautiful people. But it was probably fat people who said it, people who could never afford the tax. After all, wasn't the whole idea behind a floating city that it had to be light? Even if everything in the city was built of Heliofoam, foam filled with helium, and needed to be tethered down to keep it from floating to the rim of outer space, if too much weight was added it wouldn't float anymore, would it?

Three years wasn't so long. His next increment was almost here, any day now, the end of January, maybe even today. He expected 12%, maybe even a bit more. He had done well the last five years. Not exceptionally well, but it was hard to be exceptional given the cases he had been assigned. He had never been disciplined, never been brought to the attention of headquarters, and that was a good thing.

George was a plodder, deliberate and always prepared. He never took a risk that wasn't calculated in his favour and of course that was no risk at all. Defence counsel always knew where they stood with George. If you want to know George's position on sentencing, read the sentencing digests — George had. He negotiated plea bargains mathematically and only withdrew those charges that would result in concurrent sentences in any event.

He checked his mail again on the way to the courthouse, hoping — and there it was, from Deb at headquarters. He opened it, not paying any attention to the image on the screen. It probably wasn't an image of Deb anyway, it was more likely generated. No one used their own image for messaging.

"Good morning, George. Congratulations on your fifth anniversary with the department of Justice, Prosecutions Division."

The voice was flat and George wondered if it wasn't generated along with the image. He was tempted to command *Forward,* but didn't want to miss anything. He didn't have to. Deb came directly to the point.

"Your assessment was mostly positive, with a score of seventy-two. Good job, George. A score of seventy-two corresponds with a 5.5% pay increment . . . "

George closed the message, shoved the cover down on Deb's face.

2

"WHATEVER THE HELL ARE YOU SAYING?" Richard Warner stopped on the sidewalk in front of the building, and looked up at the large black bird. He'd heard ravens make many strange sounds in his lifetime in northern Saskatchewan, but never this, never this close to speech.

Raven repeated the phrases, repeated vocalizations in a rhythm that sounded like speech, as though he urgently wanted to tell someone something. He sidestepped to the left along the ridge of the metal roof and spoke his words again, with the same urgency, the same pleading.

"Check this out." Richard held out one arm to get the attention of the woman about to walk past, and with the other pointed upwards. "It's like he's talking."

She pulled her hood back to hear better, stood in the frigid morning and listened, two good steps away from the man who stopped her: safety space. "Yeah, it does sound like that."

It was nice to have a little amazement to start a day. Richard watched her relax and pay close attention to the bird. It was alone up there. That was different. Ravens usually appear in assemblies, often around garbage containers.

Richard was captivated by the sound, convinced the bird was trying to speak. "I wonder what he's saying."

"Maybe we should try a translator." She brought an N19 platform out of her coat pocket, a woman's platform with a panic button, took her thumb off the red button, slid the cover back, and held it up in front of her. "Translate." She was of course joking, making light of it.

"Language," the platform replied seriously with its programmed Sean Connery voice.

"I don't know." She spoke with careful enunciation, then held the platform up toward the bird, smiling.

The bird continued its speech, never stopping, a throaty rattle of words, clear in the cold air.

"Unable to identify language," the platform interrupted.

"That's too bad." Richard was disappointed. "Would've been something if it worked."

"Oh well." She slid the cover back, pocketed the device.

3

As she walked into the court building Lenore realized that she had been hoping that it would work, that her actions were more than a joke. "Oh well."

"Hey George, hold up." She quickened her pace at the sight of George Taylor, caught up to him just before he turned down the east wing hallway. "What do you have this morning?"

"Courtroom two." George kept walking, shifted his briefcase to his left hand because she was walking on his right. "You?"

"Oh, I have a quick application in front of Fraser in three."

"There's such a thing as a quick application in front of Fraser?"

"I know, eh." She wanted to tell George about the raven, would have worked it in somehow, but the conversation took its own direction and ended when they arrived at the door to courtroom two.

"You have yourself a good day, Lenore." His smile was only half there as he reached for the door.

"You too."

She checked her messages before she reached courtroom three, half hoped there would be a delayed translation waiting. There wasn't. But there was a new message from Uppsalla University, Hildi Abrahamson, Registrar, with a class offering *An Examination of Privacy in the Age of Loneliness.* Looked interesting. She stood at the door to the courtroom and read. *In the late twentieth century, Agnes Gonxha Bojaxhiu, better known as Mother Teresa, hypothesized that "the greatest sickness on earth is loneliness." This class will examine privacy law and its concomitant social isolation. If privacy is really a concern, why do people share so much personal information in online forums?*

No time to read further, she spoke to the platform. "Interesting. I'll call you later, Hildi. Hold a spot for me." And then a clear command, "Reply," before she slid the cover over, put the device back in her pocket, and with the other hand opened the door to the courtroom.

4

Daybreak bloomed across the eastern sky, spread petals of red and orange and peach above the horizon, prepared the earth for the coming sun. The tall buildings along the shore of Lac La Ronge reflected the sunrise, refracted it, shattered it with glass and concrete until the light that fell to the street below held none of its former magic.

This city had been a village, with a church and a residential school and the James Roberts Indian Band. Then it became the Town of La Ronge and a regional headquarters and resource extraction point, and there it might have stayed if not for the southern exodus, the surge in search of the Promised Land.

James Lovelock had been right when he warned at the turn of the century: "There is nothing you can do about global warming. Move north and when you get there build nuclear power plants because the people will want electricity." The man who conceived the Gaia hypothesis was old when he made that statement, too old to act on his own advice, and like when he'd told the world that the biosphere was a single complex entity, Gaia — no one listened. Populations did not begin to shift until the south became too uncomfortable, until the Great Plains began to become the great desert.

There were still people who lived in places like San Diego but they didn't come out in the summer, stayed huddled in air-conditioned spaces and waited for a cool breeze off the Pacific. But places like Phoenix and Houston were completely empty. The determined ones tried to stay, tried to keep their cities alive, but nothing lives without water and when the reservoirs dried and the aquifers drained, the people left. Those with portable wealth left first, those with land tried to stay, but when heatstroke became the leading cause of death, they too followed the exodus north until only the very poor remained, and the sand and dust from the desert came on the hot wind and buried them. By the time Arizona got its solar power projects up and running, it was too late. Even with power for their air conditioning, people couldn't live without water.

La Ronge became a city, small at first, manageable, mostly a tourist centre, a place where people came to get out of the heat, and resorts ringed the lake. There had been political and legal battles, some hard fought, mostly over energy and resources that the corporations won easily — won the land on the shore, won hotels and spas, won fishing concessions and water rights.

More people came, people who couldn't afford to indulge in the resorts, people who came to stay, brought their families with them, wanted homes and schools and hospitals, and with their mass of numbers crowded out the resorts and reclaimed the buildings as condominiums.

And more people came and filled the spaces between the buildings, and spread into the forest. The trees they didn't take to build their homes fell in the storm winds. Sometimes a tree didn't fall, come crashing to the ground, sometimes the winds plucked it up — twisted and spun it across the sky.

5

"Hey Bob, got a minute?"

"Anytime." Robert Lane turned away from the screen, toward the door. "What's up, George?"

George found a chair on the other side of Robert's cluttered desk. "I wanted your opinion on my assessment."

"What'd you get?" Robert smiled, anticipating good news.

"Five point five."

"Oh." Robert's smile faded. "That's not so bad. There's some in this office who got less."

"I was expecting more."

"Honestly, I think you should have got more. I gave you a good assessment." Robert leaned back into his chair. "What I like about you, George, is you never complain. No matter what files I assign to you, you just smile and get it done. That, and I can count on you. I don't have to follow up."

"I've got good results. My conviction rate is over 70%."

"What's the penalty rate?"

"I'm not sure, it should be good. I don't go easy on them. When someone deserves it, I push for longer sentences. Not extreme, like some of the guys here, but definitely fair."

"That's what we have to keep in mind. We have to be fair. That's what this job is about. But you know headquarters, they're all about statistics. Let me just check here." Robert turned back to the screen, pointed a finger at it, flicked, made a motion with thumb and forefinger to open a new page, flicked, flicked again. He stopped to read. "Well that's not so bad. Pretty good in places. Your conviction rate is definitely up there. Your penalty rate is right on average. It's not low by any means." He turned back to George, gave a little shrug. "I agree, you should have got the full increment."

"Then what was it? Did I piss someone off?"

Robert paused, thought about it. "Not likely. You're not the kind of guy to piss people off." He leaned over and shut off his computer, flipped the lens cover on the camera. George understood this to mean that this was going to be a private conversation. You never knew who might be watching through a camera. He watched Robert open a bottom drawer to the desk and bring out a small bottle of single malt and two glasses.

Soon George's belly was warm from the whisky, and the tension was gone. They were just two friends in an office and Robert wasn't the regional manager anymore, at least not for the next few minutes until the glasses were empty.

"You might consider going to church more," Robert offered.

"Church?" George wasn't sure what this was about.

"Yeah, all those guys from headquarters are there; just show up, let them see you, stand around afterwards and shake hands, that sort of thing. It really goes a long ways."

"Church?" George thought about it, looked into the amber at the bottom of his glass.

"You don't have to join all the committees and clubs and such. You can if you want, that's up to you. But just come to church, be seen at church. How do I put this?" Robert looked toward the ceiling for a second, then back toward George. He tasted the whisky again. "It's good for the career."

6

Richard handed the court clerk his platform. She scanned in his *Notice of Fine* and gave it back. "If you don't want that directly deducted from your account, you have twenty-four hours to register for Fine Option. You can work it off."

He looked at the notice — eight hundred dollars. If that was deducted there wouldn't be much if anything left. "Where?" he asked.

"Third floor."

He never saw her face. She never looked up.

The girl at the Fine Option window had a nice face, smiled at Richard when she registered him, scanned his platform, downloaded directions. "It's about a hundred hours. I gave you inside work. Kind'a cold out there this time of year to be picking garbage."

"I don't mind the cold." He read the directions — Scattered Sites. He'd heard of it, a soup kitchen across the river. Not so bad, and his schedule was decent, all evening work.

On his way out of the court building he looked for the raven that had been there that morning, the raven that talked to him. It wasn't there.

He looked away from the building, out across Lac La Ronge. It was calm, a bit of ice on the shore, the ice's whiteness in sharp contrast to the grey-black water. There was a time when this lake would freeze completely across. He'd even seen pictures of trucks on the ice. Not anymore. By April he'd be back to work out there. Paid work. He was one of the lucky ones, employed. Well, employed during the summer.

He drove a skimmer, his own, harvested algae, brought loads of it to the depot where they turned it into animal feed and fed it to cows at the cow factory. It was beautiful work, out on the water all day, and there was a sense of purpose to it. Not just the product, the payload, it was more than that. He was cleaning the lake, something it couldn't do itself anymore, too much nitrogen, too much heat, not enough species that ate algae. Left alone, Lac La Ronge would become a stinking green slough like the other lakes, the ones that were too small to harvest, their surfaces covered with a thick green layer that choked the life out of the water beneath.

But that would be April, maybe earlier, maybe later, depended upon the weather. Richard checked the sky — mostly clear. It was one of those days when an arctic high-pressure system drifted this far south. No wind. That was a good thing — no wind. It didn't seem like there was such a thing as a gentle breeze anymore. If there was wind, there was a storm. If there was a storm, get your ass into a shelter.

He looked back toward the court building once more — checked to see if the raven might have come back — before he turned south on La Ronge Avenue and walked away with his hands in his empty pockets, thinking about the raven.

7

When Lenore came out of the court building she too looked to see if the raven was still there. It wasn't.

8

George ran a calculation through his platform based upon 5.5%. The program automatically assumed interest rates, inflation, and hundreds of other variables pursuant to standard accounting principles. It projected seven years.

He closed the platform. Seven years. That may as well be a lifetime. Seven years. He had no idea where he would be in 2091. Anything could happen in that time. A storm, cancer — war could break out again. He put the platform in his breast pocket before he got to his vehicle in the parking lot. He thought about not driving, about the two glasses of whisky with Robert, decided he was sober enough — the vehicle almost drove itself anyway.

He was on the eight-lane headed east, just a bit north of Egg Lake, needing a piss.

"Next exit."

"Little Hills Village in six kilometres," the vehicle replied.

"Make exit at Little Hills Village."

He let the vehicle make the lane changes, and the exit, and only resumed control once on the side street. The sign said *Carsil Organic Recreational Vehicles.* The business looked like it would have a public washroom.

The heavy glass security door opened slowly after George scanned in his platform and the system determined he wasn't a threat. He was fully aware that it also read all his personal data, which would include his financial situation and whether he could afford their product.

The sales representative who met him before he made three steps into the showroom was only slightly disappointed when George asked directions to the washroom.

"Just past the Hummingbirds on the left, sir. You'll see the sign."

The salesman had positioned himself to catch George on the way out. Obviously his platform had told the man that this potential customer was solid green.

It might've been the whisky, might've been the need to talk to someone, might've been the dread of going home to an empty apartment. Whatever it was, George was happy to be led around and shown the various organic recreational vehicles, ORVs.

The sales rep — Paul, he said his name was when he shook George's hand — was good at what he did, knew his business, knew its history.

"It started with robotics, with the move away from hydraulic or electronic systems into organic systems. Carsil was the first to develop functional synthetic muscle. It evolved from simple prosthetics to exoskeletal vehicles, to what you see here — Leonardo Di Vinci's dream realized."

"I don't know. You'd have to be in pretty good shape to fly one of those." George stepped back a bit to better see all of the bird. It was larger than he'd imagined. Then realized — of course, it would have to be for a person to fit inside of it, put your arms out inside the wings and fly.

"It's not your muscle that drives it." Paul spoke easily, friendly. "The bird flies itself; all your arms do is give direction. That's the beauty of it. Synthetic muscle coupled with microelectronics. Imagine that this was a living bird, which it mostly is, and add computer controls. Carsil doesn't build ORVs, they grow them. Now take this . . . " Paul indicated a Raven, all black with a strong hint of blue along its back. "This ORV has all the genetic properties of its original. New this year. We've really come a long way with genetics."

"I still don't know." George stepped back another half step. "If I was to do this, I don't think it would be a Raven." He looked around the show room. "More like that." He pointed high on the back wall.

"An Eagle, well of course, that's everyone's first choice — prestige, power, symbolism. Only problem is they don't handle the cold weather." There was snow outside today and both of them knew that it would likely melt within the week, knew that winter wasn't winter the way it once was winter. Maybe Paul was relying on the temporary cold spell to make a sale of an ORV that didn't sell well on its own, or maybe he really saw that George would be better suited to a Raven. "Eagles are migratory. Did you know that? Ravens on the other hand are capable of living anywhere from the High Arctic to the desert, mountains, coastal, everywhere."

"Ya, but they're scavengers." George was still looking at the Eagle, white head and tail, perched high on the wall.

"So is the eagle." Paul stepped in front of him, perhaps to block his view. "Sure, eagles scavenge too. Most birds of prey will take free food when they find it. Now the raven as a scavenger is a positive. Keep in mind that this model is very genetically close to its original. It has that same heartiness, that same ability to thrive. That's what makes it such an excellent choice."

George didn't buy the Raven, but he kept thinking about it.

9

THE APARTMENT HAD A STRANGE SMELL to it, one George couldn't quite place; maybe a neighbour was painting. It annoyed him. He felt the grouch within him rise, the grouch that would ride him for the rest of the evening, suck the joy out of his life. He knew the grouch. It came often enough, turned all thought to darker versions, took his energy so that all he wanted to do was sit and stew. He experienced it somewhere within his chest, like a void, or maybe a dark wet cloth over his heart that shut out the light.

Damn Rita. Her stuff was still everywhere. He should phone her and tell her to come get it. Maybe box it all up and have it delivered. He could see her face when it arrived. Good for her, she deserved a bit of suffering.

She was using him. That was bullshit, that "I think a bit of time apart would be good for us." She wasn't coming back, and now he was just a storage place for her shit. He didn't want to think how long it had been. He poured himself a tall glass, two fingers, his usual. "Fuck it." He tilted the bottle up again and poured another finger, thought about pouring a fourth and decided against it.

He moved a meal from the freezer to the warming oven. Not that he was particularly hungry. He simply needed to eat for nourishment. The package said it was beef, but you could never be sure. There might be some bovine genetic material in the reconstituted substance. George didn't really care, never gave it more than a passing thought. His thoughts swirled like the whiskey in his glass and came around to Rita again.

He didn't package up all her stuff and send it to her. But he did move it around, out of the way, at least her stuff in the kitchen, the matching wooden salt and pepper grinders, the rack of wine glasses. He took the silk place mats off the table; what a stupid idea that was, silk place mats, the damn things never stayed in place. He rolled them up and left them with the rest of her stuff in a collection at the end of the counter.

Her stuff in the bedroom, in the closet, he didn't touch. Maybe he wasn't ready yet, not ready to move her out of there, maybe the memory of the warmth of her body prevented him, maybe between the grouch and the whisky he simply did not have the energy.

The La Ronge Ice Wolves were playing tonight. George thought he might watch a bit of it, tuned in to the game, and sat sprawled on a leather couch. *Ultimate Hockey* was more fighting than hockey. It satisfied something. Maybe people needed violence, needed the arena, needed to see blood on the ice to get their own blood to pump again for an hour. The Ice Wolves were playing the Flin Flon Bombers. It was an ancient rivalry and the Mel Hegland Sports Centre was filled to capacity with people who came to be part of it, people who brought their own energy, or borrowed the energy of the crowd, or whose energy was magnified by the acoustics of the arena, their inhibition dissolved by the alcohol.

Sometime during the first period a thought entered George's head, seemingly from nowhere, unattached to the game. It simply came and asserted itself, loudly: *Bombs look different looking up at them than looking down.* He immediately sat up and shut off the game, got up and walked away. He put his glass on the counter. It still held most of the whisky. He grabbed a coat, a thin one, then ran out the door, down the elevator and into the night.

The night was warm, above freezing, the snow on the sidewalk melting and slushy. He followed the walkway along the shore out toward the end of Nut Point. This area had once been a provincial park and a bit of nature survived here, black spruce and moss and Precambrian rock. The night air was moist, a bit of wind off Lac La Ronge. It helped George to breathe, cooled the hot embers in his chest.

Because he refused to think about some things, he was forced to think about other things. He chose to think about ORVs; it would be a nice night to fly, out there across the black of the lake, into that dark sky. He was alone, so he spread his arms, looked up a little into the night above the water, raised and lowered his arms slowly, imagined that he was flying out there. He leaned over from the waist and the bird in his imagination banked gently toward the north. He banked right and somewhere in the graceful turn he found a bit of peace, of forgiveness.

A sliver of the moon, the beginning of the first quarter, hung in the western sky, a new moon, the start of the next cycle. His imaginary bird circled it. It felt right. He circled it again, just because it felt so good. Then he walked home. Tomorrow he'd buy the Raven. He didn't think about why he picked that ORV over the others. He just did. Maybe the salesman put it in his head. Maybe he chose the Raven because it fit so nicely into the black sky. Maybe Raven the Trickster picked him.

10

"So what powers it?"

"Oh, here . . . " Paul showed George two small flasks connected together at one end; one flask red, the other yellow. "The red one holds the plasma. It circulates through the ORV and comes back to the yellow."

"Yeah." He got it. "It's the same as the blood system."

"Exactly. The plasma carries the energy to the muscle. We've basically eviscerated the bird, that's how we made room for you. Stomach and gizzard and liver and all that is the heavy part."

Paul showed him where the flasks clipped in to the ORV. "When the red flask is empty the yellow should be full. You just bring the flasks back here to have the plasma regenerated."

"So how long."

"How long does a flask last? About four hours. Depends on how hard you push it. If you're in a strong head wind and you're really working it, maybe a little less. If all you're doing is soaring, quite a bit more."

"So, if it runs out while I'm up there?"

Paul smiled. "No, you are not going to come crashing down in a tumble of feathers. It's the same as if you didn't eat all day, you slowly run out of energy. You have to be careful of that. Don't run the flasks completely empty. If the cells are not getting oxygen and fuel, they will deteriorate. Sure they'll regenerate some when you refill it, but if you do it too often or for too long, you can permanently damage it." Paul paused, his hand resting on the rail in front of the display. "It's like starving it."

The first helmet Paul had George try on was a little bit small, tight across the temples. The second one was better. It obviously wasn't made from real leather, but it had that look.

"I really like the way we've been able to hide all the circuitry. That looks good on you. To activate it, touch the edge of the goggles by your right temple."

George touched, and instantly felt a slight buzz run around his skull. He staggered, off balance for a second.

"Bit of a jolt the first time." Paul's voice was calm. He was clearly a little entertained. "You're seeing through the bird's eyes. That's why you feel like you're about three meters tall."

The strangeness of the experience dissipated. George looked around the show room. The ORV's head, a meter above them, swivelled as he turned left, then right. "That's pretty clear vision."

"Ravens have good eyes."

"Really good eyes. This is great." He looked down, saw himself from above wearing the leather helmet, but now the goggles were black. They had been clear before he activated them.

"How far does it work?"

"From the bird? Maybe a dozen meters, depends on interference."

"I like this."

"Wait until you're up there. You're going to love it."

And he did. One second after he stepped the Raven off the roof of the Carsil ORV building and spread his arms, the second that the updraft caught him and lifted him, before he even began to flap, he was in love.

Paul had been right. It didn't take effort to flap the wings. His arm movements simply provided the ORV with direction. It did the work.

Altitude; he wanted altitude. How high will this thing go? Fully fuelled and fresh, the ORV Raven climbed quickly. Soon he could see the water of Lac La Ronge and to his right Bigstone and Egg Lake; the city spread out away from the downtown high-rises toward the south and west. That's where he wanted to go, west. He wasn't sure what motion he'd made that turned the ORV Raven, whether he'd moved his arms or not. It banked easily and headed out across Egg Lake.

"Wow!" he spoke aloud.

"Kaww." The Raven replied.

"Holy shit."

"Kaye kit," the bird echoed.

Egg Lake rippled black and grey as he approached, a sharp contrast to the snow-covered ice along its shore. *Wouldn't want to fall in there, it looks cold.* He banked left and followed the east shore southward. He wanted out of the city, away from the sprawl of buildings and roads.

He thought he knew La Ronge, had driven most of the streets, he'd been around. But now, flying low over it, he saw things he'd never seen before: the buildings behind the buildings, the hidden parking places, and the things people didn't want to show to the street such as the old cars, the boats covered in tarpaulins, the junk that people keep.

To see it all from a hundred feet up, clearly, through the eyes of a Raven, gave him a whole new impression of La Ronge. He didn't know it. Not at all.

He reached the south shore of Egg Lake and turned west. Here the houses were smaller with more space between them, and there were gardens. It seemed everyone had a garden.

Black dirt showed through the mostly melted snow, dormant soil waiting for spring. Some were cultivated in straight neat rows. Others were left covered with potato tops and corn stalks after last year's harvest.

George knew about Regis, every prosecutor knew, had read files about the fights, the violence and chaos. He'd never seen it. Never driven through it. Suddenly he was over it. The neat residential area came to an end at what George could only guess was Highway Creek, and on the other side Regis began. The more substantial structures had metal roofs. Most of the shacks were just plastic and scraps of lumber. There were no streets. No wonder the police hated coming here. There was just shack after shack, nothing planned, nothing laid out. People built with what they could scrounge, borrowed a wall from someone else's home, put up a roof and tried to survive. They heated and cooked with wood. But where did they get it from? He couldn't see a single tree. Not for miles. Nothing lived here except people. There was no grass between the buildings, just yellow sand. Sand that soaked up the piss and shit and puke and blood.

This wasn't what he wanted to see. This wasn't what he spent all that money on. He'd bought an ORV to experience the better things in life, the sky, freedom. He flapped hard, drove the bird south toward the Thunder Hills. The Two Forks River area lay beneath him, beautiful, wetlands that people had left alone. He stayed above it and played, experienced the Raven, experienced the thrust and glide of flying. And below him there was something nice, something natural, a soft place to crash into if by chance something did go wrong. He tried a swoop, a shallow one, too nervous, too uncertain, too inexperienced to really push it. Someday, he told himself, after he really knew the Raven, someday he would do a loop.

He tried another swoop, a little steeper, a little faster, the smooth rush of the descent, and then reach out with the wings, head back and the g-force of the change in direction pumped the heart faster and a "Whoooee!" escaped from his lungs. The Raven called back, a long "Kawwwee."

"It's not supposed to be able to vocalize." Paul seemed surprised at George's off-hand remark that he really enjoyed that aspect of the ORV. "It wasn't designed in. But you know how these things work, we start with a bit of genetic material and we grow the bird. Sometimes we don't get what we hoped. Other times we get a bit more. Looks like your bird grew that bit more."

11

RICHARD WALKED BACK TO THE ASHRAM at Rabbit Creek, occasionally thinking about the raven on the roof of the courthouse that morning. As he crossed the bridge he noted that the Montreal River was low. The water that ran over the stones was not much more than a trickle at the bottom of the concrete floodway. He wasn't at all fooled by the low level; at any time the sky could turn black, the clouds would roll and boil and drop a hundred and fifty, even two hundred millimetres of rain in a single event and the river would roar again. But not in winter. Winter was sanctuary from the storms. Everyone knew what caused storms: heat and high humidity.

It was early afternoon before he reached the compound, tired and thirsty. Katherine found him at the well, a dipper in his hand, cold water still dripping from his chin.

"So how'd it go?"

"Eight hundred."

"Do you need help with that?"

"Naw, I got it. I'll work it off in Fine Option."

"Up to you, we've got a bit of money in petty cash if you want. That's what it's there for."

Richard thought about it. If he borrowed from the Ashram, he wouldn't have the long walk every day. But then he would be indebted. No, he would pay his own way, make a bit more than his needs and give that to the fund.

"Thanks Katherine, really, I have it."

"Shitty deal all the same." She smiled at him with that way of hers, that easy way that made everyone trust her immediately.

He returned the smile, looked back into her eyes, noted how clear the whites were, as though even the pollution in the air treated her differently.

"The law says we can have it, we can grow it, but we can't sell it," she said.

"Yeah, they're the only ones who can sell it, but who wants to buy GMO weed? Think about it, weed and GMO don't go together. If it's a weed it can't be genetically modified. To be a weed it has to be natural, free, know what I mean?"

"I fully agree with you, my friend. But you know what's going to happen if you get caught selling too often."

"I know," he replied, and he did know, knew they would put him on a recognizance that prohibited him from growing marijuana, maybe even with a condition that he couldn't possess it either. And he hadn't really *sold* anything. There was no transfer of money. Surveillance at a protest he'd attended showed Richard on the fringes giving a joint away to a young woman. A simple act of taking it out of his shirt pocket and passing it to her because she'd asked. Some cop had apparently reviewed the video and decided a charge was appropriate. It seems, in law, trafficking included giving. Now he had a criminal record for being generous.

Katherine patted him on the shoulder before she walked away, long strides, straight back, but not militaristic, just confident, comfortable in her own skin.

Richard watched her cross the compound, thought about what it might be like, and pushed the thought away. It would never work. Maybe in the short term, an affair of sorts, but he could not imagine being with Katherine *until death do you part*. She was definitely attractive enough, kind, intelligent. What would she ever want with him? He was almost twice her age, not handsome, not brilliant, and with a whole lot of baggage.

She had never been there; she didn't know, wasn't scarred, tempered, remade in the image of the warrior. The wars were over before she'd come of age. That was the big difference. That's what separated them.

Richard looked for work as he walked around the Ashram, past the bison herd. The fences were fine, tamarack posts that were naturally rot resistant and long, straight black spruce rails. Twenty-three very large animals. He knew them as a family, as a village, maybe even as a tribe. There was the chief, a huge shaggy bull that was always off to one side, separate. He was the sire of all the younger and none ever challenged him. Then there were the cows with calves, then the cows without calves, then the younger males, the warriors, the protectors. At any sign of threat the herd withdrew, the cows and calves stayed back and the young bulls formed a line between them and the threat. A four-year-old whose hair between his horns stood straight up always led the bulls, always in the front, stomping, pawing, face-first into the enemy. Richard imagined him as captain.

There had been fights over the bison, or rather, over the ten hectares they occupied, fights between the carnivores and the vegetarians who wanted the land for vegetable gardens. But the bison had been here since the Ashram began, back near the turn of the century, they had seniority.

He wondered if Katherine might be a vegetarian. He'd never seen her eat meat. But then he could not remember if he had ever seen her eat. She lived with the women. She probably wasn't. She couldn't be. She looked after the rabbits. But yet maybe. The rabbits weren't just for meat, they were quick compost machines, turning aspen into pellets for the gardens, the producers of perfect natural fertilizer: scentless and compact and rich in nutrients. There was no sense in checking out the pens, Katherine would have already taken care of cleaning them.

Richard found work, good, simple, hard work. He stood in a trench with a long-handled spade, dug down into the warmth of the earth to lay pipes, expanding the Ashram's geothermal network. He used a pick to break through the thin layer of frozen ground at the surface. There had been a time when the ground froze down more than a meter and municipalities buried their water and sewer pipes deep, but not for decades. Now the ground barely froze and some winters didn't freeze at all.

He worked until his arms and shoulders hurt, hurt with a pleasant ache. He enjoyed it, liked the feel of exhausted muscle, liked the warmth of it. There is a difference between ache and pain. Pain is sharper. Pain tells you something is wrong. Ache is quiet. You stop and take care of pain, you work through ache to get to the other side.

But he did stop, climbed out of the trench and sat on its edge, his feet dangling, stuffed a pinch of marijuana into a tiny pipe, just enough for three good hits, and relaxed into the smoke wisps. He thought about what he was doing, about marijuana use and alcohol use. Alcohol was an escape from reality. It dulled things. Marijuana enhanced reality, gave it a deeper dimension. A person could work high, carefully, experiencing every movement, thinking their way through it. Whereas a drunk can't work, a drunk is stumbling and lost, dulled and dumb.

He slid back down into the trench when the pipe was empty. He shovelled with new energy, enjoyed the colour of the wet sand on his spade, red from iron oxide, and yellow and brown. He thought about the warmth of the earth, his mother. All the energy that humanity ever needed was here, and she loved us, provided for us, kept us warm. He stopped to pray, put his shovel into the sand and leaned against it. "Universe, I know your song, I know your rhythms; let me walk to your beat, let me stay in your song, let me be a pure note in your symphony."

12

KATHERINE LIVED WITH THE WOMEN BECAUSE it was simpler; five women in an Earthship. She liked her home, liked the thermal mass of recycled tires packed with sand that made up the walls; she liked the architecture, liked the sweep of it, how it flowed into the earth.

It was one of the first buildings put up at the Ashram, in the time of Hayden Harder, the founder. Hayden was a bit of an anomaly, a hockey player before the game became ultraviolent, then a pacifist who used his wealth to contribute to the Ashram. And of course Hayden's brother was Patrick Harder, the general who led the Canadian Forces during the Second IntraAmerican War.

There were periods in the history of the Ashram when councils were formed, when the members convinced themselves that it would be more efficient to manage their affairs through formal structures. But they never lasted for long. There was still an elected council, though it had been a long time since there had been an election and the council had simply stopped meeting. The Ashram functioned because its members worked. No one needed to be told what to do. And as for coordination, that was simple, just ask Katherine.

It wasn't that she took charge. Katherine didn't tell people what they needed to do. She worked like everyone else, perhaps with a bit more spirit, and usually with a smile. She genuinely liked people, and put you at ease with the first two sentences out of her mouth. She never sought leadership and maybe that is why it was placed on her. She coordinated the functions of the Ashram because the members wanted her to. The arrangement had simply evolved this way over the course of a few years. Now everyone was comfortable with it.

Katherine was the first to say that she had no authority. She could not compel any action. She simply suggested that such-and-such be done and if no one picked up on the idea, she did it herself, gladly. So the Ashram functioned, day-by-day, night-by-night, meal-by-meal.

There had been a time when everyone ate together in the big dining hall. It had been thought that communal meals were essential for the survival of the Ashram; not anymore. Now you ate with whomever you wanted. The meals were still communal, in the sense that people ate in groups and shared resources, but they had removed the structure. Not everyone wanted to have supper at six o'clock everyday. Now there was no set cooking crew and that change alone had removed a source of tension.

Glyphosate; how could humanity imagine such a compound? She put the soil sample down, stepped back from the little workbench at the far end of the greenhouse. Just the word *glyphosate* stirred anger in her, an emotion that she was not at all familiar with. It wasn't the droughts alone that killed the farmers. The soil died first. "Six times ten to the thirtieth power." She said it aloud. The number of bacterial cells that had existed before glyphosate. She tried to imagine it; six with thirty zeros behind it, more than half of the world's species and one compound; one bit of stupidity and now the soil was dying. The United Nations Convention on Soils had banned it. But too late; the damage was done.

How could they have done it?

How could a farmer imagine that he could spray a herbicide that killed everything, that clogged the life paths of every plant, and that that would be a benefit? The anger within her was becoming more than a stir. And in its heyday they thought the worst it was doing was creating herbicide-resistant weeds, as if weeds were the problem. It took decades to realize what it did to the soil, to the life force within the soil.

She let her anger cool, closed up the soil test mini-lab. There was no way to get those micro-organisms back. They were extinct. It was like being angry because there were no dodo birds, no dinosaurs. When her anger dissipated, she was left with only sadness.

She stopped a moment in the greenhouse doorway, just stood there and looked around the Ashram, forty hectares, a blend of nature and management, where the people were not the most important element. There had been discussions about that big pine tree in front of her. Some thought it should be taken down. If a storm came it would crash into the greenhouse. The argument that won the day — she was happy to remember — was that the greenhouse could be rebuilt; to grow a pine like that would take a hundred and fifty years.

Anyway, the Ashram seemed almost blessed. It had never been hit by storm, not directly. Sure, they had lost shingles, and big rain events had flooded cellars. But, never a tornado, never a plough wind. The Ashram had always been a place of calm.

She could see Richard working, one deliberate shovelful at a time. They could get a machine to do that, to dig the trenches. The Ashram had money, more than enough. But he'd insisted, said it was honest work. She liked that about him, that he was a worker, that he was honest. She imagined what it might be like, remembered how when he spoke to her he always looked directly into her eyes, looked into her, and how that left her feeling open. Not open and vulnerable, but open and connected.

But with Richard there was always a distance, as though he was somewhere else, as though the Ashram was simply a passage, a place to heal before he moved on. There had been many like that, people who came to put their demons to rest, found what they needed and went back into the world.

Not Katherine. She found this place when she was eighteen, riding a bicycle, heading north, everything she owned in a packsack; stopped to ask for water and never left. She'd found home, found what she had been looking for, a place to belong.

13

Lenore noticed the moon and couldn't remember the last time she had seen it, an orb of gold that shone through the top quadrant of her living room window. It drew her out, away from her studies, onto the narrow balcony. She stood there in the cold and looked up.

There is always magic to a moon. She felt the old connection, a moon and a woman and the night. There was history here. Their relationship was ancient. Lenore bathed in the moonlight and the moment and experienced a rare sense of belonging. Her bare arms and face tingled. She imagined it was the moon touching her and wished she were away from here, somewhere out, somewhere dark. This moon was pale against the city lights, without all of its strength, unable to penetrate as deeply as she needed.

The moment faded. The light on her skin became the cold of the night and she was just Lenore again, standing on a balcony in the middle of the city, and the moon was just another light. But when she went back in, she found she couldn't study anymore. She tried, she wanted to, but the material had lost its relevance. She closed it out. Hit *Save*, then *Exit*. She thought she might run a search on the moon. She could tell the computer to "find lunar-woman connection", but didn't, because she knew it wouldn't be there. There'd be no connection, just words and images. She closed the screen.

Now what? It was too early to go to bed. She checked the time: nine thirty-seven. Well maybe. Maybe go to bed early, get a good rest. If she could sleep — that's what worried her, whether she could sleep, or whether she would lie there awake, remembering. She didn't want to remember.

She chose a hot bath, a long lazy bath followed by a glass of hot milk. She was sure it was real milk, she'd paid a premium price for it.

Her bedroom was small and cramped. She liked it that way, closed in, close, like sleeping in a cubby. It felt safe. She could make it even smaller, she thought, as she crawled onto the narrow bed, maybe another floor-to-ceiling closet would fill the space, tighten it up. There was already a large wooden one that she had placed to block the window. If she bought another, she would need a smaller bed so that the closet doors would open. That wouldn't be so bad. She didn't need more than space to lie down anyway. Maybe tomorrow she would go shopping.

She slept, not the deep sleep that she preferred, not the sleep where nothing penetrated and she'd wake up without any memories of the night. Her sleep was light and filled with images of moonlight and water. The image she was afraid of did not come. She didn't see the baby's hand.

14

"You have to experience it."

Lenore thought she could imagine it, being up there, the way George described it. He had obviously found his passion, an ORV Raven. She had never seen him quite like this before, animated, alive, moved by something, something that had touched his heart. She wanted to join him in it. She wanted to be part of this new obsession of his, but she didn't speak — she listened.

"There's something about making a high turn, as you just shift your body weight a bit and the ORV responds and the wind catches you and lifts you just that much higher." He had his arms out, showing her, tilting his body to the left, then straightening and bending his knees to demonstrate a swoop. His briefcase in his right hand took something away from the image of flight, unbalanced it. Maybe if they had been outside instead of in a courthouse hallway, maybe if there hadn't been so many people around, he might have been more convincing.

She thought what it might be like to fly wingtip to wingtip with George, to share flight, share the freedom. The thought didn't grasp onto anything and slipped away as George continued his solo flight.

"I thought I knew La Ronge, been here all my life, well most of my life, but up there, flying low, you get a true perspective of it. You see its other dimensions."

Lenore had never seen La Ronge from anything other than street level and even though she believed George, that she might be missing something, something exciting and new, she couldn't imagine it because it was beyond her experience.

"Hey, I have court in about three minutes in seventeen."

"Oh yeah." George looked at the watch on his left wrist. "I'm in nine. Judge Fritz." He made a sour face.

"Lucky you." Lenore offered him one of her nicer smiles, something to carry him through his morning. But she knew he didn't need her smile. He had his own joy to keep him buoyant.

She turned to look once as he walked away, his back straight, an easy stride. She noted that his fingers on the hand that didn't hold the briefcase were spread and stretched back. George was imagining that he was curling up the wing tips of his ORV. He was flying.

15

COURTROOM SEVENTEEN WAS ALMOST FULL. LENORE tilted up the screen at the prosecutor's desk and skimmed through the docket list. None of the names meant anything to her. The charges were mostly all the same: *Unlawful Participation in a Gathering.*

Those who had hired a lawyer were dealt with first. Most wanted an adjournment. She couldn't help but think that the reason given, that the lawyer needed more time to review the evidence, was a ploy to bill for a second court appearance. But, to be fair, maybe counsel was simply being thorough.

Those who weren't represented were dealt with quicker. Most pled guilty and took a fine, some angrily, some with defiant smiles. Others, like this Richard Warner, tried to argue and were told by Judge Ferris to talk to the prosecutor during the break and she would hear them later in the morning.

"What's your evidence?" he asked, standing at the prosecutor's table.

Lenore got to her feet. She didn't like having a conversation while she was seated and the other person stood. "You were at a demonstration and you have a recent criminal record."

"That's the charge. What's the evidence?"

Lenore ran her finger down the screen, stopped, tapped it lightly once, then again. "February seventeenth you were at a demonstration, and . . . " she touched the screen once more. "And, you were convicted on January thirty-first of trafficking in marijuana." She looked up, looked at Richard. He was well-built, lean, nice teeth, his hair was a bit on the long side, thick and dark and a little wavy; a likeable person. He wasn't the least upset; in fact he had a tiny smile as though he was having some fun with all of this. She checked the screen again, just to make sure. “Other than the trafficking charge, you have no other criminal record.” Then she did something strictly for her own information. She checked his birth date. He was the same age as her.

When she looked up this time she returned his smile, and a bit more. “The evidence, sir . . . ” she emphasized the *sir*, used it in mock formality, “is found in the facial recognition software used to analyse the security photographs of that little demonstration you were at on Saturday.”

Richard had his hands on the table, leaned forward a little. “Do you know what that was about?”

She admitted, “Not really.”

“We were trying to stop them from ripping up another RAN.”

“Ran?” She wasn’t sure what that was.

“Representative Area Network. They were set up a century ago. Small areas that were never supposed to be developed. Just little pieces of nature for the sake of nature.”

“Oh.” Her answer was just one word, but she filled the word with meaning. It meant that she understood. She got it, got the importance of the demonstration.

“Anyway, who recognized me?” Richard was still having fun.

“Facial recognition software.” She was having a bit of fun too.

“Really, software can recognize a person. I’m not sure that’s really possible. Isn’t recognition an experience? Only people can experience things, not computers. I recognize you. I met you in front of the courthouse a couple weeks ago. Remember the raven that spoke?”

She didn’t. She didn’t remember a raven or Richard. But a connection had been made. It softened her. “Listen, Richard, you don't have much of a criminal record. Tell you what, you enter a guilty plea and I will tell Judge Ferris that prosecutions would be satisfied with a reprimand."

"But I didn't do anything wrong to plead guilty for. I was there, I added my body to the demonstration. That's it. I wasn't shouting or causing any sort of disturbance. As far as I am concerned it was a peaceful, legal demonstration." Despite his obvious seriousness, the tiny smile was still there.

"It's not just that you were at a demonstration. It's that you were at a demonstration and you have a recent conviction." That was the law and Lenore knew the law. She also knew that as a prosecutor she had considerable discretion and it was his smile more than his words that won the day.

When Judge Ferris returned, and court was again in session and formality ruled and Richard Warner's name was called, Lenore stood and spoke to the record. "Prosecutions will enter a stay of proceedings on that, Your Honour."

During the lunch break mass exodus from the courthouse, she met up with George again, and again he could only talk about his ORV Raven.

"Because they're so unique, I was able to scan it and do a total search. I found its inception date, growth rate, everything, even who designed it. Ethan J. Beeney."

She interrupted, "Someone designed a raven? I thought nature designed it."

"Well, not the physiological aspect. Ethan designed the microprocessing."

"He put the wires to it."

"It's more than just wires." George sounded a touch defensive. "To connect neurological signals to digital circuitry isn't so simple. It's not like driving a motorcycle. Not only are there connections between the control computer and the bird, there are connections between you and the computer. I swear this thing does what I think."

"Mind control, that's expensive. Careful, you know that it can work both ways."

Everyone knew that. Everyone knew when they put mind control devices into automobiles that not only did the driver control the vehicle through brainwave function, there was a feedback loop that controlled the driver. Maybe it was urban myth, but Lenore believed it. It was easy for her to accept that there were people out there who would try to manifest mind control. The concept blended itself seamlessly into everything she knew about the society that she lived in.

"No, no, not like that. The connection I'm talking about isn't in the circuitry. It's more of an intuitive connection, like the connection that people have with each other, or a person and a pet, more like the connection you might have with a best friend, where you know what they are going to say before they say it."

She wondered whether George ever had that sort of connection with another person; he had been in a long term relationship after all. What would it be like to be connected like that with George? It was a thought she'd had many times, imagining her and George together, a team, a partnership. Since she'd found out that Rita had left him, she'd even imagined sharing a bedroom with him, a larger bedroom, one with a different sort of intimacy than her cubby-hole, a different sort of snugness. They'd come close a few times, when their conversation became personal, moments when it seemed like . . . well, it seemed possible.

This wasn't one of those moments. If George were experiencing any sort of connection it wasn't with her. It was with his Raven.

16

Lenore ate lunch alone at the Blackwater Café, a sandwich and a coffee. The coffee was good, as could be expected in a place that grew its own. Climate control: the plants took as much space as the tables. It was a not-so-subtle guarantee of freshness when a customer could reach out and pick a coffee bean, or pluck a leaf of green tea. She came here often, maybe because the air was better, maybe because the tables were small and the place was cramped and she felt safe in its closeness.

While she ate, she ran a search on her platform for Richard Warner. She'd been right, not only was he the same age as her, he'd served. And not only had he served, he'd served in the seventh. So he'd been there, the same as her — she in the fifth regiment, he in the seventh.

She'd been right to stay the charge against him this morning. Servicemen deserved a break.

Oh, this was interesting — his present address. She didn't even know that there was an Ashram at Rabbit Creek. That was sweet. This guy seemed to have got it together. *Good for him*, she thought, good that he was able to find peace after all of that.

Coincidence, fate, chance, whatever; as she was leaving the Blackwater Café on her way back to the courthouse and a busy afternoon, there he was, sitting at a table at the front of the café, tucked into a nook with only a pane of glass between him and the street. She had to — not just because she had just searched him and knew his history, but because he was reading a book, a book made of paper.

He looked up when she asked, "What is that?"

"Oh, this." He turned it to show the red cover of a thin, worn paperback. *Virgil's Little Book on Virginity.*

"Virginity? Really. What's it about?"

"Oh, a little of everything." He smiled easily. Maybe he enjoyed the content of the book, or maybe he liked it that a woman would approach him, or maybe he even liked her.

"Tell me." She didn't ask if it was all right or seek his permission first. She just slid into the chair across from him and waited for him to tell her what the book was about, not because she found the subject so fascinating, but primarily because it was made out of paper. If he had been reading it on a platform she might not have cared.

"We don't know much about Virgil, who he was, where he came from. All we have is this little treatise that we assume was written around the turn of the last century. The premise of it is simple: perpetual virginity. Here, let me read something to you." Richard flipped pages, back toward the beginning, and began to read:

"*Everything you have ever done, and everything that you ever will do, you once did for the very first time. It is this state of perpetual virginity and the surrender of it that allows you to grow. Only a mind in constant virginity can learn.*"

Richard flipped pages, couldn't find what he was looking for. He closed the book and used his memory. "Virgil says if you want a long and happy life don't worry about the beginning and the end, stretch out each and every moment. It's like a bead necklace. If each bead is as long and full as you can make it, the whole necklace will be longer."

She wasn't convinced. "That's a bit simplistic, don't you think?"

"But that's his whole point. It is simple. It's us who make it complicated."

She looked more closely at him, at the clothes that he wore. There was nothing obviously plastic. Of course you could never know for certain whether a fabric was really 100% cotton, or if cashmere was really cashmere. They could make plastic look and feel like whatever they wanted. But Richard looked real enough, the shirt looked flannel, his coat looked wool. The pack that she'd not noticed before, maybe because it seemed so much part of him, was now on the floor by his foot.

She would like to have stayed, spent the afternoon with Richard in the café, had another coffee and maybe even a pastry, and more conversation. She imagined it would be easy because Richard was easy to be with. But she knew she had court in three minutes because her platform in her pocket had just vibrated.

Even though she knew she'd have to rush to get back in time, she avoided leaving the table. She looked outside at the sun and the wind and the people.

She found herself wondering what people might think, what her supervisors might say if they found out that she was seeing someone with a criminal record, even if it was just a single count of trafficking.

But didn't everyone have a criminal record, something? Even her — insubordination, behaviour unbecoming. She'd even been court-martialled for refusal.

17

HE'D THOUGHT ABOUT TAKING THE RAVEN for a little ride during lunch. But he had court at 1:30 and it would have taken too long to drive home and back. Maybe he should fly to work and keep the ORV on the roof of the building. It would be safe there. If he could get permission — probably not, security would never allow it, not even for a prosecutor.

Instead he went across the street to the Blackwater Café for a sandwich, a quick bite and then review the files again before court.

She didn't see him. She was sitting with some odd-looking guy at a booth at the very front of the café, caught up in quiet conversation.

It shouldn't bother him. But for some reason it did. Lenore with another man. He purposely kept out of sight, wondering who the man was, and what they were talking about. The man had a book and he was showing it to her, which was okay, a little odd, but okay. What stirred George wasn't the man, it was Lenore; Lenore leaning forward, paying attention, her hands flat on the table, reaching out, as though reaching for him.

It was a bit uncomfortable. It felt like he was hiding, spying. He wasn't. He was just sitting there at a table at a public place that he had a right to be at, eating a sandwich, having lunch, perfectly normal. If they couldn't see him — well, that was because they were only looking at each other.

It was none of his business. The sandwich in his hand was nicely toasted and warm and the cheese lightly melted, but it couldn't keep his attention. What were they talking about? Who was he to her?

Hey, it's none of your business, he reminded himself and took a bite from the sandwich, an overlarge bite that filled his mouth and forced him to concentrate on chewing. But it didn't satisfy. Oh, the bread was nice, the tomato fresh and the meats were of good quality, but the taste just wasn't there.

He looked up again as she was about to leave, standing there beside the table, obviously reluctant, saying a few more words in a conversation cut short because she had to go back to work. It was clear she didn't want to leave. But she did. And when she did, he felt a bit of relief — just a bit, enough to allow him to enjoy his sandwich and cranberry juice.

18

There will be no curiosity, no enjoyment of the process of life. All competing pleasures will be destroyed. But always — do not forget this, Winston — always there will be the intoxication of power, constantly increasing and constantly growing subtler. Always, at every moment, there will be the thrill of victory, the sensation of trampling on an enemy who is helpless. If you want a picture of the future, imagine a boot stamping on a human face — forever.

Lenore stopped reading. George Orwell's famous paragraph from his novel *1984* had punch to it. It took her breath. Karen Kwiatkowski had cited him in her article "If war is the Health of the State, What is Peace?" It made Lenore think. She wasn't supposed to think. She was supposed to be studying, filling her evenings with something worthwhile and earning another degree.

She thought of both the boot and the face, couldn't help but think sympathetically of the face as hers. She knew the boot. She had been the boot.

She closed the platform, shut away the words on the screen, but could not close her mind. Had there ever been peace? Or was war all there was? Weren't they always at war of some sort or another? There'd been the war on poverty. Everyone agreed it failed, had become a war on poor people with forced labour camps that created more suffering and ended when the costs — not the costs in lives, but the financial costs — became too great.

They had gone to war to fight for peace, she and nearly everyone else her age. Then it had become perpetual war for perpetual peace, until it couldn't be stomached anymore. Even though the mass killing had subsided and the big machines of war were silent for now, were they really at peace? Could this state of existence be called peaceful? Or was it just a lull?

She poured herself a glass of cold tea. She needed something to wash her mouth with, to rinse that tiny taste of bile that was rising.

Maybe Richard was right, maybe the answer was in nature. Maybe everything was interconnected and interrelated and peace was its normal state of being and humanity as a violent species could never learn to co-exist with itself or with the planet until it could accept that it too was part of nature. But wasn't nature cruel and violent as well? Kill or be killed, survival of the fittest. Maybe, but nature had never designed killing machines, and if wolves killed deer, they didn't kill them because they were the wrong colour or spoke the wrong language or prayed the wrong way.

But those were just excuses. Race and colour and language and religion weren't the reason. The only reason that she could imagine for her three years in Guatemala was because they could.

But she didn't want to think about that. She didn't want to remember. She didn't want to drag herself back through it all again. She didn't want to open the pot and look in. She should never have lifted that lid. She should have walked out.

19

"I AM NOT GOING INTO REGIS, and I am not going to send one of my men in there." The sergeant moved his hands from his hips, away from his belt, his holstered pistol, baton, and pepper spray, and crossed his arms across his chest. He stood just inside the doorway.

"I need that witness." George had already said that. He didn't know what else to say.

"If we go in there, we go with a dozen armoured vehicles and fifty men, and I am not authorizing spending that much money to serve a subpoena. Forget it. You'll have to figure out some other way."

"Let me just explain what I've got." He ran a finger down the screen. He didn't need the file. He knew the details of it well enough. He turned back to Sergeant Williams. "Susan McLeod says she was walking home from the neighbourhood pub at night, alone. Someone comes up from behind her and pulls a bag over her head. She never sees him. All she can say is that he had her on the ground and he's trying to tear her clothes off. Then someone comes along and she hears him yelling at her attacker. By the time she gets the bag off her head, they're both gone . . . Then we have an officer who can testify that she was driving down Brad Wall Avenue and saw a man being beaten by another man." George looks back at the screen, he'd forgot the officer's name. "Constable Harten arrests Kevin Starr for assaulting Philip Charles. If we don't have Kevin to tie it together — that he came across an attempted rape, he chased the guy and was indulging in some street justice when the officer came along — we can't prove that it was Philip who attacked Susan."

"What about Harten, couldn't she testify?"

"She can say she arrested them both. But she can't testify as to what Kevin told her, that's hearsay."

"Let me explain who Kevin is." Sergeant Williams's tone softened. He uncrossed his arms. "Kevin lives in Regis. He was out hunting."

George interrupted. "Hunting?"

"When we searched him, we found wire snares."

"But, that's a residential area. There's nothing to hunt there."

"Cats and dogs."

"You're not serious."

"They're meat. Everyone knows that if you live within walking distance from Regis that you keep your pets in the house or they're going to end up in someone's cooking pot."

George didn't want to let himself think about the implications of that. "I still need him as a witness to a rape. Could you send someone in undercover, plainclothes or something?"

"Not a chance. Nobody would go, and I couldn't blame them. If an undercover ever got caught in there, they'd simply disappear. And just to serve a subpoena, it's not worth it."

George ran a finger across the screen, closing the file. "Then Philip walks."

Williams crossed his arms again. "Then I guess he walks. I'm not putting officers lives at risk. Not for this."

Now George regretted withdrawing the charge of assault against Kevin. At the time it seemed right, an award for performing a civic duty. That, and he didn't want to run a trial on those facts and have a judge scowl at him and defence stand up and make a speech about charging the wrong person.

If he'd waited until after Philip's trial was concluded before he withdrew the charge against Kevin, then Kevin would still be wearing a tag and it would be no problem for the police to find him. They wouldn't even have to go into Regis to get him, just wait until he came out, maybe on another hunting trip, and the radio tag would show them exactly where he was.

People did remove them. Some even cut their flesh to get them off. There were two yesterday charged with Breach of Undertaking and Damage to Government Property for just that, and they each got the minimum ninety days in custody.

After Sergeant Williams left, George ran a search on Regis, but all that came up were advertisements for cheap wine, a rich red sherry with 20% alcohol. He tried a couple variations on the spelling before he realized that Regis was not an actual name for the huge slum to the south of La Ronge. The place did not have an official name. It wasn't recognized by any government body. The colloquial name came from the wine that was commonly consumed there.

He remembered flying over it, at least a thousand hectares of metal and cardboard and sticks and plastic; hundreds of thousands of people that officialdom did not recognize enough to give a name. He found a satellite view and panned over the area. He thought about measuring it. How many kilometres long? How many kilometres wide? But he didn't. It didn't matter. It was big and it was there, but it wasn't part of his world.

20

SATURDAY MORNING HE THOUGHT ABOUT FLYING past Lenore's apartment. He knew exactly where it was: 1707 Hastings Avenue, not far from downtown, twenty-eighth floor facing east, facing the lake. But there was security. He could fly by the building but would not be permitted to get close enough to actually see anything. He might have anyway, flown as close as allowable until the building security system identified him and warned him away.

It was only because there was a club meeting that he didn't. They weren't very imaginative with the naming: The La Ronge ORV Club. They met every second Saturday morning at nine-thirty. George owned an ORV and thought that was a good enough reason to join the club. That's how everyone referred to it. *The Club.* "Club meeting this weekend, George. We going to see you there?"

"For sure, Eddy, wouldn't miss it."

This morning the talk was the rumour that the Hummingbird might be out soon.

"I thought it already was out. I'm sure I saw one in the Carsil display room."

"That's just promotion," Rueben explained to George. "The thing doesn't fly." Rueben flew a Swan.

"We have just about everything else, why not Hummingbirds?"

"Well, we don't have everything," Rueben corrected. "None of the small birds. Swans and Geese and Eagles, and of course your Raven and the like; but the little guys, the sparrows and the robins haven't happened yet. Why? Genetics. You have to multiply the size of whatever material you start with. Eagles and Swans are easy. Well, not that easy, I guess, you still multiply by twelve. Those smaller birds you'd have to multiply by fourteen, maybe even sixteen, and we're not there yet. Close, but not quite."

George was thinking, not saying anything. Rueben had started talking and kept going. "For me, I'm not really interested in the Hummingbird. Just doesn't strike me or something. Everyone is excited about the ability to hover. No. If we do start to get some of the smaller birds, I'd be looking for a purple martin, *Hirundo subis.* Now that would be something."

George didn't really know what a purple martin was, had never heard of it. He assumed it was one of those rare birds that was either extinct or nearly there. "Why that?" he asked, looking for a bit more information without letting out his lack of knowledge.

"Oh, man. The aerobatics, speed, agility. aesthetics. Everything about it says fast. The forked tail, even the colour. It's black with this blue sheen. Well, you know. You have a Raven. Same thing, that black that's so shiny that it looks blue. But this thing is *fast.* This is a swallow that just loves to tuck its wings in and *dive.*" Rueben was showing George with his arms and upper body and his voice how much he wanted an ORV Purple Martin. He'd trade in that big old clumsy Swan of his in a heartbeat.

George caught some of the enthusiasm, thought about the possibilities, not just of the Purple Martin, the big aerobatic swallow: he tried to imagine himself flying a Hummingbird.

"The only thing about the Hummingbird is that it can hover. It's not that fast." Rueben kept on talking. "Fast is the Peregrine Falcon, but man that's big money. If you want fast and affordable, you gotta check out those guys with Spur-Winged Geese: one hundred and forty kilometers an hour. Those things just go flat out. There's a few Ducks in the club. They're pretty fast. Sid over there . . . " Rueben pointed across the room at a table of three. George wasn't sure which of them was Sid. "He's got a Teal. Just a pretty little thing. He's got it up over a hundred, hundred and ten. And he has it over the Spur Wings. He's not just fast, that Teal can maneuver."

George finally felt he had something worth saying. "Why's the Peregrine so expensive? You'd think it's the same technology in a Duck or a Raven. Why's a Peregrine three times as much? And it's the same thing with Eagles. I don't get it."

"Prestige, man. It's all about prestige. They charge big money because people will pay it. Nothing more than that."

21

WHEN ALL OF THE CLUB MEMBERS finally arrived, when the visits were over, when the coffee or power drinks had been consumed, twenty-three of them, mostly men, climbed to the roof of the building. On the way up the stairs, George remembered an old joke his father had been fond of telling:

So Raven swallowed this frog, see, and then it took off. As it's flying away, Frog sticks his head out of Raven's ass and asks, "Hey Raven, how high up are we?" Raven, all proud, says, "Ten thousand feet." Frog says, "You wouldn't be shittin' me now, would ya?"

He wondered what his father would have thought of him — not this part, this ORV thing, the old man would have approved, might even have joined in. No, he wondered what his father would think of him going to law school and becoming a lawyer. While it seems cliché that the daughter always becomes the mother — his father had always told him that if you want to know what a woman is going to be like after you have been married to her for thirty years, take a look at her mom — with men it is different. Men don't become their fathers. No matter what success the father has, no matter what achievements, the son will find his own path, make his own mark, and he does this deliberately because he doesn't want to walk in his father's footsteps and be in his father's shadow.

There had been no animosity between him and the old man, nothing bitter. He'd wanted his father's approval of the things that he did, and he'd usually received it. Except the last time, when he'd told him that he had joined the armed forces and was shipping out. He'd seen disappointment in his father's face. But back then, he had really believed that he would come back a hero and make his father proud. It hadn't happened. He hadn't come back a hero and he'd never seen his father again.

The club held a ritual departure based upon seniority. Senior members stepped off the roof of the building first, a Teal, then a Spur Wing, a Ring-Billed Gull, an Albatross. The lone Eagle in the club was near the end of the line near George, who was the most junior and last to leave. He noted that Rueben's Swan wasn't very far ahead of him either. Would he become like that with members who joined after him — talk as though he knew everything just because the person he was talking to lacked experience?

He felt a bit nervous here, self-conscious. He was the new guy and still mostly an outsider.

During the pre-flight meeting — with no sort of formality, just a bit of talk between tables — it had been decided that they would fly to the Wapaweka Hills and regroup at the Last Pine Lodge. George wasn't exactly sure where the lodge was in the hills, but no problem, he'd just follow the others.

It wasn't long into the flight that he decided that club flying wasn't for him. He wasn't into flying fast or racing, testing whose bird was quickest. Nor did he care about aerobatics, diving and swooping, and his ORV Raven felt completely out of place when he tried flying in formation. Formation flying is for Ducks and Geese; Ravens fly solo.

It wasn't even so much the way that they flew — the speed and the tricks — it was the constant chatter inside his helmet that irritated him the most. There was a definite deliberate silliness to it: "Catch me if you can." "Hey, check this out." Or just someone screaming "Wheeeee" through a dive.

He did have to admit, though, that the woman with the Ring-Billed Gull was good. She didn't say much. She showed them, and she showed them with grace. A high perfectly executed arc turned into a spiral that tightened with her descent until she became a blur of white speed. Then, mere metres from the black waters of Lac La Ronge, she levelled out into a long low glide. It was the men whooping and cheering that ruined it.

"Way to go, Ruby."

"Good one — good one."

George banked away from the cluster, turned more southerly and sought altitude. How high can a Raven fly? His fuel pack was full. Four hours average, depending upon how hard he pushed it. He noted that his chest and arm muscles had improved in the short time that he had owned the ORV. It wasn't from the effort. The bird did the work. It was from the repetition. And his breathing was better, easier.

He put the ORV Raven to its task, tilted his head toward the sky and forced the wings to power him upward. He didn't ease up when his muscles began to warm with the effort. Instead, he pushed himself and the bird harder and higher until, even with the Raven's excellent sight, he couldn't see the other club members' ORVs. He paused once, levelled off into a long flat spiral, wings outstretched and the feathers' tips splayed in the sunshine.

Bel Arial hung high in the southern sky, a large silver oval that dangled in the morning sunshine. At forty thousand feet it was beyond his ability. The Raven could not fly to that altitude.

He caught his breath, gave himself a moment's rest and then continued the deliberate climb.

George was well aware of the record — whooper swans at twenty-nine thousand feet, seen over Ireland by an airline pilot back in the last century. That was when there were still whooper swans migrating to and from Greenland.

He wasn't sure of his altitude and didn't want to speak to his computer to ask because he was still tuned into the club communications system. He didn't want to draw attention to himself and what he was doing.

He was definitely higher than he had ever been before. It was dizzying up here. His lungs had an empty feeling to them despite how deeply he breathed. He levelled off again, stretched his wings out as fully as he could and relaxed into the glide.

22

GOVERNMENTS WERE CRITICIZED WHEN THEY BEGAN to print paper money. There was more criticism when the gold standard that backed the paper was eliminated back in the twentieth century. The argument was that with government free to print at will there was no control, they could do whatever they wanted. Prior to paper money, if a government wanted to go to war they had to increase taxes to pay for their war. The people then had some control, or at least a way to resist, by becoming angry over the higher taxes. Income tax, of course, was instituted precisely to pay for a war. The people's ability to pay, or not to pay, limited the ability of governments to engage in war.

But with paper money and central banking, governments were freed from relying on people to pay; they could print all the money they needed. Of course nothing is free. Every time they turned on the printing presses, the result was inflation. The greatest example of inflation caused by exuberant printing of money was Germany between the two great wars of the twentieth century, where the mark fell by one-trillionth of its former value, and the German people didn't blame the government, they blamed the enemy.

The people still had to pay for the government's wars, but not directly, they paid with lower value for their money. The government became addicted to the presses, and like an addict it made irrational choices and the people suffered through the resultant wars.

Lenore stopped reading the course introduction and let the information sink in. She had never thought of this, government monetary policy and war. It was new to her. She started into the next section of her course, a talk by Llewellyn H. Rockwell Jr. given June 6th 2008:

The US central bank, called the Federal Reserve, was created in 1913. No one promoted this institution with the slogan that it would make wars more likely and guarantee that nearly half a million Americans would die in battle in foreign lands, along with millions of foreign soldiers and civilians. No one pointed out that this institution would permit Americans to fund, without taxes, the destruction of cities abroad and overthrow governments at will. No one said that the central bank would make it possible for the US to be at large-scale war in one of every four years for a full century. It was never pointed out that this institution would make it possible for the US government to establish a global empire that would make Imperial Rome and Britain look benign by comparison.

She stopped reading again, this time to think about the implications of what Rockwell had said. 2008 was a long time ago. A lot had changed, and a lot had not. No one used paper money anymore. All commerce was, of course, digital. Was it true that the government switched to digital currency to free itself from the printing press? When the Canadian government got rid of the penny, and then the nickel and then the dime, were those the early steps to freeing itself from the limits of hard currency?

She looked at her palm, at the tiny tattoo in the shape of a simple key. There was more to the mark than ink under skin. The tattoo was embedded to "enable" circuitry that connected to her platform. Anyone who stole her platform, and with it all of her banking accounts and everything else, would have to take her hand as well.

It was a choice: did you put the enable circuitry on your hand, which could be easily cut off, or did you put the mark on your forehead? Of course a robber could also cut off your head. The choice depended upon your view of humanity. If you believed that people would not likely kill you by cutting off your head in order to steal your money, you put the enable tattoo on your forehead where it could be seen. Robbers would know that they would have to kill you for your money and leave you alone. If however, like Lenore, you believed that people would kill you for your money, you put the enable tattoo on your hand; it being more preferable to lose a hand than your head to a robber.

As she was looking at the tattoo on her palm, it tingled, once abruptly, then again, signalling that there was an important message for her. She checked her platform. It was from Michael. It didn't register at first. Which Michael? Then, as she read it, she remembered. Michael Stonehammer from law school. He'd been a friend to her and George.

It was an invitation, quite formal, written in an expensive private font. "Your attendance is requested." Seems Michael had done well for himself, purchased a condo in Bel Arial. A good old-fashioned housewarming party.

Would she go?

Of course.

The invitation was for her and a partner.

Who to take?

Richard?

Would he want to go? The idea of Richard and Bel Arial didn't seem to fit together. She could ask.

He might.

Never know.

But then there was George. Of course, George would have his own invitation. The idea of her and Richard and George didn't feel comfortable. Her and Richard, or even maybe still her and George.

No, she wouldn't invite Richard. She would go alone.

What to wear?

What to wear?

She had to go shopping.

She was almost to the door when she remembered to RSVP. "Of course Michael. It will be good to see you again."

Shoes. She needed shoes.

And a gown.

Was it formal?

Of course it was formal. It was Bel Arial.

She had never been before.

Imagine that, Lenore Hanson was going to a ball at Bel Arial. She felt like Cinderella.

It was an old-fashioned dress shop, the kind that still had a person working there. He said his name was Juha. Finding the right size wasn't any bother; her dimensions were of course in her platform, which was read when she used it at the security scanner to gain access to the shop. It should be just a matter of selecting the style.

But, on second thought, "I don't remember the last time I scanned my dimensions into my platform." She looked at it in her hand. "I don't think I've gained any weight . . . "

"That's fine. We always use the security scan from when you entered the shop."

The viewing booth was large and comfortable; several large padded chairs, side tables for drinks and snacks; no, she didn't want a coffee; no, she didn't want anything stronger.

"A glass of wine perhaps?"

"No thank you, I'm fine."

"Well, if you change your mind . . . "

"Can we just get started?"

"Of course, Ms. Prosecutor."

"It's Lenore, please."

"Of course, Lenore. You said something formal. Might I suggest . . . " and with that the show began. She watched an image of herself walk towards her on the full-length screen that filled one whole wall of the booth. She was wearing a long flowing thing that dragged on the floor behind her. The image of her smiled and turned gracefully. She could almost imagine herself walking like that, her hips swaying, her head back, quick steps, but she couldn't imagine wearing that dress. It was too much, way to much.

"No."

"Something more conservative?"

"Much more."

Juha made a downward motion with his hand at the screen and the brightly coloured flimsy gown fell away to a pile on the floor before vanishing. For a brief instant the image of her — the exact image of her, including the scar on her thigh — stood naked in full frontal view on the screen.

She felt her face redden slightly. Juha was at least ten years younger than her, still in his testosterone age. She looked over at him. His face didn't change. He didn't smile or smirk — very professional. But he didn't take his eyes off the screen either. He motioned crosswise and the image of her was again fully clothed, this time in a black dress. "Perhaps something like this."

"Better, but not quite."

After watching herself parade a dozen dresses, she sat down. This was going to take a while. Juha followed suit and took the chair beside her.

"I think I'll have that glass of wine now."

"Of course. Red or white?" He stood again quickly.

"Red." She would have preferred a rosé but it was only April and too early for that.

He opened a side cabinet. "We have a nice Rothschild in red."

The wine helped. Seeing herself occasionally naked, or rather having Juha see her occasionally naked, became easier with each sip.

He suggested, "Maybe something by Jessica."

Jessica's fashions were closer to what she imagined herself able to wear, more conservative but not uptight. She watched the full lineup, relaxed into the chair and the wine. This would be a fun place to spend an afternoon with a couple of girlfriends.

She really liked the way the image of her walked, that quick step, that confidence. She could walk like that. She imagined herself at Michael's little housewarming party; head back, making an entrance.

In the end she didn't choose a design by Jessica. They were nice enough, but she didn't want nice. She wanted to show Michael and friends that Lenore was a success, and sexy, and brave, a trend-setter, without going too far, too outrageous.

After she chose the dress, there was the matter of the fabric. She chose something with a high thread count. She liked the feel of the sample. It was heavy enough to hang nicely and not cling where it shouldn't and soft enough that she would enjoy wearing it.

She had another glass of wine — her third — while Juha printed the chosen dress in the chosen fabric to her precise dimensions. When the printing was done and the dress had cooled, she tried it on, not to see whether it fit, or how it looked — she knew both of those — she tried it on to experience how it felt, the touch of it.

23

With her belly still warm from the wine, the new dress package on the seat beside her in her EV Eight that mostly found its own way through the downtown traffic, Lenore decided she should go and visit Richard.

She didn't think her decision completely through. Maybe it was because she had decided that she was not going to invite him to Michael's little party in Bel Arial and felt guilty and wanted to make it up to him in some small way. Maybe she just wanted to go and see him, to see where and how he lived.

Maybe she wanted to borrow a book. Maybe she just needed a friend. Or, maybe she had some deep-rooted plan to make Richard into her lover, a plan that was still in its seed stage in her subconscious mind and hadn't found enough nourishment and warmth to generate into a conscious thought.

At any rate, she didn't know what to expect when she turned east off Highway 2 toward the Ashram. Her personal platform, docked in its place on the dash of her EV Eight, said this was where she should turn. The gate was open, no one around, no security. The narrow lane she followed simply ended at a collection of houses. Her confusion was answered by her platform. "You have arrived at the Hayden Ashram."

She spoke to the first person she met. "I'm looking for Richard Warner."

"Richard? He's around somewhere. Probably find him with the buffalo." The tiny and very old woman pointed northward. Her white hair with a very light tinge of orange had obviously once been red.

Lenore looked in the direction the woman was pointing, but all she saw was the glass of a greenhouse in the shade of a large pine.

"There's a path. You can't miss it."

The old woman smiled and offered her hand. "I'm Geneva."

The grip was stronger than Lenore had expected. "I'm Lenore." But that wasn't enough. She felt she needed to say more. "A friend of Richard's."

He wasn't with the buffalo. She stood at the fence and watched them, nearly forgetting her reason for being there.

She expected to be challenged, *What are you doing here? What do you want?* as she wandered nearly the full extent of the Ashram. It didn't happen. She met a few people. There was a couple working a garden plot together, probably a newly formed couple given the attention they paid each other.

"Richard?" the man replied to her query. He turned to his partner. "Have you seen Richard today?"

"Yeah, he's around. I'm sure I saw him this morning."

"Have you checked the buffalo?"

Then there was a boy playing by himself in the sand, building a village with lanes and houses.

"Richard? He lives in the house made out of logs. I can show you if you want."

He wasn't there either. But he arrived while the boy — "Michael" — was still scratching his head wondering where else Richard might be this time of day.

"Hey, you. Just the person I wanted to see, been thinking about you all morning."

"Really?" She hadn't quite decided yet what reason she was going to give for driving out there.

"Yeah, I finished Virgil's book. You seemed interested in it. But there's no court on Saturday and I didn't know where to find you."

"You could have searched." She felt the platform in her pocket. Of course, everyone knew where everyone was all the time. It was as easy as saying their name and "search". She'd just done it as she left the dress shop. That's how she knew he was at the Hayden Ashram.

"Well, a couple of things. First, I don't know your last name, and second, it feels a bit disrespectful to search someone. But never mind that. You're here. Come on in." And with that he led the way into the log house.

Minimalist, was her first thought upon entering. But she liked it. Lots of light and lots of wood. Walls, floor, ceiling, all without paint or stain. And the furniture likewise, old wood, obviously well crafted. And no clutter. Richard lived simple.

"Here it is." He took the book from a shelf that was just a plank attached to the wall with not more than a couple dozen volumes on it.

She skimmed through it, not reading, just letting the pages slip past her thumb for the feel of paper. "It's Hanson." She looked up at the man in front of her, at his lean build. He had not shaved and his face was bristled. There were a few strands of grey in his hair. He was a bit taller than her, not much, maybe a couple of centimetres. And he was smiling, happy with himself. "My last name is Hanson."

She stayed through the late part of the afternoon, followed Richard around the Ashram on a guided tour; saw the buffalo again but this time learned their names, met the rabbits and the goats, rabbits for meat, goats for milk. She stayed when Richard asked her for supper, got down on her knees in the dirt and helped to pick the new asparagus. It was fresh and mostly white; only the tips that poked from the dirt held a hint of green.

Wild mushrooms, elk steak, and asparagus.

"Where'd you get the elk?"

"Went south in February. I've got a friend trying to live down there. His family were organic farmers from way back in the last century. He's still on the family farm, grows a bit of grain between the droughts and the hailstorms. The elk like to eat whatever he grows, so he appreciates it when I come down."

"I didn't think there was anything on the prairie."

"Well, there's hardly any people. But it's not all desert. There's still a few places left that nature has taken back where the soil isn't dead. I wouldn't want to live down there though.

When that black dirt gets blowing around it's darker than night."

She knew something about this. She'd read the case law. "That lawsuit is still ongoing."

"Don't know how the farmers can sue the chemical companies. It was the farmers who sprayed the stuff. You have to admit, they're just as responsible as the people who sold it to them."

"That's harsh. Those people lost everything, and how could they know that those sprays would kill the soil?"

Richard didn't sound callous or cold. His answer was simply matter of fact. "The farmers weren't trying to raise food for people, they were trying to make a profit. That's why they bought in. The chemical companies promised huge profits and the farmers got greedy."

The woman didn't knock. "The Net's down." She paused when she saw Lenore at Richard's table. "Just going 'round letting everyone know."

Lenore dug in her pocket for her platform.

"Hello." She spoke directly into it.

It didn't answer.

"Hello."

Nothing.

She watched the woman check the warm frying pan on the stove close to the door. There were still a few wild mushrooms, nicely browned. The woman picked one with her fingers and tasted it.

She obviously wasn't in any hurry to leave. She seemed to enjoy her presence here, as though it was her territory. Lenore, on the other hand, frantic over her platform, felt out of place, as though she was the intruder. The woman didn't say anything. She simply occupied the space that she clearly felt was rightly hers.

Richard made introductions, clumsily, nervously. "Katherine, this is Lenore. Lenore, meet Katherine."

"How do you do?" Katherine stepped forward, hand outstretched.

Lenore looked up from her dead platform. If things had been different, if she hadn't been so concerned about the Net, she might have been more assertive.

"What am I going to do?" She held her hands out, palms up, the dead platform in her right.

She couldn't go anywhere. The EV Eight needed the platform to function. And even if she could get home, she couldn't get into her building without the security codes. And even if she could get into her building somehow and managed to get into her suite, nothing would work. Everything was connected to everything and everything was the Net. A sudden thought brought a little wave of panic. "It could be a military virus."

Which meant only one thing — war — again.

A sharp electric squeal suddenly erupted from near the door. Richard took the tiny device from the nail it hung on and thumbed a switch that shut off the sound.

"Is that connected to the Net?" Lenore was hopeful.

Richard answered with an apologetic, "No. It's independent, battery operated." He looked at the display. "It goes from bad to worse. Storm warning. Barometer dropped five points in the last hour. It's going to be a big one."

24

George turned the belly of the ORV Raven toward the sun that hung in the southern sky, his arms were outstretched, his fingers splayed. The right wing pointed at the ground and the left aimed at the sky. The bird banked in a long smooth turn. He was thinking maybe this was as high as he wanted to go — this time. Maybe start a spiral descent, back down to the others. They had been strangely quiet for the last few minutes. The constant chatter had simply ended and he was alone in the heavens. He liked it like that, just him and the ORV, distant horizons, and the whole of the atmosphere to himself.

But before he began his descent, he needed to know his new record.

"Altitude."

Even though he knew that he was addressing the control computer, somehow he felt that he was speaking to the bird.

It didn't answer.

"Altitude, please."

Silence.

As he levelled the ORV, wondering why it didn't answer, he felt a sudden surge lift him. He arced his wings to ride the strong wave of air. It carried him for a few seconds, then dropped him. He reached, spread his arms wide, tried to catch something to hold on to. Then the next gust hit him. Harder. Almost tumbled him over.

He spoke the universal words of people in trouble. "Oh shit."

Why hadn't he seen it? Big, black, and mean, coming out of the east. He should have seen it. How the hell does a person not see a storm that size?

He needed to get down, needed to take cover, find shelter.

"Stupid, stupid."

He could only guess at his altitude — ten thousand feet, maybe; he really had no way of knowing with any certainty. Not that it mattered, it was a long way down and it was going to be a bumpy ride.

All he knew was that he was being banged around and the ORV was almost impossible to control. The only direction that he sought was away and down, but the wind kept spinning him back facing toward the storm. He didn't want to see it. He wanted to point his tail feathers at it and sail away. He didn't like the look of it, black and boiling, and he especially did not want to see the flashes of lightning.

"Ride it out."

The wind felt like punches, big fists in boxing gloves. An uppercut to the stomach drove him upwards. A roundhouse to the ribs, a jab to the face, another to the face, then the storm stomped on his back, with both feet. The ORV wasn't built for this. The space that he rode in was comfortable in normal flight, but in this — this beating, this constant slamming — the ORV didn't protect him, it contributed to his bruising. The goggles gouged his temples and forehead. His chest and stomach began to ache with the pounding.

"Relax. Don't tense up. Ride it out."

He tried. Forced his muscles to relax, ease the tension in his shoulders. But the next kick to the belly tightened everything up again as his body instinctively tried to protect itself from the beating.

"Ravens are tough birds. They can handle this."

"Nothing to worry about."

"They're built to withstand this."

But *this* wasn't recreational flying, *this* wasn't a sunny summer Saturday morning, out with the boys for a little play. This was the fight of his life.

"You're going to be okay."

"The plasma tank is still mostly full."

"You're going to be okay."

Gravity didn't care about George or his ORV. It was too busy holding on to tree roots and buildings. It was his own fault anyway. No one told him to fly that high. No one told him to buy an ORV and fly it into a storm. He was as inconsequential to gravity as the millions of new spring leaves torn from trees or the bits of paper garbage the wind swept from the streets. Even if he folded in the ORV's wings, pointed its beak at the earth and dove, gravity would not help him. He was there of his own choosing and there he would stay until gravity remembered him.

The storm grabbed the ORV Raven and threw it hard to the left, sent it sailing, wings useless, then caught it, dribbled it like a basketball, kicked a field goal with it, and tumbled it beak-over-belly. He was thinking about the plasma tank. How much was really left? How much had he burned up trying to achieve altitude? It had been full when he started, a brand new tank for the day with the La Ronge ORV Club.

"Half, maybe better."

"It will last longer if I relax and ride it out."

"Glide and soar, don't fight it."

Then the storm was on him and the day went dark. George did relax into it, quit flapping, quit fighting. It didn't matter if his wings were outstretched or tucked in, the beating continued. Like a man on the sidewalk being stomped by a swarm of teenagers there comes a point where resistance fails and the victim goes limp to each kick. But this wasn't a swarming, they didn't take his wallet, give him one last boot to the face to remember them by and flee into the streets. This beating continued long after he'd given up. His surrender was meaningless.

25

"CAN WE EAT IT?"

"You don't want to eat that."

"It's made of meat, isn't it?"

"Eat that and you'll be able to shit through the eye of a needle at forty paces. Let's see if we can't get it down. Give me a hand, would you?"

"There'll be a man in here, you know."

"Maybe we could eat him."

"Don't even joke about that. Grab that other leg and we'll drag it out to the clearing."

"Fuckin' thing's heavy."

"Careful with it, watch that wing there."

"Maybe we can pull it by the head."

"Naw, we might pull it off. How about if you take that wing and I take this one."

"There. How do you open it?"

"I don't know. How about we flip it over on its back?"

"You're right, there's a man in here. But he's too skinny to eat."

"Stop that. Is he all right?"

"He's breathing."

"Anything broken? Can you tell?"

"Check for yourself."

"He's awright, probably took a real shit kickin' though."

"How we going to get him off this mountain?"

"Maybe I could fly this thing and carry both of you."

"Don't fuck with that."

"Huh?"

"Ravens are sacred. You know that."

"This isn't a raven. This is somebody's toy."

"Damn glad we're carryin him down the mountain instead of up."

26

"You just rest now, easy. Drink this." She put a cup to his lips.

It was hot, a familiar taste that he couldn't identify, and oily.

"Fish broth. It's good for you. Lots of nutrients, and you need hydration."

"Where am I?"

"Two Bears Camp. You're safe. Nothing to worry about. Roby and Allan brought you in. Here, drink some more."

"I've got to get back."

"Your world is going to be there. It's not going anywhere, much as some days we want it to." She gently pushed him back down onto the bed. He didn't resist. He didn't have much left to resist with.

"I'm Sarah, that's my Christian name. My real name is Memegwans."

"Memi . . . "

" . . . gwans." She finished it for him. "That's okay, most people just call me Mem."

George stared up at the white cone, at the long poles meeting at the top. It took a while for him to figure out where he was; the shape, the size of the place at first was confusing. He didn't get it until he'd had a good look at Mem, at her deep tanned complexion and her brown eyes — bright brown — and her long black hair twisted into a single thick braid that hung over her shoulder. Mem was an Indian, therefore, this must be a teepee.

"You're going to be all right." She patted his shoulder reassuringly as she was about to leave.

He cringed.

"Oh, sorry."

"It's okay, just a bit tender there." He relaxed back into the bed. He didn't tell her that there likely wasn't a spot on his body that wasn't tender.

She returned hours later.

George sat up. "Would you know what became of my ORV?"

"That thing they found you in?"

"Yeah, it's an ORV Raven. Do you know where it is?"

"Must still be where they found you."

"And where was that?"

"Long Lake Pass, that's what Roby said. You should ask Allan though. He'd know better." She put a jug of water on the ground near the cold fire pit.

"You're looking better. Think you can walk?"

He could; with her help at first, in a circle inside the teepee, then outside. The first steps hurt, every joint, every muscle stiff and unwilling. He knew the difference between an ache and pain. These were aches. Pain is sharper. Pain would tell him if he had any broken bones. He didn't.

Once they were out the door and the flap had fallen shut behind them, he looked around at the collection of teepees and tents and log cabins. Trees ringed the clearing, large coniferous trees. Spruce, he guessed, he didn't know for sure, trees were not something he'd ever paid much attention to. These however, caught his attention. Not just the ones around the camp; there was a whole forest of them that spread in a thick, dark green carpet up the mountain.

He turned, looking upward until he'd made a full circle, amazed at the size of the mountains that surrounded him, at how little of the sky remained. He felt closed in as though the massive grey-brown rock actually leaned over him. He also felt safe, protected from the sky that was pale blue now, an apologetic blue, he thought.

He understood it. You could live in teepees here, with those mountains to protect from the storms, storms that might be hiding behind any one of those huge peaks, a big grey-black monster storm waiting for him to come out.

It was one full day, an anxious day, a day where not much happened. He met some of the people in the village, but couldn't remember all the names. Isadore, Joel, Pony, or was that Ponee? Everyone shook his hand, smiled, went back about their business. He was fed real meat, broth, and vegetables, followed by a night and a sleep so deep that dreams could not penetrate.

27

WHEN GEORGE AWOKE THE SECOND DAY he felt much better. He still hurt, but not like the day before. His shoulders and back still resisted movement, but the rest of him wasn't so bad. He raised and lowered his arms, bent over in an attempt to touch his toes, slowly, couldn't quite touch, tried again, a little closer but not there, his back still too tight.

Isadore waved him over, offered him a breakfast of tea and bannock and, like everyone else in the village, did not ask him anything about how he came to be there, simply accepted that he was there. Everyone smiled when they met him, shook his hand, even the very little ones, some shyly, others boldly. Isadore and his wife had three little ones, Keewatin, Kimowin, and the baby Waposis.

Keewatin, a boy of about eight, a little man, shook George's hand firmly. His younger sister Kimowin looked down when she offered her hand and when Betsy, Isadore's wife, introduced Waposis, she held the tiny boy out. It took a second before George understood that he should shake hands with the baby as well.

The tea was strong and brown, the bannock coarse and crumbly, and there was a bowl of cooked blackberries to dip the bannock in.

"Nice tea." He held his cup up in a salute to Isadore.

"Elk root and Labrador and a few others that Betsy likes."

"Elk root? Never heard of it."

"Grows where it's wet."

George tasted his tea again. It was very pleasant, strong but not overwhelming. It tasted of earth and water and something else, something that filled him, energized him. *I need to take some of this with me when I leave,* he thought.

"We know where to dig it, but we never show anyone from outside." It was as though Isadore knew what he was thinking.

"Why not?"

"Because they'd come and dig it all up and there wouldn't be any more." Isadore wasn't making an accusation. He said it as simple matter of fact.

The point wasn't arguable. George let it go. He tasted his tea again. *Well, that's just too bad. It would have been nice to have a cup of this every morning at home.*

"Help yourself to more if you want," Isadore offered. "I guess you'll want to go to your toy today."

"I was hoping."

"When you're ready, we'll go see if we can find it."

Long Lake Pass was, of course, at the end of a very long narrow lake that filled the mountain valley floor for miles north of Two Bears Camp. Isadore paddled the stern of the old battered Kevlar canoe. George tried his best in the bow. This was not a skill he had ever learned and he struggled with it, tried to follow Isadore's instructions.

"Paddle on the right to turn the canoe left and paddle on the left to turn right."

"Sit straight."

"Push on the top of the paddle while you pull with your bottom hand."

"Pick a spot where you want to go and keep your eye on it. The rest becomes natural."

But it didn't, not right away. George picked a large tree that leaned out over the water a kilometre ahead and paddled toward it. He had to concentrate, each movement an ache.

They were about three quarters of the way up the lake when Isadore told him to stop doing that. He spoke slowly, in rhythm with his breathing. "Quit counting. Instead of one, two, three, four, five — try, one, one, one, one, one."

And when George did, when he counted *one* with each pull on the paddle, each stroke became the only stroke. The transformation was almost instant. He experienced *now* in a whole new way. *One*, he felt the sun on his back, *one*, he could smell the water, pure water, mountain water. *One*, the wind was in his hair, *One*, he was George and his heart and his lungs were working together with his arms and his back, *one, one, one*, the paddle was his friend.

They found his ORV Raven on the side of the mountain, crumpled and battered. They stood it up, checked to see if anything was broken — there didn't seem to be anything structurally wrong with it. It simply didn't work, as though all the electronics were shut down. He eased in, checked the plasma flasks; low, very low, but still something. Enough to keep the ORV functioning in a hibernation mode.

He climbed out again, took his platform from the control slot. It too wasn't functioning.

"Hey, you can't have one of those in camp." Isadore's voice was firm.

"What?"

"That. They're not allowed. I don't care if you have a platform. You can't take it back to camp with you. No Internet, no alcohol, no drugs."

"Well, it isn't working anyway."

"Probably because of the mountains. No signal."

They climbed to the top of the pass. But the platform didn't work there either.

Isadore grinned. "The Net must be down." As if that was a good thing.

"Must be." It was beginning to make sense to George, why he'd lost contact with the others in the club, why the ORV had behaved as it had in the storm.

"It's okay, we'll come check again in a couple days, then you can use the Net to reboot your bird. It'll be all right."

George was caught by surprise by the contradiction. How did Isadore know the ORV needed to be rebooted and how did he know that the only way to do that was to contact the manufacturer and have the reboot conducted over the Net? He was an Indian, who lived in a valley where they did not allow technology. He didn't ask. He was forced to accept that Isadore knew a lot about a whole lot of stuff.

28

THEY LEFT THE ORV RAVEN ON the mountain. It was too heavy, too big to try to bring back to the camp with them. Was it really all right where it was? Nothing was going to come and eat it? There was a bit of plasma left in the flask. It was safely in its hibernation state. They hardly use any plasma when they hibernate. How did they do that? Genetically cross a raven with a frog so that the raven had the ability to shut itself down?

The plasma should last maybe a month — there was a quarter flask. But then he still needed to fly out of here again. Nothing he could do about that now.

He couldn't find that place again, that zone. He tried. Counted *one, one, one*, with each paddle stroke, but he couldn't maintain it, his mind wandered. The Net was down. How was the world functioning beyond these mountains? What day was this? Monday. No, Tuesday already. He went up Saturday with the Club, rode the storm all night, Sunday he was in the village, Monday was yesterday; yeah — today was Tuesday. It doesn't matter. The Net is down. No court anyway.

It doesn't matter, *one, one, one*.

He felt the wood of the paddle in his hands, smooth, wet. *One, one, one.*

A fish jumped. Right there, right in front of him. He saw the whole of it. He guessed it was a trout. He tried to recall the last time he'd seen a fish jump. He was sure that he had, sometime in his life. He couldn't remember. Maybe he hadn't, maybe he had only ever seen it on television.

One, one, one.

They stopped where the big tree leaned out over the water. Isadore's suggestion. "Take a break here. We're about halfway back to camp."

He was beginning to like Isadore and his quiet, easy way with everything. But he was firm, in that same quiet way. "You don't bring that thing back to camp. Just leave it here. It'll be all right." And George had put the platform back in the control slot in the ORV, and knew it would be all right. It would be there when he got back.

Isadore asked, "Do you want a drink?"

"Yeah."

"Here." Isadore took a metal cup from his pack, placed it on the flat of his paddle, and using the paddle as an extension, passed the cup forward the length of the canoe to the bow.

George took it. Looked in it. It was empty. He waited, unsure. Was he going to pass him something to drink?

"The lake."

George looked at the water.

He looked back at Isadore sitting in the stern of the canoe — patient, waiting for him.

He looked at the water again.

"You can drink it."

At Isadore again, questioningly.

"Yeah." Isadore nodded. "It's safe."

George didn't have to try to remember. He knew that he had never, in his entire life, ever drunk water directly from a lake. This was crazy. This is how people got sick. Poor people. Poor people drank ditch water and got diseases, got bugs that ate their guts. He knew about water purification. He'd been assigned to protect the truck convoys and the tankers travelling across the deserts in Mexico during the Second IntraAmerican War — water for the troops. He'd seen people die for lack of clean water, a lot of people, good people, friends bombed and shelled in the convoys. If he dipped this cup into the lake and drank, then those people would have died for nothing.

The sun was in his face. The lake sparkled where light struck ripples. A mosquito buzzed. He looked down. He could see the lake bottom, rocks — lots of rocks, grey and black — about a meter deep, maybe a meter and a half, hard to tell. The water looked clear, clean.

He was thirsty. He hadn't noticed before, but now with the cup in his hand, a bit of sweat on his back, the sun, a bit of wind, not enough to cool him, he was definitely thirsty. The spit in his mouth felt thick. Maybe he could just rinse his mouth and spit it out.

One, he dipped the cup. Felt the cool of the water on his hand.

One, he put the cup to his lips.

One, he drank.

One, he didn't spit.

"This is good." He drank again. "This is really good." He had never tasted water without chlorine, without the taste of plastic from a bottle. Now he understood the commercials, visuals of mountain streams, glaciers, pictures of mountains on water bottles. He forgot about the desert and the smell of diesel engines and the trucks with steel tanks and the bombs like rain. He dipped the cup once more, this time filled it. Not just a bit at the bottom.

He held onto the cup until Isadore's patience ran out. "You can pass it back when you're done."

He was really beginning to like Isadore, trusted him. He could tell Isadore. It was something he would probably never tell anyone back in that other world. Not his supervisor, Robert Lane. Not because he didn't trust Robert, he would just worry what Robert might think of him. Not Lenore. Especially not Lenore. He wanted to impress her, not have her think he might be a bit of a nut case.

"Hey Isadore. I saw something when I was up there."

"Yeah? What was that?"

"I'm not sure." He wasn't sure what he'd seen, and he wasn't quite sure he should be telling Isadore either. But there was something about the taste of water in his mouth, the little breeze across his face, the warmth of the sun — not hot, just nicely warm — the canoe, the wood of his paddle in his hands again. And Isadore was an Indian, maybe he knew. And he had already started to tell him.

"A bird . . . "

Isadore was patient, but not infinitely so.

"What kind of bird?"

"Ever heard of a Thunder Bird?"

"Yeah. What did it look like?"

"Big — bigger than my ORV."

"Maybe it was an ORV."

"No, you can tell the difference. The real thing flies different — truer. Nobody can fly like that, not with that skill. Even the very best can't make it look completely natural. No, this thing wasn't being tossed around like I was. It was playing in the storm. I got a good look at it in one of the lightning flashes."

He remembered looking into its eyes.

"It was close. And it wasn't an ORV. Only thing I can think of is a Thunder Bird. Black, all black, and bigger than my Raven. And it didn't have feathers, more like skin."

Isadore put the cup back in the pack. "You should talk to Two Bears. He'd know." He picked up his paddle. "Ready?"

"Yeah." George turned forward and started paddling. He felt better. Isadore believed him. *One, one, one*, he found the zone.

That night, back in camp, sitting around a fire that pushed away the darkness that could only be experienced in a deep mountain valley, he asked Isadore, "How did you know I was counting my paddle strokes?"

"You seemed the type."

29

The lyrics from the old "Bohemian Rhapsody" song filtered its way through Richard's mind while he made a simple breakfast. Lyrics about the wind and how it didn't matter. He liked this time of day, early, just before sunrise, when the earth has those soft hues, when the light is gentle. Birds like this time as well, sing to the coming light; maybe they are praying, maybe they talk to the universe in their music language.

Maybe he should go outside and pray as well, tell the universe his thoughts, ask for kindness and pity. She was still asleep, curled up under a quilt, only a bit of her blonde hair exposed, her face in the pillow. He wondered how long she would sleep. Was she a sleeper, or a morning person? Could he live with a sleeper? Maybe. He liked mornings to himself. Another person up and around might be an annoyance, disturb his tranquillity.

He decided to let her sleep and took his coffee outside. From where he stood on the front steps of his cabin he couldn't see any damage from the storm. The big pine was still there, so was the greenhouse. In the brightening sunlight, it looked as though someone had come during the night and washed and scrubbed the entire Ashram. Wind and hard rain will do that. Any litter that might have been around yesterday was gone this morning, blown into the neighbourhood downwind, or maybe siphoned into the sky forever.

Richard walked carefully, not just because the north trail was a little slippery, nor because he was conscious that he was making the first new tracks on the damp ground that looked as though it had been swept. He simply didn't want to spill any coffee from the porcelain cup with the handle that was a bit too small for his finger. He should have used the bigger mug.

By the time he reached the buffalo pound most of the coffee was gone, with only a mouthful to enjoy as he stood, elbows on the top rail, and admired the animals. He wondered how they had weathered the storm; huddled probably, faces into it. Buffalo know something about storms and life. It's better to stand and take it in the face than to turn your back and cower. Nature and life throw things at you, things that are hard to take — blizzards, pounding rain, wind, sometimes even a little hail. It was always best to stand into it, put your head down, be humble and accept that it's all part of the greatness of the universe and worthy of giving thanks for.

The words from the old song continued to linger. He heard Freddy Mercury singing about killing a man, putting a gun to his head. He didn't want to go there, didn't want to follow the lyrics back. What was done was done. Now face into the day, enjoy the sunshine. There was no sense in reliving old storms.

On his way back to the cabin to check on Lenore, he saw a familiar vehicle through the Ashram gate.

It was Robin Orr.

The universe was truly a magnificent thing. With the Web down, Robin would be the best person to have around.

"Thought I'd hang out here with you guys until things are back to normal."

Richard slid the gate open for Robin to drive his old EV through. He thought about leaving it open for the day, decided against it and not only slid it shut again, but also made sure it was securely latched.

Of course Robin could drive. His vehicle wouldn't be completely dependent upon the Net. Robin would have known how to disconnect it, bypass security and navigation settings. Robin knew computers. Sometimes he even seemed to think like a computer. Maybe he could even jerry-rig Lenore's new EV that he was parked beside. She probably wanted to go home.

"It's getting crazy out there." Robin was looking at the empty cup dangling from Richard's finger.

"Coffee?" Richard offered.

"Oh yeah. Coffee would be great. I didn't even have water. Shitty, but this caught me by surprise, and I like to be prepared. Imagine all those others."

"We can definitely do coffee, probably feed you too." Richard smiled. "You know you'll have to work for it."

"Don't mind that. I'm going to be busy today no matter where I am. There've been people knocking on my door steady since the Net went down."

"You don't know how good you have it." Robin sat on the step in front of Richard's cabin, a cup in his hand. "Your own water supply, your own power — everything basic, simple, independent."

"I'm sure we know." Richard rested a hip against the railing, a second hot cup between both hands. "Any idea how long it's going to be down?"

"No. Only way to get information is from the very thing we need information about."

"So you don't know what caused it either?"

"I can speculate, but I'd just be guessing. Military grade virus, or maybe the damn thing just got too big too fast and collapsed in on itself. Who knows. What I do know . . ." Robin took a sip, " . . . is that a lot of people are in trouble today. No traffic on the way out here. People are either locked in their apartments or locked out. Power is down, no water, stores can't open, so they can't get food. Security is down, all the cameras are out. So with no one watching . . ." Robin let Richard imagine it for a moment before he continued. "There'll be riots. They know there's food in the stores, and without cameras, how will the police prove anything?"

30

"HEY RICHARD. IS THAT YOU? HEY, It's me. It's Donnie, remember me? Come on man, let me in."

Richard knew him. Donny used to belong to the Ashram, even worked a summer with him harvesting algae.

"Yeah, no problem. What's up?"

"I'm pinned. I need a place to stay."

"What you pinned for?"

"Long story. Let me in, man."

Richard unlatched the gate, slid it open a little, just enough, and a skinny Donnie, long brown hair tied back in two ponytails that hung between his shoulder blades, scurried in.

"Thanks Richard, knew I could count on you. I need a place. Shit is going to go down and I don't want to be blamed. I got pinned."

Richard understood. With the Net down, the pin in Donnie's back, somewhere close to where the two pony tails ended, wasn't transmitting his whereabouts and actions. It was a sort of parole. The pin, surgically implanted in a spot not easy for the subject to reach or remove, told the parole board where he was and what he was doing, whether he was keeping his curfew and whether he was ingesting any illicit substances.

"Shut that damn gate." Her voice was loud and commanding, unexpected from an eighty-something tiny woman. Geneva wasn't using her walking stick. It was in her hand, but she wasn't using it for balance as she marched up to them. "You keep that gate closed, you hear me?"

Richard slid the gate shut and latched it.

"How many guests do you have, Richard?"

"Well, there's Lenore who came yesterday. I let Robin in this morning, and now Donnie here."

"You're allowed only one."

"Since when?"

"Since the First Intra. We passed rules. Only one guest." Her voice softened. "Otherwise it's like trying to feed grasshoppers."

Richard remembered the First IntraAmerican War, barely. He remembered being hungry and scared, and his father wasn't there. He remembered walking. He remembered a particular cup of water, his mother crouched in front of him, holding it in both hands to his lips, and how good it tasted and that he drank all of it and there was nothing left for her.

He remembered the Second IntraAmerican War much more clearly.

"We'll figure it out." Geneva was still being strict, calm, rational, fair, but firm. "Your one guest can be your new girlfriend. As for Robin — he'll have no trouble getting adopted by someone. And this guy . . . " she looked at Donnie. "You poor bugger, I guess you have to be my guest. But you're going to have to work."

"Thanks, Geva."

"I remember you. You made a choice when you left here. Live by the rules or go back to the world. You chose the world."

Donnie nodded.

"Come on, then." Geneva began to walk away. This time she used her walking stick.

Donnie cleared his throat, loosened phlegm.

"Did you cough?" Geneva turned on her heel, mid-step, her walking stick planted by her foot. She looked hard into Donnie's face. "You better not be coughing."

"I wasn't."

She stared at him a few long seconds. "Have you eaten?"

"Not yet."

"Okay, then, first we feed you, then you work."

The walking stick led the way — Geneva followed it up the narrow lane with Donnie quietly a half step behind.

Richard looked back toward the gate. There was a different kind of storm coming.

31

Like most people, Lenore relied on the voice from the system to tell her where to turn and did not pay much attention to her location. She couldn't remember the route home.

Her security pass would work, but it wouldn't be needed. None of the security checkpoints between the Ashram and her apartment, or anywhere else, would be functioning. There'd be no one to scan her as she drove through, no one to close gates and stop her if her security pass didn't signal that she was one of the good guys.

If the Net were up, she could tell her apartment to start supper and it would be hot and waiting for her when she arrived.

If the Net were up, her favourite music would be playing when she entered.

If the Net were up, doors would open, elevators would work, security cameras would recognize her as she came in the building. All she'd need to do was make sure she wasn't wearing sunglasses or be looking down and her iris would be read and the system would let her pass.

If the Net were up, the system within her apartment would advise her if any change in her biometric readings indicated a health problem.

If the Net were up, her personal platform would pay attention to the food she was eating and how much exercise she was getting and advise on daily caloric intake. It would tell her that her period was late, normal, early, or expected.

If the Net were up, it would calculate light intensity compared to her vision and adjust her glasses accordingly.

If the Net were up . . .

She could try to go home, but she didn't.

She checked her platform. The message still read NO SIGNAL. *Habit, that's all it was*, she told herself. *Just a damned habit*. She put the platform back in her pocket, determined not to look at it every few minutes. There would be no messages, no updates.

She felt lost. A huge part of her was missing, there was a place inside of her that wanted to be filled. It was somewhere below her lungs, close to her core. She could feel it. It didn't hurt or ache, it was just there; void, empty, incomplete.

Soup with Dianne and Walter at two, Richard had said. Soup would be good, it might fill her. In the meantime, she wandered the Ashram.

"Hey lady." It was the boy, the one from yesterday who'd showed her where Richard's cabin was. Michael. She liked that she was good with names. George couldn't keep a person's name in his head for more than a few seconds. Why was she thinking about George?

"Hey lady, they're waiting for you at Dianne and Walter's."

"Is it two o'clock already?" Of course she didn't know what time it was, her platform was dead.

"Yeah, come on, I'll show you where."

Dianne and Walter had a cozy place together. The living area was mostly kitchen, cupboards and counters and stainless steel and a huge oval table set for eight.

"Asparagus soup," Walter grinned. "Fresh asparagus, just picked it this morning. First of the season. Fresh milk from the goats, a few choice herbs, and . . . " he paused for effect, "and when Dianne wasn't looking I threw some bacon into the pot."

The protocol seemed to be that guests filled their bowls from the large enamel pot set in the middle of the table between the loaves of fresh bread. Each person in turn removed the lid from the pot, filled the bowl, put the lid back on to keep the soup hot, broke off a piece of bread, and sat down.

Robin Orr was first in line.

Then Katherine.

Then Gus.

It was obvious that Dianne and Walter, as good and proper hosts, were determined to serve themselves last, after every guest was completely satisfied. And if there were nothing left?

Lenore began to panic as soon as Robin put the lid back on the pot. Why? Why put the damn lid back on? The soup wasn't going to get cold before Katherine stuck the ladle in. Fuck.

Katherine put the lid back on.

That Gus guy put the lid back on.

Now Richard lifting the lid.

And she was next.

And she couldn't.

It wasn't going to happen.

She wouldn't do it. She could not take the lid off the pot. There was that other pot. The one in the cinderblock house, the house with the flies and skinny dirty people with brown faces, their heads down in shame. And she'd stood by the door with her rifle pointed at them. They were supposed to be searching for weapons. Just weapons and bomb-making stuff, that's all. And there was the pot on the stove, simmering, and it smelled good, and she wondered what they were eating. What were these hungry people cooking? And she looked. She took the fucking lid off the pot and looked inside, and fuck . . .

There was no way on God's green earth that she was ever going to be able to take the lid off that pot of soup. Not after what she had seen in that house. She had never told anyone, not a single person in all the years since, not her fellow soldiers at the time. She had lifted the lid, looked inside, put the lid back on and her entire life had changed. Her military career came crashing down. *Insubordinate,* they said at the court martial after she refused, and she'd never said a word about the pot. She didn't have anything to say. She couldn't do it anymore. Not after that. Those people weren't enemies. Those weren't terrorists standing there with their heads bowed. They were hungry. The climate had changed and the crops had failed, cows had died from thirst and from the heat, and things done in hunger needed to be forgiven. She needed to be forgiven.

She needed to be forgiven for looking in the pot, the pot that smelled so good. She needed to be forgiven for being curious, wondering what in the world they might be eating. What was it that hungry people were cooking? She needed to be forgiven for seeing the fist of a baby almost defiantly held above the boiling water. She needed to be forgiven for putting the lid back on the pot.

The tears didn't come and the lump in her throat eased enough that she could speak. "Richard, would you please fill my bowl for me?"

Raven remembers. He has a good memory. He remembers the old man Noah and his wooden boat. He remembers forty days and forty nights. He remembers that he was the first to fly over the water that covered the earth, even before the dove.

He remembers the island of Crete and the young man Icarus, whose father had fashioned him a pair of wings and warned him before their escape to neither fly too low or the sea spray would soak him, nor to fly too high or the sun would melt the wax that held the feathers in place. He remembers the splash as the boy fell into the sea. Why didn't he listen? Why do they never listen?

He remembers Leonardo da Vinci and the wing. He'd held it out, modeled it for him as the young Italian sketched. Now there was a man with dreams, good dreams. He'd dreamt that he could fly.

And why not?

Humans needed to learn to fly so that they could learn to dream.

32

His poor mother, George thought. He'd never seen a man so wide at the shoulders before. *No wonder they call him Two Bears. He could be three bears or even four bears.*

Isadore had brought him here, to Two Bears' cabin, introduced them and left.

"You have something to ask me?"

"Yeah."

Silence followed.

"Um." He wasn't sure where to start.

Two Bears obviously wasn't going to say anything.

"Um, on my way here I saw something."

Silence.

"I think it was a Thunder Bird."

Why does this man make me feel so damn nervous? I'm not afraid to speak. I can stand up in a courtroom full of people and make long submissions without ever stumbling. George inhaled deeply, tried to start over. "It was in that storm. I was getting hammered around pretty good and then I felt like I wasn't alone up there anymore, like everything was going to be okay. Then in one of the flashes of lightning I saw it, right in front of me. I only saw it briefly. But it's something I won't forget. It was black, all black, and the eyes; maybe it was from the lightning, but the eyes were red. It didn't look like it had feathers either, but I'm not sure. Maybe it did. Maybe they were just wet. Then it was dark again and that's about the last thing I remember."

Silence.

A long silence.

"Are you finished?"

"Yeah." He wasn't sure what else to say.

"So, what's your question?"

He had to think about that. It took a moment. "Was it a Thunder Bird?"

"I don't know. I didn't see it." Two Bears shook his head, swinging his long black braids.

What the hell am I doing here? This guy isn't going to help me. He's just trying to make me look ridiculous. George put his head down, looked at his feet, thought about how he could leave. Maybe walk away without saying anything more.

"Whatever you saw up there, that's yours. Nobody on this earth can tell you what you saw, or what you didn't see." Two Bears' voice wasn't at all kind, there was no sympathy here. "If you say you saw a Thunder Bird, then I guess you saw a Thunder Bird. Now let me ask you a question. Did it say anything to you?"

"No, nothing."

"Did it give you a gift? Some kind of power?"

"Uh," George wasn't sure what he meant. "No, not that I know of."

"Well if you don't know, then nobody does."

"I guess what I wanted to know is if there is such a thing as a Thunder Bird."

Two Bears sat back, looked hard into his face. There was another long pause, uncomfortably long. George would have spoken again, to fill the void, but couldn't think of anything to say.

"There were Thunder Birds a long time ago and our people had relationships with them. We could talk to them, call on them for help." Two Bears spoke slowly, carefully. He picked his words with caution. "There is a story about how the Thunder Bird came to be, how the Creator gave him to us, but I am not going to tell it to you. We used to tell you people our stories and you ran off and put them in books and made yourselves famous. Then our people had to pay to read the story. That's also why we quit telling you about medicine. You took our medicine and sold it to the big companies and when Indians got sick we had to pay for something that was ours in the first place. I am not mad at you . . . " His voice softer. "George, there's a whole lot of stuff I can't tell you. I won't tell you." His voice firmer. "About the Thunder Bird, there's a whole lot of stuff you can find on the Net, about people seeing them, up in Alaska, in the States. You might even find pictures there."

George blurted it out before he had a chance to think it through: "I might not look it, but I'm part Indian." He was. Or at least his official genealogical chart said he was. His DNA profile proved it. On his father's side.

"Really." Two Bears smiled for the first time.

"Yeah, one thirty-second Ojibwa."

"You are one dumb fuck, you know that?" Two Bears was still smiling.

"What?"

"No Ojibwa would call themselves that. They're the Anishinabe people. Or maybe you're Nahkawininiwak. You know what? You're all fuckin' Indians now. I don't think there's one of you bastards that doesn't have some Indian blood in you." He was almost laughing. Then his voice changed, became more serious.

"That's what we're doing here. We're trying to save Indian people as peoples." He stressed the *s* in *peoples*, dragged it out. "I am one of the few full bloods left. We're almost wiped out. You didn't get us with Christianity. You didn't finish us with Small Pox. You couldn't assimilate us with your government policies. No, what done us in, is we interbred with you. Now there's hardly any of us left." He wasn't smiling anymore. "That's why we're hiding here in the mountains, trying to save ourselves." His voice was almost sad. "There was a time when this land gave us everything we needed. Everywhere you looked there was your food and your medicine. We talked to the Creator everyday, all day. You could drink from any stream, eat the food that was everywhere. Now we have to search for it. It's like it's hiding from us.

"When I think of you people I get angry. I try not to. I tell myself, *they don't know any better. It's not their fault.* But it is. We've been telling you for centuries. You just won't listen. You think you're smarter than the Creator. You're so smart I can't even explain to you what the Creator is. I have to use the word *Creator* so you understand a little bit. I can't explain to you how the Earth and the Sky are related, how you and I are related, because you're too smart to understand.

"Now you come here in that toy of yours. You take something that's sacred and play with it. And I'm not talking about the raven. It's a sacred bird. It has special significance to us. That's not what I'm talking about. Even if it was, you would never understand it. You'd think it was a quaint story, an Indian myth or something. No, what you're fucking around with is life herself. And you're just casual about it. No respect. You don't respect anything. The Earth gives you everything you need and you piss on her. All the food you ever wanted was right there and you fucked it up. Now you've killed her. The soil is dead where you had your farms.

"You take sacred things and you play with them. You took a raven and made it a toy. You took the buffalo and you made it a cow. Now you come here and tell me you saw a Thunder Bird and want me to help you. What would you do if I told you, if I told you all the stories about it? Would you learn anything? Or would you do like you always do and play with it?"

33

"Did he give you shit?"

"Yeah."

"Well, that's good."

"What do you mean, good?"

Isadore's smile widened a little. "That means he likes you."

"What does he do to people he doesn't like?"

"Oh, he don't talk to them. Not at all."

George thought about that, the implications and it didn't fit within his reality. Why would someone give you shit because they liked you?

"Did you say thank you?"

He felt sodden, heavy. "No."

"You should've."

"What for?"

Isadore took a moment. "Because he gave you something."

"Yeah, he gave me a blast."

"No, no, he gave you some time and some words, words that will help you. If someone takes the time to scold you, uses their personal energy to set you back on the right path, you should thank them. That's how we do it when we get a scolding, put our heads down, remember the person scolding us is trying to help us, and when they're done, we say 'thank you.'"

"You're serious."

"Yeah."

"You think I should go back in there and say 'thank you'."

"Yeah." Isadore looked straight into George's face, into his eyes. His voice was soft, serious. "If you do, and if you're sincere, he'll probably help you."

"Right now?"

"Before it's too late."

"Just go back in there and what, walk into his cabin, look him in the eye and — "

"Something like that, just be honest, say it from the heart. It'll be all right."

So he did. Walked back into the cabin, not because he wanted to, not because he thought there was any point to it, but because for some inexplicable reason he trusted Isadore; something about a day of paddling and walking, about Isadore sharing his food with him, and something more. Isadore had done something to him that he could not remember another person doing to him, not ever. He tried to remember, consciously thought, *when was the last time*? And was forced to conclude, sadly, *never*. He could not remember a time ever when a man put his arm around his shoulders, gave him a little hug, then patted him on the back.

That bit of encouragement carried him through the door and gave him a voice. "Thank you for your words." He spoke as sincerely as he could.

"Uh huh," was the only reply he received.

34

"THERE USED TO BE A GLACIER up at the end of the valley. It's mostly gone now." Isadore pointed west, parallel to the ridge of jagged mountains. "Most of it was still there when I was young."

"So, you've been here all your life, then?"

"Around the end of the First Intra I was about ten." He was quiet for a moment. "There were four of us kids, the others were older, teenagers; looked after me." He paused again.

George looked at the mountains, at light and shadows crossing grey rock streaked with brown and, at a place where the sun struck full force, the colour of salmon.

Isadore walked ahead a few steps. "I'm the only one still here."

George waited, then followed.

"I never really lived in your world. Mostly I've been here."

"And Betsy?"

"Second Intra. We took care of a lot of people." Isadore smiled at the memory, looked around. "This was a big camp. Tents all up the lake."

The smile and the obvious fondness of the memory contradicted George's experience. He looked around again at the mountains, at the camp and the brilliant aqua-green water. The Second Intra to him was about that, about water, lack of water. Ten years of extreme drought, and these people had lived through it all, here beside a glacier-fed lake.

"Betsy's from farther south, Montana Cree. Her whole family came, aunts, uncles, cousins, all of them at once. Good times. They liked to powwow. We danced almost all the time. Any reason and someone would bring out a drum." That

Isadore liked this memory showed in his face, and his voice was lighter, easier.

"Why didn't they stay?"

"You come from a powerful world. It pulls people back. It's okay. Their choice." His voice a little heavier, harder. "This camp has been here for almost a hundred years, since Two Bears' grandfather. He was a medicine man too."
"What was his name?"

"Two Bears."

"The same?"

"Not really. His grandfather was William Two Bears or Billy Two Bears. Our Two Bears is just Two Bears. He doesn't have a first name."

"You say he's a medicine man?"

"Yeah."

"What exactly does that mean?"

"Means he's one of those that can walk between this world and the other."

"And you believe that?"

"Got nothing to do with belief." Isadore looked directly at him. "It's about understanding. If you pay attention long enough, you get a little understanding and from that you can develop until things like the connection between this world and other worlds make sense and logic doesn't."

George had no response, couldn't think of anything to reply with. The two men stood without speaking, listened to the crows argue; each "caw, caw" shattered the mountain air. There was violence to the sound. It irritated him. He looked into the tree tops, tall slender lodgepole pine, into the canopy for the noise makers. The sound came from all directions at once and he couldn't locate the culprit birds.

Isadore saw him searching. "Don't worry about them. They think their voice is beautiful. They call like that just to hear the sound of it."

"Someone should tell them it's not as beautiful as they think."

"Naw, there's no point. They'd never believe you." Isadore began walking again. "There's people like that. Talk all the time, love the sound of their own voice and you'll never convince them that quiet is better."

They weren't long back at Isadore and Betsy's place when Two Bears arrived. He came directly to George. Stood in front of him, massive, blocked out his view of the mountains. Standing, he didn't appear as wide. George tried to guess at his height — seven feet easy, maybe seven-two, seven-three.

"The Net is back up."

The comment took him by surprise. *How could Two Bears know?*

"You can feel it. The world has been quiet for a few days, now it's all buzzing again."

"Oh."

"I guess you'll be leaving now. I thought I might give you a story to carry you on your way. This was given to me by Danny Musqua, long time ago. It's helped me. Maybe it will help you. If it helps, use it in a good way. If it doesn't then just leave it here." Two Bears paused. Started again: "Danny said you were a spirit travelling across the universe, just a little dot of blue light, then you met the Creator and the Creator was both spirit and physical at the same time and you said, *I want to be like that.* So you came to this world so that you could experience the physical. While you're here, you should keep the Creator in your mind all the time. Never let anyone come between you and him, and never come between someone else and the Creator. That's what Danny told me. I respect him, he knew lots." He paused again, looked around at the lake, then at the mountains, then upward toward the narrow strip of blue sky, then directly at George. "It's a journey. If you are really lucky, you'll have maybe a hundred years. Don't waste even a moment of it. Keep your thoughts pure, don't ruin this beautiful journey with anger, or gossip. In the end, all you will have is your memories. If you spend your life drunk and blacked out, you won't have anything at the end of your journey."

35

George waited for someone to ask him about his experience of four days without the Net. No one did. He wanted to tell the story, but for some reason could not bring himself to say, *You'll never guess what happened to me.* Instead he listened to others' experiences: locked out, or locked in, no water, no food, no transportation and, for most, an overwhelming sense of complete loneliness, loss, not knowing what was going on.

His journey back had been uneventful. Isadore had helped him reboot the ORV. They had said their goodbyes on the top of a mountain. Updrafts over the foothills had carried him to Edmonton, or what remained of that city after the oil had run out. He purchased another flask of plasma and flew home on a west wind, straight as a crow flies, assisted by the on-board global positioning system. He arrived home tired, the plasma flask in the ORV empty.

There had been some discussion about the weirdness of a storm that moved from east to west. George too thought about it briefly; the predominant weather pattern was from west to east and the storm that carried him to the mountains had defied the rule. But weird weather was just something everyone simply accepted. What was weather if it wasn't weird?

Court resumed. He put on a suit and tie and went back to work. There had been violence during the dark days, break-ins, looting, and mobs of teenagers with nothing else to do. The police had been busy, charges laid.

Proof was going to be difficult with most of the files that he'd received. All of the security cameras had been down and he doubted whether, without video evidence, he could get convictions, and for some reason new to him, it didn't matter. He'd enter a stay of proceedings on those files where there was no reasonable likelihood of conviction, prosecute those where there was some proof, and at the end of the day he'd go home and not think about them again.

He did get around to packing all of Rita's belongings into plastic bins, sealed them up, and had them couriered to her. That part was overdue. The last thing she had said was, "I think a bit of time apart would be good for us." Well, that was a long time ago now. He thought about it. How long had it been? Months. He counted backwards. A year? Yes, it had been one full year, almost exactly.

He felt quiet inside. The constant buzz and hum and clank of the city wore against his ears, against his skin. He chose not to contribute to it with useless words. His submissions in court were concise, and mostly without emotion. In the office, he smiled often and said little.

Robert Lane noticed, the way a friend would notice. "Is everything okay?"

"Yeah, it's all good."

"You just seem, well . . . " Robert searched for the right words, "not yourself."

George wanted to say, *get used to it,* but instead patted Robert on the shoulder with a "Thanks, buddy," and left it at that.

36

"I UNDERSTAND YOU TOLD THE COURT officer that you were staying charges because you didn't have video evidence." Sergeant Williams declined the offer of a chair and remained standing. "Just wanted you to know that Mackenzie down the hall has been getting convictions on viva voce evidence." He stood near the one window in George's office. "I hope you appreciate that I'm not telling you how to do your job."

George knew he wasn't. Williams respected the division between prosecution and investigation. He was being the thorough sergeant, babysitting his officers, pushing where there was room to push. At the end of the day he'd go home to his family with a clear conscience.

"Judge Robertson actually gave out custodial sentences today based on officer testimony alone, without supporting video. Just thought I'd let you know."

"Thanks, Sergeant. I'll keep that in mind."

But he didn't. After Williams left, George went back to thinking about Betsy, about her explanation of hospitality. "When you come to my place and eat my food, you bring a blessing to my house. If I share my food with you, then I will always have food. If you come to my house and I give up my bed for you, and I sleep on the floor, then I will always have a nice, soft, comfortable bed. If you come to my house and you laugh, that laughter stays here, it's in the walls, and after you leave, my house is blessed with it."

It was beginning to make sense; not complete sense — he still didn't understand the mechanics of it, how giving something away ensured that you always had it — but he was starting to appreciate the spirit of it. Memegwans had given up her teepee for him and gone to stay with her sister Anangons. At the time he had worried about putting her out of her home. He hadn't seen her again, hadn't said thank you or goodbye.

And goodbye was another thing. Isadore on the mountain, sky and peaks behind him.

"I am coming back," George had said.

"I'm sure you will. But whenever you say goodbye to someone, you should always think, *this might be the last time I ever see this person*, because none of us know where our journey ends." He gripped George's hand in both of his, pulled it up and held it over his heart. "You fly that thing safely now, have a good trip home. And when you come back this way, you are welcome in my house."

He got up and shut the door to his office, shut out the sound, shut out the chatter. He sat again and stared out the window, past the buildings, through the gap between two of them, at the lake, at the water and the sky. "I was a spirit travelling across the universe, just a little dot of blue light . . . " he recited to himself.

37

THE LARGE PINE CAUGHT THE AFTERNOON sun in its branches, held the light with its needles and cast a shadow away from the greenhouse. Richard sat with his back against the trunk, enjoyed the play of light, the cool of the shade, a few moments of quiet and contemplation before he found something else to keep him occupied.

He experienced *alone* the way a single man looking forward sees forty approaching, with a bit of urgency. He felt the singularity of self, but not lonely. There was no sadness accompanying the feeling. He was alone and aware of it. That was all. She had gone back. *Four days*, he thought, *and four nights.* Now she was back in her other world; the Net had blinked back on, normalcy had resumed. She'd be in the courthouse, or just leaving now. And he was here, on the Ashram.

No regrets. That's what Virgil had written. Don't waste time looking backward. But the memory of her was pleasant; quiet conversation, sharing space, sharing food. They could be good together. He had to admit, she was attractive, intelligent, and she had a solid career. It could be good.

Don't hope. Something else Virgil had written. *Hope is a robber, a thief of now. Be hopeless. If you spend now hoping, you waste now and you never get this moment back. All you really ever have is this moment, this now. Past and future are merely distractions.*

He plucked a blade of grass from amid the pine needles beside him, crushed it, and held it to his nose. It smelled green, like life. He inhaled it.

Joy and sorrow are the same thing. Without one, there is no other. If you hide from sadness, you can never experience gladness. A world of constant happiness will quickly become routine, normal and empty. If you never know thirst, you will never appreciate water. Food tastes better when you are hungry. Embrace your sorrow, if that is what this moment gives you.

Experience it fully. If you try to flee from it, drown it in alcohol, jump up and dance, it will follow and find you. The only way past it is through it. Enjoy your sorrow, say "this is mine." And once you own it, once it is completely yours and you have examined the depths of it, it will turn itself over, show you its other side, and give you joy.

He thought again about Lenore, the way she walked, the length of her legs, the way she stood, back straight, and the way her blonde hair framed her face, an earlobe showing. He smelled the crushed blade of grass again, this time with his eyes closed.

38

"That's it, isn't it? The fact they aren't saying anything implicates them."

"Well, what I think they said is that they don't know."

"No, what the minister said this morning was that they were still studying it. That's different."

"Solar flares — that's what I heard."

"No, it couldn't be. They solved that a long time ago. Solar flares can shut down the power grid, but I don't think it could hurt the Net. Magnetic energy used to build up in the really long power lines and overload stuff. It was bad back in the 10s and 20s, but that's been fixed now."

Lenore nibbled at a sandwich, looked out the window of the Blackwater Café, out toward La Ronge Avenue. She wasn't listening in on the conversation in the next booth — two younger men and a middle-aged woman. They were simply so loud that she couldn't help but hear every word.

"I think it was military. We were hacked and hacked good."

"But if it was military, the government would be pointing fingers at the Brazilians, or the Chinese, or whoever."

"I agree, and especially if they thought it might be the Brazilians. Any excuse."

"Four days, complete shut down, and no one is saying a word. Something's not right."

"I don't trust them. Even if they gave a reason. I don't think I'd believe it. If they said it was an attack, for sure I'd think there was something technically wrong, a glitch that got out of control. And if they said it was technical problems, I'd be certain it was a military hack job."

Lenore tuned them out, stopped listening, her memory took her back to the Ashram, to Richard — soft light in his cabin and easy conversation. *"If we could get beyond democracy we might have a chance. What we have now is too easy to highjack. Special interests capture government, government rewards its supporters, the supporters gain strength, and then new interests try to overthrow them. No one's working for the betterment of humanity."*

"Well, the alternative . . . "

"The alternative is to become independent of government. The less dependent we are the less power they have. If we rely on them for everything . . . If we rely on anyone, not just government, as soon as we need, or think that we need them, we aren't free anymore."

She liked that about Richard, his determined self-sufficiency, his apparent ability to survive.

"The way I see it, and this is me now, nothing to do with Virgil, I see us like a village of hunter-gatherers, the leaders are supposed to scout ahead and make decisions about the best direction for the people to move. The people trust the leaders and go in that direction or they don't trust and follow someone

else. But, what we have now aren't leaders. They watch which direction the people are moving and run ahead and pretend they're leading. If public opinion says 'this is good, that's bad', then the politicians will say 'this is good, that's bad'."

"So, who's leading then?"

"The artists."

"You can't be serious."

"Oh, but I am. The artists imagine the future—fiction writers, movie directors, poets, musicians, all of them — through their art they imagine the direction. Then the people who read, or watch, or listen, move in the direction that's imagined for them. The problem is when the artists only imagine pornography and violence, we end up in a pornographic and violent place."

She'd thought about it, didn't quite accept it; it might be true, but it was too easy, too pat. *"So, then, what we have to do is regulate the artists."*

"Won't work. Never has. Every time we try to interfere we only mess things up. If we act in one place, we cause something to happen in another place. It's like trying to push water."

"Well . . . "

"It's up to the people. Ultimately it's always up to us."

"I can't buy that. The people aren't in charge." She'd sat forward. She liked his utopian perspective, but reality was different. *"How can they be, as long as we have mega-corps?"*

Richard had taken his time to answer. *"Mega-corps don't exist, or at least they wouldn't exist if we didn't buy into them."*

"Bullshit. It wasn't that long ago. You're forgetting about the militias."

"No, I remember them all too clearly. I was in a militia before I joined the regular force. It wasn't the corporation committing war crimes. It was us on the ground."

"Acting on orders."

"Doesn't matter. It was still us. We give them the power they have, we carried the guns. The corporation only exists because we believe it does. We used to believe in dragons and unicorns, now we believe in Monster Incorporated." He wasn't being argumentative. He'd obviously thought this all through and wanted to share it with her. *"Why did you join up?"*

The question had surprised her. She hadn't been ready for it. She'd answered quickly, *"Because everyone else was, I guess. Something to do with home and native land. You?"*

His answer was blunt. *"For the money."*

She hated to admit it, but that had been her reason as well. At the start of the Second Intra, work prospects hadn't been very good, actually, they were non-existent. Regular meals, a paycheque, and guaranteed clean water had seemed like a good deal.

Richard continued, *"Yeah, I bought in. Just like everyone else. I justified it with words like honour and duty but I was there so I could eat. It was my choice. I gave the government its power. Not anymore, though. I'm through with it. From now on I don't give my power to anyone. I'm not holding up anyone else's ideal. As long as I can grow my own food, look after myself, as long as I'm independent, I won't have to go and hurt other people, and if everyone did the same, I wouldn't have to worry about anyone coming to hurt me."*

Richard's ideas made sense on the Ashram. It was different there. There, a person could imagine freedom and independence, taste the food that came from the ground, be with like-minded people. Here, in the real world, the strength of those ideas diminished. Here, if she didn't do her job it would all be chaos. Like that guy this morning, the one that got the two-year sentence. He'd beaten another man with an empty wine bottle, fighting over a few dollars to buy another.

What would Richard do with him in his perfect independent society?

She pushed away the partially nibbled sandwich, wasn't hungry, she told herself, but she was. It was just that she couldn't bring herself to eat.

She wanted to believe, wanted to live in that possible world Richard described. Choices: career and a steady pay cheque, or independence and Richard's utopia? Richard or George? Or maybe neither, she could continue on alone. She told herself that she was okay with alone for a little while longer. But, at the same time it could be good with George. If he was interested the way Richard was clearly interested.

She also wanted to go to Michael Stonehammer's housewarming party in Bel Arial. Two more hours of work, then take the rest of the afternoon off, put on that beautiful dress and those shoes, drive out to the tether, and an elevator ride. She felt a twinge of hunger; not to worry, there'd be food at the party, she'd eat then.

39

It wasn't so bad going to the party alone. It gave the impression of self-determination, of not needing a partner, of not being tied to someone. Once up there, good manners would dictate that no one would comment, whether they thought about her status or not.

This was all new and slightly exciting. There were old-fashioned real people at security down on the ground. Not an automated turnstile that wouldn't open the door until you passed the scanners. They were polite, professional, and thorough.

The elevator ride up the tether took longer than she had imagined it would. It was a long way up. And the view — incredible. The curvature of the Earth expanded as the elevator cage rose until the horizon turned blue and disappeared. This really was a land of lakes, Lac La Ronge with island clusters at its north end. She could pick out Wapaweka, long and narrowing toward the east. The smaller lakes she didn't know.

Then a thin layer of clouds and the land disappeared. She had a moment of concern as the reality of her height registered. Was the carbon fibre tether really strong enough? It didn't appear to be more than a black ribbon that disappeared below her. She knew the science behind it, borrowed from a spider's web, knew that the tether was strong enough to hold the entire floating mini-city and therefore strong enough to hold the elevator. But logic was not as powerful as perception. It didn't feel like it was strong. It looked flimsy. She stepped back from the elevator's glass front and took a seat at the back where she couldn't see downward.

Michael Stonehammer's cabin was forward and on the starboard side, forward being whichever direction the wind might happen to be blowing from. It wasn't one of the most prestigious cabins in Bel Arial. It was only on the second deck. Real class occupied all of the topside. She was thinking about Richard when Michael met her at the door, courteously invited her in. "Look around, enjoy the food. Please try the shrimp, they're real. Wild Arctic shrimp from a little fishing village in the north of Greenland." Then he was shaking hands with the couple coming in behind her.

The place was luxurious, with Heliofoam moulded and coloured to resemble log construction. The designers had tried, and mostly succeeded, to give the impression of knotty pine. There was even a large fireplace that would require very close examination to differentiate it from real stone. She liked it. It was good. It felt comfortable. Somehow the rustic look seemed to work. She walked around with a glass of wine, skirted groups of guests and conversations about nothing. Yeah, maybe she should have brought Richard. He'd fit in here. Well, he'd fit in with the décor; he might not fit in with the people. She couldn't imagine him in flowing formal black tie. She kind of wished that men's style would change again. She wasn't fond of the loose fit. It looked sloppy. And she couldn't really see Richard living in the sky. He was too closely connected to the Earth. Now George, on the other hand, George loved the sky, loved his ORV Raven, loved to soar.

The view — she looked toward the large windows. This was the selling point, this was what drew the buyers from the surface. The entire outboard side was glass. Every room looked out across the world, looked down on the clouds, looked down on the chaos and struggle, looked down on anyone without sufficient financial means.

Two famous artists, Liz and Nevaeh, were there. Lenore knew about them, the sisters. Early in their careers, critics had compared the two: some acclaimed Liz as superior, others favoured Nevaeh. For the past thirty years each had sometimes signed the other's artwork, so by now no one knew which sister had painted which piece.

Michael Stonehammer's housewarming party was also an art exhibit, with the artists as much on display as their paintings. Liz and Nevaeh stood together, casual, but not looking entirely comfortable. They must have been paid to be here. Something an agent had no doubt arranged. Lenore watched them nibbling the expensive food, avoiding the alcohol, smiling at the guests, explaining something about the idea behind a painting.

The shrimp made up the centrepiece of the table of hors d'oeuvres, large, pink, stacked in a spiral. When she approached the table she intended on trying a few of the offerings. The plate looked like porcelain but it weighed next to nothing. She almost dropped it, fumbled in front of the young man dressed in white chef apparel, his hat so white it almost shone. A caterer, obviously. A single stylized purplish patch over his heart proclaimed him an employee of Sabrina's Real Foods Inc. He smiled at her, or maybe he was smiling at her clumsiness. She smiled back out of politeness, a little embarrassed.

Faced with the mass of food, the variety and the smiling young man — she pointed at the shrimp. He pronged one, placed it on her outstretched plate, reached for another but she shook her head, indicated no, looked at the other food and walked away.

The shrimp was good. It had a crunch and a definite sea flavour. But she couldn't say for sure whether it was better than farmed shrimp.

George Taylor was there, quieter than usual, standing with a group of mostly men. She went to stand beside him, he nodded at her, not disrupting the conversation.

"I really thought it was nothing more than a condominium. It's not. It's really a small city."

"I wonder if we could look around. I'd really like to go topside."

"When they built it, it originally had a public viewing area topside and forward, but it's private now."

"Yeah, some son-of-a-bitch wanted it. Paid enough, and they sold it to him."

"Too bad, that's really too bad." The woman in the red dress punctuated her lament with a sip of wine. Several of the group drank in agreement.

A caterer, purple patch over her heart, came near. Lenore held out her glass, the woman poured rose-coloured wine into it. Stopped when the glass was half full. Lenore continued to hold the glass out. The woman poured again, slowly. Lenore nodded when it was three-quarters full. The woman tilted the bottle upwards, smiled, and stepped away.

Four days in an Ashram, a day and a half at the office, then here. Maybe the Ashram ruined it. It should be more, she thought. She should be enjoying herself more. She should be happier, a little more excited. These were her friends, her crowd. She belonged here. These were people from law school, from her profession. Judges Rommel and Ferris, Defence Counsel, and not just the regular sort; Trevor Smith himself was here, standing obvious, the full force of his powerful personality surrounding him.

There was a flute player, and very good if you stopped and listened, paid attention to the flow of sounds he produced; he could touch you, or touch something within you, if you stopped and listened. Or you could, like most of the people here, accept him and his art as background music and focus on mingling, on conversation.

It should be more. It would have been more if she hadn't spent four days with him, four days and four nights. The food he gave her was real, she'd seen where it grew; she trusted that the elk was elk. She trusted what he said because he was not trying to impress her, he wanted nothing, nothing more than to share concepts of universalism, concepts that he was passionate about.

Maybe that shrimp came from the Arctic though you could never be certain unless you went there and caught it yourself. It might be a scam — farmed shrimp sold at a premium because of a label. Maybe the conversation here was true, maybe they were all enjoying each other's company. But she suspected that a lot of what was being said was nothing more than words spoken simply for the sound of the speaker's voice, to show how much they knew, how smart they were, how connected they were.

If she hadn't gone to the Ashram, if she'd come here directly from her life, wearing her new dress — she looked down — and her nice shoes, it would not have been such a contrast. This was such an obvious fiction. He'd ruined Bel Arial for her.

The lady with the bottle was passing again. Lenore held out her glass.

She looked at George, the new, quiet George, wearing a slim smile, with a glass of whisky in his hand. He was looking past the group, through them and beyond. She followed his gaze to the windows. He was looking out, at the blue, at the stringy wisps of cloud. Now she smiled. George was imagining what it might be like to launch his ORV from here.

The group they were standing with were mostly friends from university. Most practised private corporate law, worked for one or more of the large firms, or were in-house. George and she were the only ones in criminal law and did not have much to contribute to most of the conversation.

Michael Stonehammer joined the group, a glass in one hand. He slung an arm around the shoulder of one of the men. "Heard Tysson took a big hit this morning. Cheer up, buddy, Monday will be a new day." He gave the man a little shake. "So, how's everyone else? Enjoying yourselves?"

"Oh yeah, great party, Michael."

"Like your place."

"Good job, Michael, well done."

Glasses raised. Whisky sloshed, whisky drunk.

Lenore too gave him a salute, took a sip, a bigger sip. A smile for Michael, a smile for his success.

He'd come a long way. They all had. The University of Saskatchewan was almost ten years ago, nearly half of the graduating class had been war veterans: she, George, Mickey, Eta, Sketch . . . What was Sketch's real name? She couldn't remember. Didn't matter, he wasn't here tonight anyway. Michael was a leader even then. One of the bright and connected, a committee member.

"Hey Michael, tell me now, what's the best part about living here?"

"That's easy." Michael's wife wedged herself in between him and the man who'd asked the question, claimed the arm that didn't hold the glass of whisky. "No dust."

Lenore remembered her, almost. Tanya maybe, or maybe it was Tanja with a j, or Sonja, or something. She was the right woman for Michael, right in all the right ways, pretty, petite; she looked good beside him and he looked good beside her. She was from the same class, the same caste. They presented to the world that look of success, of the rightfulness of success. Shit, they even dressed so that they complemented each other; her gown matched his suit, both black and of the same fabric, with the same gold highlights.

No dust, yeah, right. Lenore looked around. And no birds, no insects, no squirrels, no trees. She looked toward the window. George had it right. It would be good to jump from here, but without an ORV, without a parachute.

The thought shocked her. She could hear her heart pounding, a rush of blood roared in her ears. She needed to breathe, needed water. Flushed, she slipped out of the group. No one noticed. Her glass was empty again. She looked for the woman in white with the bottle.

40

Why wasn't he impressed? He looked again out the windows at the same blue, the same wispy clouds. It hadn't changed. There was no brilliant sunset. Tonight Michael Stonehammer's cabin was on the wrong side of Bel Arial. It faced north. There might be a stunning view from the other side, but George doubted it. This was just like one of the preferred scenes depicted on those huge screens that people without windows displayed on their inner walls. Even some people with windows chose to have them covered with vision screens. Why look out at the ugly building across the way, when you could have a mountain view, watch for the elk to appear, or a seaside and watch the surf or, if you had aspirations of extreme success, a Bel Arial vista.

It was made of Heliofoam, lighter than air. Sure it was safe. You could fire a rifle through it and the helium wouldn't leak out. The bullet would puncture a few tiny bubbles in the foam and make no difference. But the mass of it, the amount needed to keep it afloat, was far greater than he had imagined. It was nothing more than a giant glob, with tiny apartments carved into it.

Granted, when the Net went down, everything here still worked because they were on their own independent system, completely solar powered, the outer skin mostly covered in photovoltaic cells. But there was more to life than connectivity. You still needed food and water. Maybe they could get water from the clouds. He wasn't sure. But there were no gardens, at least none that he'd seen. So they were dependent and vulnerable, just like everyone else.

Why are you being so negative?

You used to want to live here, remember?

Is it because you can't afford it?

Is it a big case of sour grapes?

You can't have it so you don't want it?

It didn't feel that way. George didn't feel small and petty. He felt better than he had in decades. Strong. Yeah. He thought about it. It was strength that he was feeling. Not muscular, a different kind of strong, a strength of spirit.

Spirit, really? That wasn't one of his words. It was something new. Probably from Isadore. No, from Two Bears, definitely from Two Bears.

I was a spirit traveling across the universe, just a little dot of blue light.

It's all about the experience, isn't it?

George came back into the group, his friends — people, humans, spirits even. He should enjoy this. It was good, the food was good, the whisky was good. He felt his smile tweak his cheek muscles, felt the warmth in his stomach, the calm in his mind — and mixed in with it all an urge to put an arm around Lenore's waist, draw her close, share the moment.

She wasn't there. He looked around, sighted her near the door, sitting by herself on the little landing, one step down to the main level, her knees up, her legs crossed. Even from here they were nice legs.

Sitting in near foetal position, she looked like she might be hugging herself, except for the very full glass of wine she held in front of her with both hands.

"Hey." He couldn't think of anything else to say.

She looked up. "Take me home." Her eyes met his. "Please George."

41

SUNSET. THAT MOMENT BETWEEN TWO WORLDS, when day and night meet and shake hands over the western horizon, when it's not one and not the other; a time when the exceptional becomes possible. Richard understood this, not completely, but enough to know that if he put thoughts out, those thoughts or prayers would flow through the gap of space and time, between dark and light, and travel. He did not pray to God or the Creator. He prayed to something greater than those simple concepts. He had no delusions about a bearded man sitting on a throne throwing lightning bolts at him. He needed his prayers to reach the farthest possible, but he didn't really have a name for it.

Long ago he'd prayed, "*Creator, God (whether you are a woman or a man), Jehovah, Great Spirit, Great Mystery, Allah, Buddha, the force that flows across the universe, the force that holds the universe together, life, whoever wrote our original instructions, our DNA codes, I am just a man and do not have the capacity to understand you in your entirety, yet I want to talk to you. I seek to know you more and know I can never know all of you. When I talk to you, when I put my thoughts out to you, what name should I call you by?*"

He'd never received a concrete reply, no single word ever entered his mind in response. Instead he'd experienced an overwhelming sense of peace and calm, wherein he'd heard his own heartbeat, his own breath rising and falling in rhythm. Joy had been the best word to describe this otherwise indescribable thing. His communication had been successful. But he still did not have a name for that which he sought to understand.

Now when he put his thoughts out there, when he prayed — if you could call what he did prayer — he first tried to find that space, that place of calm and peace, and once he was there, which was becoming easier and easier every time he did it, he started out with a simple, "*Hey you . . .* " or more often just, "*Hey . . .* "

"*Hey, this is me, this is Richard. Thank you for this beautiful day . . .* " No matter what the weather had been that day, no matter what might have happened. If he was alive at the end of it, it was a beautiful day. "*Thank you for my life.*"

Sometimes his mind wandered as he communicated, went down a path parallel to or at odds with what he was putting out there. He didn't let it frustrate him. He simply caught those thoughts, gently, and continued putting his words into the great mystery.

He was getting good at it, enjoyed it. He looked forward to sunset and sometimes waited awake through the last hours of dark before sunrise in anticipation of when he would go to his special place and connect with something wondrous. It made a difference to both his day and his night. He slept better and he walked gentler. He paid attention to where the sun was, where the moon was, and the relationship between the two.

It was cloudy, high, thin clouds blocked the sun. He judged its position by the light, by its intensity, or rather its lack of intensity. *Maybe another half hour,* he guessed, *until sunset.* What would he pray for tonight? Blessings for the Ashram, its people, blessings for the environment, for the earth, for all its inhabitants, for the microbes that looked after the soil, for the life that came from there, for Lenore.

He took out Virgil's book. He'd loaned it to Lenore, but she hadn't taken it with her when she left. He'd found it again on the little shelf by the bed. Maybe she wasn't interested. Maybe she'd been simply in a rush when the Net came back up. Now it was something to fill these last minutes of the day. He flipped through randomly through well-worn pages with his thumb and let the flutter of paper stop near the middle of the book where he began to read:

It is a hard thing to do, to stay in the moment, stay always in the now. We were given a mind with the capacity to imagine. With this wonderful mind of ours we can go into the past and into the future. But we were not given it so that we could wallow in regret or waste our lives with hope. We have the ability to remember the past so that we learn from our mistakes, so that we learn action and consequence. We can imagine the future so that we understand that whatever we do in this moment will have repercussions later.

A mind is not an easy thing to control. Its only limits are those we impose. Left to itself, it will seek out its potential. It will remember and it will anticipate. Perhaps when it goes into the future we should use it to look back on where we are. Whatever the crisis we find ourselves in in the moment, it is going to look different if we project ourselves into the future and look back on it. What will the circumstance of your now *look like in a hundred days? Probably smaller, not so urgent? What will it look like in a hundred months? Maybe something to be smiled at. In a hundred years, will it have any significance at all?*

And if our mind takes us into the past, perhaps we might look forward from there to here and ask, "What did I hope for then for myself now?" because even though it is always better not to get caught up in hope, not depend upon it, not abandon now for it, our minds have such capacity and, despite our best efforts, we will hope. It is part of who we are; it simply should never be all, or most, of who we are. Use it. When your mind takes you into the past, remember what your hopes were then, and come back to this moment to see if they have been realized.

Richard closed the book, his finger marking the passage. If he was to hope, what would he hope for?

42

HE DIDN'T HAVE TIME TO DECIDE what it was that he hoped for; Geneva interrupted. "Katherine has a cold."

"What?"

"You heard me. I said Katherine has a cold."

"Where is she?" Richard was thinking: *Colds aren't common, people die from colds, she needs to be isolated. Colds spread. A lot of people could die.*

"I've got it. She's home." To Richard this meant she was at the Earthship along with four other women, which then meant that there were four more at risk. "I'm looking for somewhere for Tasha to stay."

"Of course." That was obvious. She could stay with him. "What about the others, what about you?"

"Got it covered. Tasha is here with you, Emily is in with Walter and Dianne, Vivienne jumped ship at the first sniffle, she's gone to her sister's apartment across town."

"And you?"

"I'm going to stay and look after her."

"Are you sure, Geneva?" What he was really asking was: *Are you ready to risk your life for her?*

"I'm an old woman. I'm eighty-six years old. Seen lots, done lots." There was a distinct finality to her voice. She was not to be argued with.

Tasha moved in, threw a little pack onto the cot. Gave a quick, "Thanks Richard," and left. All she needed was a bed, she didn't need his company. She was always like that: curt, decisive, and direct. He didn't know her well, thought about it, realized he didn't know her at all, probably no one did.

A cold. Damn. There was no cure for a cold. There was nothing to be done. Absolutely no sense in taking Katherine to a medical centre. They'd just isolate her until she died then sterilize and cremate the body. Much better that she died in her own bed. At least Geneva would be there.

Richard paced. She might not die. Some people pulled through. Maybe it wasn't that serious a strain. Maybe it was one of those cold bugs from before they began messing with cold bugs. He knew it wasn't. That never happened. If someone got a cold it was always the killer strain, the one they'd accidentally created when they tried to manipulate the virus, played with its DNA. They'd actually sold it to people, promised the cure to the common cold. Bastards. He kicked the ground because there was nothing else to kick, sent a little clod of earth flying.

"Aw, man. Oh man." He felt the hurt beneath the anger. "What to do?" And the answer, of course, was nothing. Nothing could be done.

He found himself at the buffalo pens, slipped through the pole fence to walk among them. He hadn't planned on coming here. He'd been walking around angry and when the anger dissipated he found himself among these animals. Maybe that's how it happened. Maybe his anger brought him here, or maybe he knew somehow that anger couldn't survive for long among them.

The rock where the buffalo rubbed themselves sat in a hollow gouged by hooves and large bodies that rolled and tossed. Most people believe that they rubbed against the rock to relieve an itch, that it was just a scratching rock, a louse killer. Richard had formed a different idea. He'd watched them and it didn't seem like that was what they were doing. It seemed more like they were trying to get closer to the rock; they rubbed against it the way a cat rubs against a person's leg, but not quite. Cats rub against people to put their scent on them, to mark their territory, to say *this person belongs to me.* Buffalo came to the rock to get closer to it somehow; it was more ceremonious, something akin to worship, as though the rock was an altar, something sacred, and rubbing was a form of prayer. But those were just his ideas.

He spent the night there with his back to the buffalo's altar, touched it sometimes, ran a hand over its smooth parts, greasy from the tallow of their hides. He'd found that special place within just before sunset as the light became dim, and he'd spoken to the universe. "*Hey you, it's me, Richard. You know I never ask for anything for myself, all I want is to understand. But today I need a favour. I need some help here. I know you don't interfere much, let us make our mistakes and adjust the universe accordingly. If you could, if you would, please look after Katherine, give her good health. Help her get through this. And look out for Geneva too, would you?*"

The dim light had turned to dark. There was no moon tonight. It was in that final stage, the dying stage. A sliver might show itself before dawn, but not likely given the clouds. With the darkness had come silence and both now felt thick, smothering. There was depth to the darkness, almost solid, so solid that sound didn't penetrate. Occasionally a buffalo stirred, moved around, something blacker than the night; something, it seemed to him, only slightly more real than the dark.

He stayed, not moving, waiting perhaps, waiting for light. He pulled his knees up and hugged them for warmth in the last hours before dawn, sat huddled and shivering. There was no reason not to go to his cabin and the warmth of his bed. He thought about it. No reason at all to stay here. But it didn't seem right. It seemed better to be here with the buffalo at their altar.

He tried to imagine what Katherine might be going through. It wasn't good.

Twenty-four hours, they said. Twenty-four hours was all it took. Quick. One day good — a sniffle, a little cough — and the next day gone. Today, after the sun came up, today she would walk out of the Earthship, or they would carry her out. He tried not to hope, consciously tried to stay in the moment, in the dark, feel the cold on his skin, the moisture in the air, but he couldn't. The moment always turned to daylight, to hope.

He spoke again to the universe in those moments of light as the sun began to rise. *"Hey you, thank you for everything, thank you for today. Know what I'd like to see today? I'd like to see Geneva and Katherine today, that's what I'd like."*

And he did. Early afternoon she came out, Geneva at her elbow. "I needed some sunshine." Katherine's voice was a bit weak still, but she was obviously past the worst of it. Geneva helped her into a reclining lawn chair. She leaned it back and stretched out full in the heat of the sun. "Now I know why they call it a cold. It felt like my bones were in a freezer, just couldn't get warm."

"Do you need anything?" Richard was the only one near other than Geneva. The rest of the Ashram kept back, out of range of a cough or a sneeze.

"Yeah," she sat up, "my hair feels a mess. Could you get me a brush?"

"Just happen to have one." And he did. In the pack, the pack that he carried everywhere, that had become so much a part of him.

He'd intended to offer the brush to her, simply hand it over, but when he got to her chair and looked down at her sitting there, still weak, slouched slightly, he changed his mind and began to brush her hair. It was one of those things, unplanned, a simple act of kindness, that changed both of their lives forever.

Raven remembers his cousins Huginn and Muninn, the ravens of Odin. They sat on his shoulders and spoke into his ear. They told the God King all the happenings, all the doings of men. They were his spies; flew out into the world and gathered the gossip, gathered the lies. But more than the words, more than the mutterings, Huginn and Muninn could hear the thoughts, hear the silent cries, hear the hate that burned behind men's eyes. They returned and croaked in whispers, of words and deeds, spoken, thought, and done.

And sometimes, very rare, a Shaman man did seek to learn their language, speak their tongue and learn from them who flew the whole world, one wise word to use. One word from Huginn, one word from Muninn, to change the shape of things, to shift between the worlds of man and beyond.

Raven remembers those old times, those days of Odin, when men sought to learn his language, to speak, to converse, and to learn.

43

Not like this.

They shouldn't have done it like this.

They should have gotten Robert Lane to summon her to his office, sit her down, show her the video and then tell her in person.

But this, this was an insult, to send her a message.

Someone didn't have the courage to say it to her face.

Conflict of interest, bullshit.

Richard wasn't a conflict.

Lenore closed her platform carefully, deliberately, not slamming it on the desk, not letting her anger rise. But it wasn't all anger. There was hurt there as well.

And there was no signature to the message. It came from no one, from higher up, a superior with no name. And the evidence was a video of her and Richard in the Blackwater Café. Not disputable. A video of her going to the Ashram.

Conflict of interest because he had a criminal record, and because she had prosecuted him.

Continued association with the subject can have permanent repercussions with regard to your appointment as a prosecutor. Conduct yourself accordingly.

It wasn't right. They didn't know Richard. Didn't know anything about him other than he had a criminal record and that she had stayed charges against him.

She picked up the platform to read the message again, to make sure those were the exact words.

But no.

She changed her mind and put it down again without opening it. The truth was there was a conflict, but it was inside herself. Continued association with the subject would have repercussions for her and George.

Maybe the reprimand was a good thing.

A blessing.

Did George know?

Probably not.

Confidential communication from head office, encrypted, sterile. Maybe it was better this way, that they didn't have Robert Lane do it — the less people who knew, the better.

Her mind spun.

George, in her bedroom until morning.

Her career. She still had one, but with something like that on her record . . .

She'd kissed Richard, on the cheek, and said, "I'll give you a call." She remembered the feel of his bristly face on her lips. And that was the last she'd seen him, the last time she had touched him.

The message solved things.

The spinning slowed.

Where to from here?

Obviously, to George. But then what?

"I guess that's up to him." She spoke aloud to the empty office, her voice quiet. She would from now on conduct herself accordingly.

And she did.

That night, over supper with George in his apartment, she ate the pasta, and even laughed. Richard wasn't a secret.

Richard belonged to "before". She wasn't keeping anything from George. Their relationship started the night he'd brought her home from Bel Arial. She didn't expect him to tell her about every woman he had ever been with, and her past was likewise, simply her past.

It was easy. George started the talking. "If science hadn't been interfered with, we might be further along than we are. If the church hadn't censured Galileo, for example, and Copernicus' ideas about the sun being the centre of the universe had been allowed, who knows what else might have been discovered."

"Yeah," she agreed. "And if Prime Minister Harper hadn't fired the scientists in 2012, we might have seen it coming."

"Exactly, that's exactly where I was going." George looked pleased. They were connecting. They were on the same page. "And in both instances it was religion that interfered. With Galileo it was the Catholic Church, with Harper — everyone agrees that he was motivated by fundamental evangelical ideology."

"I read something," Lenore offered. "Can't remember who said it, but it goes something like this: From the time of Christ to one thousand AD, man's knowledge of the physical universe doubled once, between one thousand and the time of Galileo, about five hundred years, it doubled again. Then two hundred and fifty years later, by the time of the industrial revolution, it doubled again. Each doubling took half the amount of time. By the year two thousand it was doubling every six months, and now knowledge, it's doubling every week — soon it will double every day, every hour, every second."

George was quiet. The expression on his face indicated that he wasn't buying what she was saying.

"Yeah, the numbers are silly, but the idea still has some merit." Lenore felt defensive. "It goes along with what you were saying. Imagine where we would be if no one interfered, if the development of ideas progressed at its own pace."

"Well, it wasn't just Prime Minister Harper firing the scientists in twenty-twelve. They were making predictions, but I don't think anyone could have stopped what was coming."

She knew what he was talking about, everyone did. "The First Intra."

"The ecological collapse that led to the First Intra," he corrected. "That's what the scientists were warning about. I don't think anyone could have predicted all hell breaking loose. Maybe you're right. Maybe that doubling isn't out too much. But everything changed at the First Intra. Everything we have now is old technology, just put together in new ways. Sure, we have sky cities and ORVs and everything is faster, but . . . " He paused, perhaps for emphasis. "Everything we have now was possible fifty years ago. All of our fighting didn't advance anything. It set us back. We can't even imagine where we might have been if science hadn't been distracted. And it's not just technology. We're no further ahead now than we were fifty years ago when we consider human rights and justice and peace and truth."

Lenore didn't really care, she recognized the conversation as simply the putting of words into the air; nice safe conversation simply for the sake of conversation. She forked a bit more pasta, not thinking about it, put it in her mouth. She pushed aside the image of the simmering pot. She wanted her mind filled with George, with ideas.

She wanted his mind to be filled with her; wanted both of them filled with a sense of togetherness, of shared ideas, shared thoughts; maybe she wanted a shared life.

44

HE RAN HIS FINGERNAILS OVER HER bare knee. She stretched out and put both her feet on his lap and leaned back on the arm of the couch. She looked like a cat wanting its belly rubbed. He took in the full length of her. It was the first time he had ever really looked at her, all of her, filled his eyes with her. He rubbed her bare foot with his left hand, massaged it. His eyes followed the bones in her shins, a little dent and a scar just below the right knee; a fall, he imagined, when she was a little girl learning to ride a bicycle. The hem of her pleated skirt lay just above the knee, something tartan, with reds and browns; her legs were thin, raw-boned. Her white blouse was loose, probably cotton, open at the throat; short sleeves showed her sinewy arms. There was another scar there as well, jagged across the left bicep. Second Intra, he guessed, shrapnel. That arm lay across her midsection. Her other elbow rested against the back of the couch, in her hand a small glass of wine, a glass of whisky in his right.

He liked what he saw. Her nose was a little too long, maybe; it jutted, and her skin was beginning that transition from smooth and supple to showing the first signs of grain and thin lines.

In this intimate moment, with each of them relaxed in the other's company, George felt the need to tell her. "I know this guy . . . Isadore," he began. "Really interesting. Some of the things he told me . . . " He faltered, then caught the thread of what he wanted to say and told her the story of getting caught in the storm, of the beating he took, of Isadore and Betsy and their children, and he told her the story of Two Bears.

Lenore listened without comment, let him tell the entire saga.

"And Two Bears said, 'You were a spirit travelling across the universe, just a little dot of blue light, then you met the Creator and the Creator was both spirit and physical at the same time and you said *I want to be like that.* So you came to this world so that you could experience the physical.'" George recited Two Bears' words from memory. He'd repeated the story to himself several times in the last weeks, tried to find the meaning in it, tried to experience it, imagine himself as a dot of blue light. He was, for a few moments at a time, able to imagine his life as a journey.

He wanted to share that idea about life as a journey with Lenore, wanted her to join him on that path the Indians talked about: the good red road. The moment was nice, the whisky in his belly warm, and his hand on her foot . . .

"'While you're here, you should keep the Creator in your mind all the time. Never let anyone come between you and him, and never come between someone else and the Creator.' That's what Two Bears told me."

Light began to show on the eastern horizon as George climbed into the ORV Raven. Half an hour, that's all he wanted, to be there in the sky when the sun burst free of the night. He stepped the ORV from the roof, let himself fall a fraction of a second longer than usual before he spread wings, tilted his head back and felt the force of the swoop against his body. He banked right, gently, in a long easy turn to avoid the building across the street, then, once out over the lake, he put the ORV into a steady spiralling ascent, rising over the city.

The clear sky promised another hot day, even with the wind that came across from the west and rippled the water. But that would be later; now he was up where he wanted to be, soaring. And there was the sun, an arc beginning to rise from the horizon. It always amazed him how quickly it came up. It only took a minute from when it first showed until it was a complete circle, free from the Earth.

He let the ORV glide, tilted now and again, just an easy gentle ride to start the day. Sky, lake, city, and Lenore down there still asleep in his apartment. He'd wanted to tell her about the Thunder Bird. He'd started to tell her and ended up telling her the story of Isadore and Betsy instead. Maybe it was that look on her face when he told her about Two Bears, that look of disbelief.

Maybe he should let her fly the ORV. Maybe after she'd had a few hours up here. Maybe then he would tell her. It might make more sense then, maybe. And if she discovered that she liked flying, maybe they could buy an ORV for her, then there would be two of them in the sky to meet the sunrise. He turned his head a little to the right and lifted his left arm, stretched it back and the ORV turned in a gentle bank and began a spiral down, back to the city, and another day of work.

45

"Never heard of Tarasoff's Farm? Come on, Gus, how long have you been here?"

"Eight years."

"And, you've never heard of Tarasoff's Farm?"

Gus shook his head. "No."

"Thought everyone knew about that place. It's a very old organic farm. Peter Tarasoff runs it now," Richard explained. "He tolerates a few visitors at a time, feeds you, shows you how to grow your own food, and how to look after soil. It's Katherine's idea."

"So, it's a research project, then."

"Something like that. If Peter accepts us."

"Oh." Gus smiled a big Gus Grafos smile. "So, just the two of you?"

Richard understood the question and chose not to answer it. "It's for the Ashram." He slung the leather bag over his shoulder so that it hung in its familiar spot. Never forget the bag.

46

PETER TARASOFF WELCOMED THEM AT THE gate. "The couple from Hayden's Ashram. I wanted to greet you personally." He offered his hand to Katherine.

"And we definitely wanted to meet *you*," she replied.

Richard nodded and smiled as he shook Peter's hand, noting his extremely gentle grip.

"Well, come up to the house. I suspect we have lots to talk about." Peter Tarasoff turned and led the way to the two-story multi-windowed building.

"How was harvest?" Richard looked at the stubble-covered field that sloped away toward the south.

Peter stopped as though surprised by the question and spoke very earnestly, "As you no doubt know, harvest always provides something to be thankful for. This year again, the Earth has provided us with what we need, and a little extra that we might share."

Not quite the answer that Richard was looking for. He'd meant quantity and quality. That was wheat stubble on the field and it looked like it had grown thick. He wanted to know bushels per acre. What was the yield? Perhaps he was not going to get that sort of answer from Peter. Perhaps Peter was beyond the simplicity of numbers, beyond economics.

There were twelve guests for the week. They would all stay in the big house, except for Richard and Katherine. Peter showed them to a small guesthouse with thick walls. It was nothing more than a single room with two beds, a wood stove and a counter under the only window with a basin and ewer. Richard checked. The ewer was filled with water.

"I thought as Ashram members you'd be more comfortable here."

Katherine was gracious: "Why thank you so much, Peter. How thoughtful of you."

"This was our first experiment with straw bale construction." Peter rapped the wall with his knuckles.

"I don't know it," Katherine admitted.

Peter took his time, as though he had been granted more time than an ordinary person. He explained about building a frame of timbers, and filling the frame with flax straw formed into bales. "Flax straw because it doesn't rot." Then a thick layer of plaster over it all, weather proof, naturally insulated and all local materials. He made a small hand gesture at the room. "There are no nails in here."

"Really?" Richard looked around. He knew something about construction and to build without nails, well, it was possible. "But why?"

"To see if we could do it. An act of defiance, to be completely independent." Peter had a little smile on his old wrinkled face. "Check out the floor. I bet you've never been in a building with a dirt floor before."

"No, I haven't." Katherine knelt and ran a hand over it. "Dirt? . . . Really? But how?"

"Carefully . . . put down a layer of soil. Tamp it. Another layer, tamp it, then another and another and the final layer is clay and over top of that you build a fire and bake it, then sand it all smooth, and then Doreen Kalmakoff comes with her paints and does her artwork." His pride came through his words.

"It's beautiful." Katherine stood again. "We should have taken our shoes off at the door."

Peter left them with an "enjoy it", and leaning heavily on his diamond willow walking stick, made his way back toward the main house.

"A house made of straw," Richard joked, "Makes you think of the big bad wolf."

47

Supper was late. It was already quite dark. The last guests had just arrived, three women from the university. Peter took his place at the head of the long dining table. "If you'd been any later, there might not have been any crabapple cider left."

"It's very good." Richard lifted a heavy glass toward the women. It was filled with golden cider. And it was very good; there was a distinct rich sweetness beneath the sharp tart taste of the recently pressed crabapples.

"Everything you are going to eat over the next several days has been grown here at Tarasoff Farm." It sounded like Peter had made this speech many times before.

Katherine took Richard's hand under the table and squeezed it.

He liked that, liked that Katherine was happy.

There were eighteen people at the table, all dressed similarly in clothes for work, with no attempt at fashion. They ranged in age from a teenage boy who ate in a frenzy, his plate piled high — Richard guessed the boy was a resident — to the very old Peter, eighty and maybe even older than that. The woman at Peter's left seemed to go out of her way to take care of him. She might have been his daughter, Richard wasn't sure. Maybe she was his wife.

"Each of you have your own reasons for being here. Some have come to learn about soil, some have come to learn history, others have come just for a holiday . . . " The teenaged boy stopped eating, put down his fork, and paid attention to Peter's opening statement.

"There has been a Tarasoff on this land since 1899. My great grandmother pulled the plough that first broke the prairie soil. We have to forgive them, they simply didn't know any better. In their day, the Saskatchewan River flowed full and they dug their homes into the riverbank. So I can say we were cave dwellers. My ancestors were cavemen and cavewomen." A thin smile showed on the old man's face. "In the early years we farmed not too much different than everyone else. The prairie was broken, the buffalo bones were picked and sold. Then in the time of my grandfather and my father, about 1980 or so, they changed and became what was then known as organic farmers, which simply meant that they rejected the use of chemicals, quit using pesticides and herbicides, and farmed the soil." He stopped for a taste of the apple cider.

"It was that decision that saved this place. That is the reason Tarasoff Farm is an oasis in the middle of a desert. Our neighbours, like most of the other farmers, quit thinking about the soil. The earth to them was simply a platform that they put seeds into and sprayed fertilizer over. They farmed the chemicals, not the soil. They got away with it for a long time, then the soil got sick. Most of them still didn't figure it out. They thought the soil was blowing away because of the drought. Hardly anyone realized that it was dying. They kept trying to farm it the same as before, put more chemicals onto it until they completely killed it. All that grey land that you drove past on your way here . . . "

Peter wasn't telling them anything that Richard didn't already know. Dead zones, where nothing would grow, where there was nothing but dust that wouldn't hold a seed, and when it rained, nothing but mud. Then the dead zones got bigger and bigger and connected with each other and the farmers abandoned their fields and their homes and moved to the city.

" . . . And they not only made their own soil sick. If they had only killed the soil on their own farms it might not have been so bad." Peter stopped again. He lowered his head as though remembering the death of a relative. "Over the next few days we are going to show you how we resuscitated the soil, how we've breathed life back into it. We share with you, hoping you will take these ideas home and put them to use. Everything is free. All of this is our giving back something to the Earth, because the Earth has provided for us all of our lives, and the lives of our ancestors. We wouldn't be here if not for her."

The teenaged boy bowed his head.

Richard remembered old photos and videos of the Saskatchewan prairie, of wheat fields golden and waving, of grain elevators, and combines, and busy little towns. He tried to keep that image of what once was, but despite his efforts the image was replaced with the reality of the journey here, across a grey desert that stretched away as far as he could see. The slightest wind lifted the fine dust and swirled it in grey ghosts that danced across the dunes. Their vehicle had hit drifts heaped across the roadway; the dust behaved like feathers that blew away with their passing. It wasn't until now, until Peter's words, that Richard recognized the dust as the corpses of living entities.

48

RICHARD WAS INTERESTED IN THE MACHINERY, the work involved in farming. Katherine was here to listen to Peter expound upon the ideas of farming. He tried to listen to what Peter was saying, tried to be interested for Katherine's sake, so that later, in the cabin, when she, in her excited voice, went back over the lecture and its implications, he could participate, or at least have something relevant to say.

But the morning light pulled his mind toward the river, just a trickle now. The glaciers in the Rocky Mountains were gone. There were no ice fields to feed the Saskatchewan River or the Athabasca or the Columbia. There were years when the Saskatchewan didn't flow. But there were also years when extreme rains fell in the mountains and foothills and the river flooded, tore away homes, bridges, and swept that huge valley clean of any cattle that might have been grazing there. After a dozen major flood experiences, people had learned to avoid the valley.

"Soil is a cycle, it's a life, it's a complexity of relationships. It is not a thing." The sheer force of the old man's words drew Richard back to what he was saying. "There are cycles within cycles within cycles." Peter had his hands to his head, his fingernails to his temples. "The simplest is the nutrition cycle. Everyone should know this one. A plant dies, falls down, rots, we call that compost. The rain carries the nutrients from the decaying plant material deeper into the soil. Then new plants reach down with their roots, collect the nutrients and carry them back to the surface, then that plant dies and falls down and becomes compost again. You see, there's no need for a plough. People thought it was up to them to turn the soil over. It wasn't. The plants were doing it themselves and much more efficiently."

"So, if you're not turning the soil over." Katherine stepped forward a quarter step to ask her question. "Does that help the soil, I mean as a living organism, is it hurt by machinery?"

"I think the question is . . . " Peter was addressing the entire audience but he turned to face her, "does turning the soil over, running a plough through it or cultivators, or rototillers, hurt the soil? I think it does. Everything depends for its life on water, right? Turn the soil over and it's much more likely to dry out. But I'm really of two minds on this. I don't like ploughs and cultivators and I especially can't stand the violence of a rototiller. Somehow they just seem abusive to the earth. If we think of the soil as though it was a living body, then slicing and dicing and chopping certainly must be harmful." He paused. "The soil is at once a single living body and at the same time it is also trillions of microbes living in complex communities, and soil has history and memory, and experiences emotions. It mourns, knows sadness, and it also knows joy and desire. Who was the first farmer of the prairie? Who first deliberately planted? Selected which grains he was going to grow? Where he was going to plant? Who first cultivated the soil?" He looked around the group. "Anyone . . . "

Peter didn't hold out long for a reply. "The buffalo . . . imagine millions of Bison across the prairie, their hooves cultivating the soil, churning the top layer. Now the thing about most grass seeds is that the grass puts a hard shell around her tiny little babies, designs them to pass through a bison. So after the bison cultivates, it plants and at the same time fertilizes. And so he's our first farmer. But he doesn't work alone at this. He has an agreement with the grass that he prefers to provide good quality seed that meets his digestive requirements. He has a contract with the dung beetles to spread things around for him. And he has a contract with the soil, that everything he takes from it he is going to put back.

"What do you think was the first crime committed by the first European settlers here?" Peter searched the little audience for an answer, received none, only head shakes and shoulder shrugs. "The first crime was to pick up the bones. The bison had an agreement with the soil that the soil would provide for him, and in the end the bison would give his body back to the soil. Humans interfered in that contract, picked up the bones and loaded them on trains for a couple of dollars. And maybe the demise of the bison is in part because of that broken contract with the soil. But I have nothing to really substantiate that, so we won't go there."

Richard's attention was drawn by a flock of snow geese away toward the river again. He tried to guess at their numbers. A hundred, maybe more? It was almost autumn after all, they should be migrating. But, where to go? Sunlight caught them as they lifted momentarily above the rim of the valley, showed them in their finest white, brilliant against the mostly grey landscape.

Only the river valley and the draws, the deep places where humans did not destroy the soil, continued to sustain plant life. The green places, just beginning to show their autumn colours, a few yellows and reds, created a wandering pattern over the earth. Richard knew there would be deer in there, and rabbits, and maybe even grouse. He took Katherine's hand for no reason other than in that moment it felt right.

"They say the farmers pushed the Indians off the land," Peter continued his lecture, "but the land didn't belong to the Indians. Even they would tell you the land belonged to the Buffalo. When the farmers came and divided up this prairie, the Indians were already put away on reservations, and the buffalo had been hunted down for their hides, loaded on trains and sent east." Peter's voice was matter-of-fact. "That's just the way it was. To the farmer, history started with him, he was the pioneer, the hero of this place. In his mind he saved the land from the wilderness, improved it, made it productive. There was a family every quarter mile." He gave an expansive wave of his arm toward the horizon. "A rush of a million people just to the Saskatchewan area, homesteaders, and the beautiful soil grew crops that astounded them. They were truly in the land of milk and honey, they built roads and schools and towns and railroads. A time of plenty. And then the rains stopped." His voice lowered. "And the winds came from the west, and the soil they had turned over, exposed to the sun, dried out and blew away. That was the first exodus from this land, the 1930s, the dust bowl.

"But do you think we learned anything?" Peter's voice full strength again. "Not on your life. That first hit drove most of them off the land, into the cities. The farms got bigger. At the height of farming here, the average size farm was up to about twenty square miles.

"How does one man look after that much soil? Try to imagine it. Twenty square miles and he's farming it with monster-sized machinery. He has no relationship with it. All he's doing is driving a machine that puts seeds down, and nitrogen, and more nitrogen, and then when the plants begin to grow, he sprays them to kill the plants he doesn't want, and he sprays them again to kill any bugs that he doesn't like. And he never gets out of the machine. He has more of a relationship with his tractor than he does with the soil."

Peter shook his head, sadly. Katherine snuggled against Richard's side.

"But that's okay." Peter continued. "The soil didn't need to have a relationship with the farmer. It was already in a complex relationship with the sky and the Earth. This entire biosphere . . . " he waved both arms outward," is an interplay between the mineral earth and the atmosphere — between ground water and sunlight. There's a spiritual connection here — between Mother Earth and Father Sky. And that's where we are . . . "

Richard missed the rest of what Peter was saying. His mind drifted. He tried to imagine himself as spirit, disconnected from the physical. He understood the sky part better than the earth part. He did after all pray to the universe, to the beyond, to the greatness of everything out there, to the mystery. He'd always imagined his spirit as somehow intermingled in the equation of space and time. Now he tried to imagine it as part of the earth that he stood upon. He usually imagined his spirit as something that came out of his head, something that went with his prayers upward, outward. Now he thought about his feet.

It didn't work.

Nothing happened.

He could not experience his spirit flowing downward. He looked at his feet, at his boots, good solid leather with a durable sole, deep treads, and a steel shank for arch support.

49

THE SOFT LIGHT OF A LATE summer dawn filled the cabin. It woke Richard with its pressure as it poured through the east window. He was still tangled with Katherine, arms, legs and blankets. His first thought was that he was late, that he had missed his morning prayers, had not stood out there and spoke to the sunrise, to the universe. He considered getting out of bed, pulling his arm out from under her, probably waking her up if he did. He even began to ease the wool blanket off his shoulder but changed his mind when the cold air touched his nakedness.

Instead, he said his prayers there, in the bed, in whispers, with her wrapped around him, and for the first time included her in his communiqué with the great mystery, for her good health, her happiness, and a "thank you for this person to share this adventure with."

"I heard that." He felt her breath on his shoulder, her voice still sleepy; with a soft "Mmmmm" she moved closer against him.

The knock on the door was sharp, like someone was hitting it with something. Not the soft muffled rap of a knuckle.

It was Peter, walking stick in hand. "Not too early, I hope."

Richard, barechested, pants scrambled into, belt undone, its end dangling. "No, no, not at all."

"Sorry, I took you two for morning people. You just seemed the type."

Katherine casually pulled on a knit sweater, unashamed of her exposed skin. She spoke once her head was through. "We usually are. That's a really nice bed there, hard to get out of."

"Especially when you're young." Peter smiled an old man smile, all wrinkles and amusement.

Katherine shared his humour with an easy and bright smile. “Well, we’re up now.”

“Come for a little walk with me.”

There had been a frost overnight, one of those rare occurrences in September when the sky is clear and a high-pressure system brings cold air down from the north. A lone raven watched them pass, stood still on the edge of an outbuilding. Only its eyes moved.

“Something I wanted to show you.” Peter led the way. “This isn’t part of the normal lecture, not something I share with those people from the university, you know. It’s because you guys are from an Ashram. I thought maybe you’d understand it.”

“How’s that?” Richard wasn’t sure what the old man meant.

“An Ashram by its very nature is a spiritual place.” Peter stopped beside a small two-wheeled trailer with a galvanized metal tank on it. “When I saw your names on the list, I knew you were the ones. What I’ve learned I want to pass along. And like it or not, you’re the ones I chose.” He spoke with the blunt authority of an elder. “Let me go back a wee bit.” He leaned his stick against the trailer and sat down beside the tank. “When I was just a little guy, this Indian came to visit my dad. His name was Alec Whiteplume. The one thing I remember him saying was the soil was alive and that if he staked me out on the ground, within a couple of weeks the soil would start to eat me. For some reason that has stuck in my head all my life. Now you take that idea and you blend it with my Doukhobor background and you get a Christianized slant on things. Now don’t get me wrong.” He looked directly into Richard’s eyes. “I know that if you take two religions and you mix them together all you get is mixed up. But, this idea that there is a God, and that the earth is also part of God just seems right to me somehow." He looked away toward the horizon, at the first yellow leaves on the aspen. "Alec said that he belonged to the land because his ancestors were part of the soil, that when they died they went back to the earth and the plants that grew had his ancestor's atoms in them. And he ate those plants, and he ate the animals that ate those plants and he was part of the cycle. Now from the Christian side, there's the Genesis story. Remember this one, about Cain and Abel?"

Katherine shook her head.

Peter explained. "Cain was the first born of Adam and Eve. He was the first farmer. His brother Abel raised sheep. They both made an offering to God. Cain offered vegetables and Abel offered the first born from his flock. God favoured Abel's offering over Cain's. That got Cain pissed off and he killed Abel. Now usually this story is told about the first murder. What I find intriguing is that God wanted a blood offering." He patted the tank beside him. "From the abattoir."

"You're putting it on the soil." Richard looked around, looking for evidence of it, for redness.

"It's the only thing that I've found in my lifetime that works." Peter stood up. Took his walking stick. "God wants a blood offering, or the earth wants a blood offering. I don't know which. All I know is that if you put blood in the soil, it comes back to life."

Richard looked out at the dead prairie, at the grey sifting dust. It was going to take a lot of blood to bring it all back . . .

"I think I understand." Katherine broke the long pause, put words out into the cold air. "It's about life. We eat too much dead stuff." She stepped a bit closer. "Like all the chemicals they once used here." She waved at the grey prairie. "When they farmed this, they put stuff in the soil that had never been alive, nitrogen and phosphates that were the leftovers from industry, from oil and gas. The plants grew, but they had no life in them. Now if soil is a living thing, like you say . . . " she nodded toward Peter, "then when it's healthy, the plants that grow out of it will draw that life up. It will be part of them."

"And when you eat those plants," Peter added, "you take that life into yourself. And if the soil is healthy, then the plants are healthy and full of life and when you eat them, then you are healthy and full of life, and when you die, as all of us must, then you go back to the soil."

"Yeah." Richard started to get it.

"Now take it a little further, back to the idea of God and earth being related. We know that there is a whole lot of life under the soil, right?"

"Well, there used to be a lot more," Katherine answered.

"Granted, but even so, there's still about fifty thousand different species living under the surface. There's more species under the surface than above. See those aspens over there?" He pointed toward a coulee that extended up away from the river. "How many trees do you think are in there?"

Both Katherine and Richard shook their heads. There were too many and they were too far away to count.

"Probably just one." Peter answered his own question. "One single organism connected through a web of roots. Most of it is underground. All we see are the parts that harvest sunlight. Now that's what's amazing. If there is a God and he is somehow connected to Mother Earth, then those plants know that. They live in both worlds. They're the only ones that do. Us surface dwellers only know one dimension."

Richard looked down at the grass between his boots. He was beginning to understand how the universe was put together at a new level — a little closer than the cosmos. He heard: "That's why plants are medicine," and then he wasn't listening as Peter went on. His mind returned to the bed and the night before. She had simply walked naked across the room from her bed to his and crawled in without saying a word. Not that any words were needed.

Did he love Katherine?

Probably.

But did he love her the way she loved him? Hers was a romantic love. His was more practical. He could live with her for the rest of his life, however long that might be.

Did it matter? In the long term would it make a difference?

Her romantic notions would diminish in time and she would end up loving him the same way he loved her.

50

EMILY WAS SPEAKING AROUND THE PINS in her mouth, "That's the most romantic thing I've ever heard of Today was the day, him brushing your hair like that."

"It's because he wasn't trying." Katherine turned so that Emily could pin the hem of the long black dress. "If I'd thought for one second that he was trying, it probably would've turned out different." She looked toward the window, deeply recessed into the wall of the Earthship. The light struck the floor at a low angle, not steep as it had at the height of summer, when the sun at this time of day was high overhead. In June the rectangle of light from the window barely reached the table. This September sun was lower, noticeably. The days were shorter, and the light had changed; softer, it lacked the intensity of July when the sun had definite force to it.

Where had the summer gone?

Flown away in a whirlwind, a whirlwind of falling and being.

She'd fallen in love with him before Tarasoff's. She'd fallen in love with him before the last soft strokes of the brush, before he'd put it back in his pack, before he'd said, "There, now you look all pretty again."

It was true. It was because he wasn't trying. He'd simply taken a moment to show her who he really was, a man of gentleness and kindness. He'd simply shown he cared. And then at Tarasoff's it all clicked together beautifully, naturally, when he'd gently taken her hand and held it. She remembered the cabin with the painted floor, how she'd crossed it and crawled into Richard's bed and neither of them said a word, beautifully, naturally.

Maybe, she thought, it was because she had come close to death with that cold, had looked at death, had lain freezing on a bed, shivering and afraid. Geneva had piled blankets on her, had heated bricks in the oven and put them under the heavy blankets and still she had not found warmth. A day and a night, and during it she'd sweated, poured water out of every pore. She'd lain in that wet bed without the strength to lift her head. Then it passed, as quickly as it had come, and she'd wanted to be outside because she was alive.

Maybe it was because he came to her in the first minutes of her new life. Maybe that was what it was about, about life, more than companionship, more than sex.

Maybe it was because she had been afraid, afraid to die and never see the people again. She remembered her fear, and her anger at the scientists who'd manipulated DNA and created a monster. The common cold didn't need a cure. That's what made it common. It had always been a few days of discomfort.

But people wanted comfort, didn't want to feel a little ache, a runny nose, a sore throat.

Richard had said that DNA was our original instructions, written in code and placed in every part of our very being. These were the rules we were to follow on our journey. You don't take the map and scribble on it and expect to find your way.

He'd quoted Max Planck. *Science cannot solve the ultimate mystery of nature. And that is because, in the last analysis, we ourselves are part of nature and therefore part of the mystery that we are trying to solve.*

Richard.

And she was going to marry him.

Thursday.

On the equinox.

The day of equality, the day of equal day and night.

She was going to wear black.

Not because it was different.

It was different.

It was definitely different.

It was because she was Swedish, and traditionally in Sweden brides wore black, and she wanted to honour her ancestors. Her great-grandmother, Pia Enocson, would have been proud of her. Her ancestors on her father's side, the Indian side, they would have been proud of her also.

"Okay, take it off now." Emily didn't have any pins left in her mouth.

"I want to see it first." Katherine took a step in the direction of the full-length mirror that hung on the inside of the heavy wooden door. She wanted to see what she looked like.

"No." Emily stopped her. "Trust me, I have it perfect, and I don't want you to mess it up moving around. Now take it off and I'll finish sewing it. You'll see it when it's done."

51

RICHARD PUT ON HIS COAT, HIS wedding coat. Today was the day.

Gus Grafos was there, happy and bouncy and helpful, the only way that Gus could be. "Let me brush that." He meant the coat.

"Sure." Richard stood still, his arms straight down while Gus stroked his shoulders, back and sleeves with a small oval lint brush.

"There." Gus straightened the tie, made it snug against Richard's collar, stood for a moment to admire his handiwork.

Under the pine tree at precisely noon on the autumnal equinox, Katherine promised the rest of her life to Richard, and four women stood behind her as she said it. And Richard promised Katherine the rest of his life, and Gus with a big proud smile stood behind him. While Richard was speaking his words of promise, looking a very radiant Katherine in the face, he felt a warmth in his chest somewhere close to his heart, and he realized that he meant the words, "All my love, all I have and all I am, and only you, forever and ever, my wife."

He paused, took a breath. "All I have is my body, all I am is a man."

52

"I'm PREGNANT."

"How'd that happen?"

Lenore laughed. "You really don't know?"

"I'm sorry. Bit of a surprise. I just assumed . . . "

"No, I wasn't on birth control."

"That's what I meant."

The conversation wasn't going well. They both knew the real question was, *now what?*

She didn't want to ask, *do you want me to keep it?* She wanted him to say first. She wasn't even sure what she wanted him to say — *My darling, let's have this baby and a family and live happily ever after;* or *We have careers to consider, now is not the right time.*

She also had to consider her age; she was way past the best years for childbearing. If she wanted to be perfectly rational, she should have an abortion. But she wasn't perfectly rational. The bubbling pot was in the way. An abortion would be the same as a pot. But could she participate in bringing a baby into the world, into a world that might collapse again at any time and someone might put her baby into a pot?

Could she hold a baby? Could she even look at a baby? Change it, wash it, feed it, put it to her breast?

George wasn't any help. "Whatever you decide." She saw that he meant to be supportive, to be courageous, to stand with her, whatever that meant. But he didn't know, he wasn't thinking it through. She could see he was caught in a whirl of emotion and didn't want to show it.

They stood facing each other, wordless, waiting.

Someone needed to decide something.

She looked into the blue of his eyes. *He damn well better be man enough to handle this.*

The moment grew. And then he opened his arms, reached out silently.

She stepped forward, into those arms; they wrapped around her. She buried her face in his shoulder. It was going to be all right. It really was.

53

"THANK YOU FOR COMING."

"Yeah, well . . . " George couldn't think what else to say. *I didn't come for this. I didn't even know that he had died. Lenore is at her mother's for the long weekend and I decided to come out here to say hello, and maybe, just maybe, pick up some little piece of wisdom to help me through the next part of my life.*

The camp was filled with people standing in groups, sitting in groups, eating, drinking tea. There was even coffee brewing. No one seemed to be doing anything other than visiting. He couldn't tell from the behaviour of those gathered that it was a funeral. There was way too much laughter. People seemed to go out of their way to tell humorous antidotes, to tease, but only in the gentlest way, just enough to bring a smile.

"You'll stay with us tonight." Betsy patted his arm.

"Of course he will," Isadore confirmed.

George was about to say thank you, when the entire camp went suddenly silent. A woman walked up to the plain plank coffin, looked down at Two Bears. She turned to face them.

"Thank you all for coming to say goodbye to my brother. Thank you for coming to stand with our family at this hard time." Her voice was strong, proud, and carried to the edge of the camp.

"Tomorrow we'll take him up on the mountain and leave him there. He loved these mountains. He loved being here. He loved all of you and this camp. This was his life. This was his purpose." She spread her hands outward, a gesture that included their entirety: mountains, valley, lake, camp, people. "He was born here. This was his home, his connection point. As you all know, he was given a gift, he could go over to that other world and get help for the people from over there. And he did. Many of you were helped by him. He sacrificed for the people. That was his love."

George missed the rest of what she was saying. Not that he couldn't hear. Her voice continued to carry on the strength she put into it. He was distracted by his own thoughts. Who was he going to ask for help, now that Two Bears was gone? His life was changing. He was going to be a father. He couldn't imagine that. It was too far away. He'd thought about going out and getting good and drunk, but changed his mind, packed an extra flask of plasma into the Raven, and had flown here instead. Now it seemed for nothing. The man he wanted to talk to wasn't here.

"That's the way we do this, at this time." The sister's voice drew him back. "We laugh and remember the good times. And when we see someone grieving, we give a hug and a smile and say something cheerful, to help them through their hard time."

George began to understand a little of what was going on around him. The joking didn't come from a lack of respect. It came from a need to overcome the sadness, to laugh despite the pain.

The sister spoke for a long time about Two Bears, his childhood, that he had never married. "He carried his burden alone."

George wondered about the two words. Sometimes she called it a gift, sometimes a burden. Which was it? Or were they the same thing? He was beginning to look for a place to sit down, his legs were getting tired. He shifted from one foot to the other. The cup of tea that Betsy had given him was long empty. The cup dangled from his finger looped through the handle, held at his side. That was good tea. It would be nice to have another, his mouth was dry.

Her speech was obviously unprepared. There was no order to it. She rambled from one theme to another, pausing occasionally, found a new thought and spoke on that until it was exhausted, then moved on to something else. Only after a long pause, when she looked exhausted, did she conclude with, "Now eat."

"His family is going to feed us now," Isadore said to George.

It was mostly Two Bears' family that served plates stacked with food, but others joined in as well. Betsy brought plates to George and Isadore. Maybe she was related. George wasn't sure. Then he was distracted by a hot cup of tea and deer meat cooked until it was falling apart, and wild turnips, a bit stringy. He wasn't accustomed to the texture, though he enjoyed their rich taste.

It wasn't until close to midnight, when the fires were burning low, that several others had spontaneously risen, walked up to the open coffin, and spoke about the man inside. After another meal as large as the first, George asked Isadore, "How did he die?"

"Went to bed and never got up."

"Heart attack?"

"Maybe. Don't know." Isadore's voice quieter: "Maybe he went over to the other side and decided not to come back."

Mountain nights are colder and darker than city nights. George didn't realize how cold he was until Betsy came up behind him and draped a blanket over his shoulders.

"It's a wake," Isadore said, wrapping himself in the woollen blanket. "That's why we stay awake. Someone has to stay with him, keep him company, until we take him up the mountain."

There were only a handful remaining: George and Isadore, their backs against a tree at the periphery of light from the low fire, another younger, more talkative group closer to the coffin, three women who sat together at a table, their voices quiet, and a young man who never said anything but kept himself busy hauling wood to the fires, boiling tea, going from group to group with a pot, filling cups.

Both George and Isadore put their hands over their cups when he came around the last time. They had had enough.

"It's okay." His voice clear and gentle and a little feminine. "I've got it covered. You can sleep if you want."

So George did, easily, leaned back into the tree a little more, wrapped the heavy blanket a little tighter, closed his eyes, and sleep grabbed him. He woke just before daybreak on his side, a tree root painfully against his ribs. The mountain peaks showed orange and rust against a bright blue sky.

There were a few more people now, moving down to the lake to wash up, some standing quiet, looking to the east. Not too far away, the young man with the feminine voice stood shirtless in the crisp morning, stood still, the light on his face and chest. It took George a full minute to realize the man was praying.

He shifted away from the root at his ribs, found a hollow that better fit his body, wrapped the blanket tighter, closed his eyes, *another five minutes*, and fell back to sleep. For hundreds of years needles had fallen from the pine in a thick layer that softened the warm earth that he let himself sink into.

Two Bears, and he was not alone. George sat up within his dream, his back pressed against the tree, held back the rising fear. Two Bears never said a word, just smiled down at him as he walked past, happy, content — free. He didn't stop or wave or otherwise acknowledge George beyond the smile. But that smile said more about Two Bears' place in the universe, and about Two Bears experiencing his new place, than if he had spoken.

Two Bears' companion also turned to look at him. George jumped, now fully awake, struggled to untangle himself from the wrapped blanket, untangle himself from the dream. It walked away like a man, then turned and looked directly at him, into him, into his very being. Two Bears' friend was a Thunder Bird, black, blacker than his ORV Raven, blacker than darkness, except for the eyes. There was light there, the light of an immense intelligence.

He wanted to tell Isadore about the dream, but Isadore had left. As the day got going his friend returned. "Oh yeah, well you were out and I decided it would be better to sleep with my wife than with you."

The right moment never happened. There always seemed to be someone around, someone telling a story, someone standing too close.

Two Bears' sister, Sakastew — Isadore said it meant sunrise, or maybe the way sunlight shone down — spoke again. "Today is the last time we will see our brother. Today we take him up there," she pointed toward a mountain, "and say our last goodbye. From today forward, we will not say his name. He will not be part of us anymore. We will carry him up there and then come back down. We've decided not to grieve for one year. We'll have the memorial today. He was a medicine man and we should not grieve for him.

"We need pallbearers. You — " she pointed at a man seated nearby, he stood. "You — " she chose another, and another. Each walked forward as they were called. Four . . . five . . . six . . . seven . . . George counted. "And you." She pointed in their direction. George turned to look at Isadore beside him.

"Uh huh, she means you."

"Me?"

"Yeah, you. Go on up there." Isadore touched George's elbow, started him walking toward the coffin.

He took a couple steps, unsure, stopped. Certain she was going to say, *No, I chose Isadore.* But she didn't. She stood there, waiting. The selected pallbearers stood in a loose line at the coffin, George took his place at the end. There was obviously a mistake. He shouldn't be here. He hardly knew Two Bears. Someone else, Isadore, should be here, not him.

"And now we'll say goodbye." Sakastew went to the coffin, leaned over and kissed her brother's forehead. Stood a long minute — quiet; then, with tears beginning to form, and a sniffle, she walked down the line of pallbearers, shaking hands with each of them in turn, accepting a hug here and there. She took George's hand, gently, looked into his face, another sniffle, "Thank you," then walked on.

She was closely followed by others that George assumed were family. They formed a line, the entire camp quietly lined up behind them. Each stopped at the coffin. Some bent over and kissed his forehead, others put a hand on his shoulder, others just stood there and looked down at the large man wrapped in a buffalo robe. Some took a long time; these usually came away crying, needing hugs from each of the pallbearers.

The line went on and on. Up to the coffin, say goodbye, shake hands with the pallbearers. Each handshake was different, some as gentle as feathers, others firm — even among the men, there were some that took his hand with an amazing gentleness. And the hugs — from people he had never seen before this morning. A skinny young girl, crying, put her head on his chest, her arms around him, and sobbed into his shirt, until he began to feel her sorrow, until he began to feel the experience becoming real.

He was the last in the line, the last to have his hand shook, the last to be hugged, the last to be thanked. When the last person came away from the coffin, walked down the line shaking hands, the first pallbearer joined in behind her, shook hands with the second pallbearer, and the second pallbearer joined in behind him, and the third and the fourth . . . until the man beside George turned and shook hands with him and it was done and George stood alone.

He helped to hold the lid in place while pallbearer number one nailed the coffin shut, echoes from the bang of the hammer repeated off the mountain.

Then, without ceremony, they picked up the coffin and started walking, carrying it on their shoulders. The camp followed. Two Bears wasn't light. The sharp edge of the coffin dug into George's shoulder. He struggled under the weight, tried not to stumble on the rough path, where there was a path.

It would not have been an easy walk, even without the load. The rock-strewn trail made walking difficult. It seemed that every step forward was also a step up. They stopped three times, put Two Bears down, caught their breath, looked out across the valley at the next mountain range; picked him back up, hoisted the mass onto their shoulders and forced their way forward and upward.

Someone had dug a grave, not very deep — but then in the rocky ground digging would not have been easy. He'd expected some sort of ceremony, for someone to say a few last words, but there wasn't one. They put him in the hole. There were two shovels. A couple of pallbearers immediately began throwing dirt and stones on top of the coffin. George and the rest stood and watched until the first two were tired and were replaced by two more. He took a turn, shovelled gravel, worked the spade into the pile and tossed it into the grave hole. Then they were done. There were a few final touches, the grave mound was rounded with the back of a shovel, a woman patted the soil down with her hands, picked out a few stones and tossed them aside. Then came a much easier walk back down to the camp. No one said anything.

"I've got to be heading back." George offered his hand to Isadore.

"No, you can't. You have to stay for the memorial." Isadore spoke matter-of-factly, as though what he said was completely obvious. His words silenced George who was about to say, "but I have to work tomorrow." Work was something far away and not at all relevant.

The memorial was a feast and a giveaway. Sakastew called people up and presented each with a gift, usually a blanket, handmade and beautifully coloured. Pallbearer number one, Allan Turns, was the first. Then another of the pallbearers, the guy who had walked directly in front of George, the guy he had accidentally kicked several times.

He waited for his name to be called. Did she know his name? Probably not. She'd point at him and he'd walk forward, collect his gift, shake her hand, maybe give her a hug.

She did not call his name, did not point at him. Had she forgotten him? He was one of the pallbearers. He was certain he should be called. The pile of blankets was getting low. All of the really nice ones had already been given out, and still he wasn't selected. Then the last one, to an old woman. He didn't understand. He'd been a pallbearer, selected and honoured to carry the man, and no gift, no recognition?

It wasn't until he was halfway to Edmonton, flying in the ORV, that he realized how much easier it was to fly now. After a year of taking the bird out nearly every day he was in good shape. No, it didn't take any effort to flap its wings, but if you repeatedly move your arms, even without straining . . .

That's what it was about. She hadn't selected him as an honour, she had chosen him to carry that heavy load because he looked like he was in good shape.

54

The concept of good and evil is a misinterpretation of the universe. It comes from a time when humans lived in caves. To them, the shift from day to night was not caused by the orbit of the Earth around the sun. It was a mystery. There was light, then there was dark. Nocturnal hunters, the big cats and wolves, would eat them if they went out at night, and sometimes might even come right into their caves. This is where good and evil came from. Cave people ascribed to the night all the terrors they could imagine — to the day they gave all the beauty that the light exposed. Hence the association of evil with black, with darkness, and white is always something good . . .

Richard's re-reading of *Virgil's Little Book on Virginity* was interrupted by Walter, and he wasn't coming over to invite Richard for a bowl of asparagus soup.

"You've been attending a lot of protests."

"I wouldn't say a lot. I've been to a few, the RAN thing and . . . well mostly the RAN thing."

"You were arrested once for that, if I'm not mistaken."

"Yeah, once." *Where was Walter going with this?* Of course he had been arrested: and released, the charges stayed. Everyone knew that. He sensed he should be careful with what he said.

"I'm not here to tell you what to do. I actually came as your friend." Walter gave a careful measured nod. "The word *expulsion* has been heard around the Ashram."

The word hit Richard hard. "Expulsion — what for? For protesting? For trying to save one little piece of the earth from destruction?"

"For putting the Ashram at risk."

"What risk?"

"People have been asked to leave before for drawing attention to us. You know as well as I do that the reason this Ashram has survived for as long as it has is because we

are not political. We don't take sides. And the world leaves us alone."

Richard sat there, his finger marking his place in the book on his lap. He had nothing to say, no answer to the threat: stop protesting or leave. He also didn't want to speak in that moment because he felt a surge of anger rising. *Who the hell was Walter to come here and threaten to have him expelled? After all that he had done, after all of his work. The Ashram owed him. He'd given as much as he'd received, probably more — more than some of the others, maybe even more than Walter.*

The silence dragged on and then Walter put carefully chosen words out. "Listen, Richard, I came as your friend. I just need you to know what's being said, that's all."

"And where do you stand in this?"

"I'm not taking sides. Like I said, I just came to tell you what's going around."

"Gossip." Richard spat the word.

"If you like, yeah, it's gossip. But you should take it seriously." Walter's tone softened. "At least for a while."

"What about Katherine?" Richard heard the irritation in his own voice, couldn't help it. It was there and it came out in his words.

"Nobody's said anything about Katherine."

They better not, was his thought. He didn't speak it, kept it. It was too packed with rawness to put into words and in any event his jaw was clenched too hard for him to speak.

But, what about Katherine? He placed a marker in the book and put it down on the table, looked at the door that Walter had left through. It was a good door. He'd built it himself from solid heavy planks. Doors were important. They were points of transition. When you build a door, you have to do it carefully, not just so they open smoothly and hang straight and keep the weather on the outside and the warmth on the inside; doors have a mystical quality, they are the physical manifestation of the passage between worlds. He'd chosen the boards for it, measured and marked and cut them with the utmost care. Now he was being told that he might have to pass through, go, leave, exit.

He belonged to this Ashram, had built his place here. Not just the door, the entire cabin and beyond. The ground out there contained his sweat, sweat that poured off him on those hot summer days when he was the only one working and everyone else sat in the shade drinking lemonade.

And, what about Katherine?

If he was expelled, so what. He could start again. He could build again. He could survive in the other world, even if it meant living in Regis. He was a man. He didn't need comfort. He could sleep under the steps of whatever house she lived in. But Katherine needed a home, a nest, a burrow. She needed a place, her place.

The Ashram was her place. He could not imagine her anywhere else. He could go, easily enough, but if he left, if he fought and lost and left, he'd have to leave Katherine as well.

55

SOMETHING HAD HAPPENED. KATHERINE WAS SURE. Something wasn't right. Since yesterday, something was up with Richard. It wasn't that he had kissed her on the forehead. He did that often enough. The kiss was the same. This morning he'd leaned over as she was sitting and gently, carefully, put his lips to her forehead. Then without a word, he'd gone out, out and about his business in the world — surely nothing different there.

It wasn't that he was quiet. He was always quiet. That was Richard's way, to not make noise, to not speak unless the words were worth uttering.

There was something in his face that worried her. The lines were deeper, it seemed. She liked that face, and the lines, and the way he smiled when he was with her. When he smiled at her he did not hold back like when he smiled for anyone else. With her it was always a wide-open smile that showed the one crooked tooth, that one on his left that jutted a bit. When he smiled at anyone else his mouth was lopsided as he consciously or unconsciously tried to hide that crooked tooth.

Today his smile had looked forced. The smile seemed obligatory, like he owed her a smile. He smiled with his mouth and not his eyes. It was a half-face smile, just the lower half, it didn't reach past his cheeks and his forehead remained furrowed.

Something wasn't right. She wondered if it was something she had done. Was he upset with her and not saying — being Richard and holding it all in? She wished he wouldn't do that, try to save her feelings. It never worked in the long run. Better to deal with issues while they were small, instead of holding them, feeding them, growing them, until they were too big and burst out.

Was he having doubts?

She liked men. They never got past being boys. Watch a man long enough and you'll see the boy in him, all tumble and wrestle and mischief. Men and their bodies –they had a different connection to it than a woman did. To a man, his body was for work, for play, for sex — a machine, a toy. It wasn't a vessel to experience life through.

Katherine contemplated her body. It wasn't young anymore. It was stronger than it had ever been, rounder, firmer. But was he already tired of it? Had he now explored it all and wanted something else, something different?

All I have, and all I am, and only you, forever and ever, my wife.

Those were his words, the words he used to take her as his wife, the words he repeated when they made love. Did he still believe them? Did he still mean them when he whispered in her ear?

"Don't be stupid, Katherine." She spoke aloud, words into the empty cabin. "You always imagine the worst. Just go out there and ask him."

But when she went to look for him, to put her arms around him and smother him, he wasn't on the Ashram. Not at the buffalo pens, not working on a fence or building something. She stood just inside the gate leading from the Ashram and looked out. From here to there was only a few steps, from here to the rest of the world, from safety and security and community to uncertainty and loneliness. Only a few steps, but what a great distance.

She remembered walking her bicycle through, tired, thirsty, hoping for nothing more than a cup of water, and maybe some shade to drink it in. Seventeen years old. Seventeen and alone.

Her mother had left first, or hadn't made it back. Katherine preferred to think that her mom had not abandoned her, had not simply walked away when times were at their hardest, in the middle of a long drought, when there simply was no food and water. Something had happened to her. To do without water was something no one was ready for. First they rationed it, only turned on the pumps for a few hours a day. Then they didn't turn on the pumps at all. She had memories of twisting on the faucet taps. The only water was in the tears that streaked her face.

Then her father had left.

"Kat, you're old enough now to take care of yourself. I heard there's work up at Yellowknife. Me and a couple of the guys are going to try and make it. Sorry kid, but I can't take you with me."

She'd chosen La Ronge because La Ronge had water. She'd left Saskatoon because Saskatoon didn't. A bicycle and a packsack with nothing much in it, strength enough in her young legs, and luck, lots of luck, and Geneva had given her a cup of water, cold water from a well, and something to eat, and offered her a bed under a roof. It wasn't so much that she'd chosen to stay as much as she chose not to leave, not to go back out onto the road. Here at the Ashram she had purpose and place.

She wasn't a refugee.

She wasn't dirty.

She remembered that first bath. When Geneva had poured a whole bucket of water over her head and laughed.

She didn't have an education. Not because she was stupid or incapable of learning, but because schools had useless flush toilets. For health reasons, sanitation, they'd closed her high school half way through ninth grade. Temporarily. Everything in a drought is temporary, until it rains again. In the second year, there had been talk of reopening the schools, to get the kids off the streets, the importance of education. But, it didn't happen. They couldn't pull it together, partly because there were no teachers. Teachers were just people and, like all the other people, they were too busy trying to survive.

All the people watched the sky. Every passing little cloud. They watched and prayed, begged. "A little rain, *PLEASE*, enough to settle the dust." At the beginning of a drought, no one plans for four years without water. "Maybe it will rain next week, next month."

"October it usually rains."

"Maybe we'll get some snow this winter."

"April showers, God — Please — April Showers."

And the South Saskatchewan River became the South Saskatchewan Creek and then it stopped flowing all together. They didn't reopen the schools, they were too busy fighting with the people upstream. It was Alberta who took too much out of the river. It was British Columbia. And they ran to the courts, and the courts made decisions that said that Alberta had to leave enough water in the river for it to flow. But it didn't flow, because it didn't rain.

Then Alberta raised a militia to defend their water. The people took charge. The government couldn't help them. The government was against them and they had a right. A human right. It was the bastards in the East again, trying to tell honest hardworking Albertans what to do. And this time the people had had enough. They picked up their hunting rifles, enough is enough. And it still didn't rain.

They went back to the courts, and the Supreme Court of Canada sitting en banc made a unanimous decision: Alberta had to share the water and if it didn't, then Canada had the lawful authority to employ the Canadian Armed Forces to compel Alberta to share. And it still didn't rain.

"Cows use too much water."

"Do you know how much water a cow drinks in a day? Enough for a human to have a bath."

"Those Albertans and their cattle ranches are just wasting it."

"Somebody ought to do something."

"It ain't right."

"Wheat takes too much water."

"You can't waste water growing flowers."

"Unless you are going to eat the flowers."

And it still didn't rain.

Then British Columbia was mining the last of the Columbia ice fields.

"It was just going to melt anyways."

"At least if we mine it and truck it to Vancouver it won't go to waste."

This was a glacier that had flowed into three oceans — the Columbia River down through Oregon into the Pacific, the Athabasca River into Great Slave Lake, then the McKenzie River into the Arctic, and the Saskatchewan River across Alberta, Saskatchewan and Manitoba, up into Hudson's Bay and the Atlantic Ocean.

They'd watched that glacier shrink for generations, measured how quickly it receded, pointed where it used to extend to and said, "That is because of climate change."

"Climate change is real."

And the people drove up to see it before it was gone, in trucks pulling trailers, in cars and motor cycles and motor homes, and left them running in the parking lot for the air conditioning while they walked up the gravel slope to see the last of the great glacier. They stopped on the way up the winding mountain highway to buy more fuel for their trucks and cars and motorcycles and motor homes. They stood there pumping gas into their vehicles as the carbon puffed from the exhaust pipes, stood and looked at the mountains, at the beauty of it all, at the last of the snow on the peaks and said to themselves. "I hope this doesn't come to pass. Somebody has to do something."

And then it had started to rain.

A month after Katherine arrived at Hayden Ashram, it rained, and rained, and rained, until the Saskatchewan River flooded its banks and bridges washed away. And it continued to rain, until the people began to pray for the sun again.

She turned away from the gate, away from the memories. Something was wrong. Richard was out somewhere in the world, and she was in the Ashram. The world and the Ashram, they lived in both, the big world and the little world, and the little world was all safe and comfortable.

But she wished he had said something before he left. Now she was worried.

56

What you're fucking around with is life herself. And you're just casual about it. No respect. You don't respect anything. George was putting a new flask of plasma into the ORV when Two Bear's words came smashing back. They hit so hard that he stopped, took a full step back and looked at the bird.

It was life, wasn't it — this combination of feather and sinew? The heart and brain might be artificial, a pump and a computer, but the bulk of it, the legs and claws and wings, were grown. It was alive, and the proof was that if he didn't feed it, it would die; the Raven would shrivel up and begin to decompose. Isn't that part of the very definition of life then, the certainty of death?

He took a moment, accepted that the ORV lived, and with that acceptance felt a kinship with it. It was no longer a thing. It became a him, maybe a her, he wasn't sure.

But, for some reason, the fact that it was alive changed things. Foremost, it couldn't be neglected. It was alive and dependent upon him. He had an obligation now, he'd taken responsibility for a life, and no life should ever be wasted or taken casually.

He reached out and ran a hand over its feathered head, looked into its black eyes. Were they made of glass? He'd always assumed so, that the shine in them was a reflection off the lens of a sophisticated camera. Now he really wasn't sure. Paul, the guy who'd sold it to him, had said something about ravens being scavengers and needing good sight.

Were those eyes part of the organics of it? Where did the computer part begin and the organism end?

What was that guy's name again? The one who designed the interface? He had to think a bit before the name came to him. Ethan James Beeney. Yeah him, how did he connect life to electricity? Or perhaps, more properly, how did he connect electricity to life?

Was it the way an arm or a leg is connected to the body, or was it more like a harness on an oxen, something peripheral, external?

He'd have to research it when he got back.

George hadn't intended to take the ORV up when he came to change flasks. It was something about the realization that this was a living creature that made it almost obligatory to exercise it. Just a quick flight out over the lake and back, stretch a few muscles.

The ORV needed a name. He couldn't think of one at the moment. It couldn't be something random. The bird needed a real name, something that suited it, something that said who this bird was, something that matched its personality.

Without planning, without setting it up first, without checking altitude and wind speed, George put the ORV into a roll, tucked one wing slightly, arched his back, turned the head to the side away from the tucked wing and let the bird roll over.

"Yeah!"

He did it. First time, flawless, smooth, not like the flops of his other attempts, a scramble of feathers and wind. This roll had been perfect. And when they came out of it, he wasn't disoriented, trying to discern which way was up. Maybe because he was relaxed going into it, not tensed up. It wasn't forced. It was natural. The way it was supposed to be.

"Yeah."

It felt good. They had worked together. The ORV had wanted to, needed to, and finally had showed him how it was done.

He didn't try another. He considered doing it again, and maybe again, to re-experience that feeling, that exuberance. But no, he'd done it, something he'd tried over and over and always failed to execute with any grace. And now it was his, he owned it. He wanted to keep the victory.

He thought of the roll again late that night, in the moments before sleep when thoughts tumble and stir before they slow and become still. He smiled to himself, what a beautiful day it had been. It was good — life was good. He reached over and wrapped an arm around Lenore, snuggled closer to her back, ran his hand down the front of her, over the roundness that was beginning in her belly.

57

The courtroom was mostly empty; George looked around. Maybe a dozen people in the gallery, relatives or witnesses — a judge, a clerk, Erin the defence lawyer with the accused beside her, himself as prosecutor and a police officer.

"Mr. Taylor . . . " The judge began to speak.

George stood up without hurry.

"How many witnesses will you call?"

"Three, Your Honour: two civilians and a police officer."

"Well let's get started then. For the record . . . " Judge Roberto spoke to the microphone, raised his voice a bit. "This is the Preliminary Enquiry of Philip Charles, charged with sexually assaulting Susan McLeod; Erin Lawson represents the accused, George Taylor for the Crown. Your first witness, Mr. Taylor."

"Susan McLeod." George spoke loudly, half turned toward the gallery. A woman, her hair cropped short, a bright pink scarf that offset her black jacket and matched her ear rings, stood and began hesitatingly to walk forward.

"Please take the stand." George pointed toward the witness box.

Susan took the oath, quietly, barely audible. The clerk reminded her to speak, "Nice and loudly now, dear, so the microphones can record what you have to tell us."

Susan Ester McLeod had just left a pub on McKenzie Street.

It was April 29th.

How is she sure?

Because that was her birthday.

Twenty-four. She'd just turned twenty-four.

She wasn't drunk, she'd had three, maybe four beer and a shot of tequila the bartender bought for her.

No, she wasn't going home. She didn't remember where she was going. "That was a long time ago now." But it definitely wasn't home. She thinks she might have been going to a friend's for the night.

No, she never saw who it was that came up behind her, pulled a black cloth bag over her head and started dragging her off the street.

She remembers being scared, really scared. He wasn't so much dragging her as half carrying her. He basically had her under one arm. Her feet were dragging.

Yes, she was struggling, kicking.

No, she couldn't yell. He had a hand over her mouth.

In the alley . . .

The clerk reminded her to speak nice and loudly.

He was sitting on top of her. She couldn't move. He was heavy. He was taking his time. Unbuttoning her pants.

He didn't have his hand over her mouth now. He had it on her throat. She couldn't breathe.

Both her hands were around the wrist of the hand that was choking her. She remembers this part vividly, like it just happened, or it's still happening. What freaks her out the most is that he is unbuttoning her pants like he has all the time in the world and she has only a few minutes left to live.

No, he never said anything.

Not in the alley.

Not at any time. Not a word.

No, she never saw who it was.

No, she never saw the accused before. She never heard the name Philip Charles before. She doesn't know him.

She's not sure. She might have been unconscious. She was just laying there on her back in the alley and he was gone. She buttoned up her pants. No, he never pulled them down. He only unbuttoned them.

Then she went out onto Brad Wall Avenue and the police were there arresting two men. No she never saw the other man before either. No, Kevin Starr is not a friend of hers. Well, he wasn't a friend of hers then. He is now.

"Kevin Starr, will you please take the stand."

"Place the Bible in your right hand and repeat after me . . ."

Kevin looked and sounded nervous. "I was just there," his voice wavered slightly. "It was late. I don't know what time it was. The sun was down for a long time already. Maybe after midnight.

"I heard something.

"I went to check it out.

"He had this woman in the alley.

"No, I didn't yell at him first. I just hit him.

"I caught up to him on the street. He got a couple of shots in, but I mostly had him by the time the cops showed up. I was holding him by the hair.

"Oh yeah. It was definitely the same guy that was in the alley on top of the woman. Yeah, I kicked him in the face."

"Constable Harten, please describe for the court what you saw on Brad Wall Avenue, in La Ronge Saskatchewan, on the twenty-ninth of April of last year."

"Well, that's a quiet area, not much happens there, so I was really surprised to see two guys fighting. "While I was arresting them both for creating a disturbance, Susan McLeod came out of the alley. She was covered in leaves like she had been rolling around on the ground.

"I took a statement from both Kevin Starr and Susan McLeod at the scene. The statements were video recorded on the patrol unit. Shall I play them for you?"

"No, that's fine," George concluded. "That's the case for the Prosecution, Your Honour."

58

"SCHIZOPHRENIA."

"So?"

"What do you mean, *so*?" Defence Counsel Erin Lawson clearly didn't like his reply.

"So, he should take his meds."

"He was on his meds. Come on, George, you know how it is. He's twenty years old, a young man, with young man ideas, he's schizophrenic, his thinking gets mixed up."

"Mixed up?"

"He thought she liked him. He bought her a drink — she drank it. She smiled. It was Philip who bought the tequila, not the bartender. He followed her when she left. He doesn't have the social skills to get a girlfriend, his body is still telling him things. Just the normal testosterone urges that every young man experiences, and he doesn't have the capacity to deal with them the way that society demands. It's not his fault he's schizophrenic."

"Doesn't matter if his thinking is mixed up." George was adamant. "You don't pull a bag over a woman's head and drag her into an alley."

"He didn't pull a bag over her head. There was no bag. I didn't see it as an exhibit. The police didn't find the bag, because he never had one."

"Why would she lie about that?"

"Why did she lie about who bought her a drink?"

"Well then, put him on the stand and let him tell his story."
"You know I can't do that."

He smiled. He did know that if Philip took the stand in his own defence, he'd get caught up rambling about disconnected ideas and conspiracies and the fear that chased him down the dark depths of neural pathways.

"So, what have you got in mind?"

"A joint submission. Provincial time, not federal. He won't survive in the pen."

"Two years less a day? No way." George wasn't being hard. He was being realistic. "Sex assault, even if he bought her a drink and there was no bag over her head, it's at least seven."

Erin disagreed. "Seven years is at the high end of the range. Come on, George. He's twenty years old. He hasn't even begun to live yet. Seven years in a federal institution will destroy him. He could do a deuce less and still be something of a decent human when he got out."

You were a spirit, a dot of blue light travelling across the universe. George wondered about Philip's life, his experience of the physical. Seven years was a big piece of that experience. What right did he have to say that Philip needed to spend a tenth — maybe a tenth, depending on how long he lived — in the pen. He might get himself shanked for being a skinner and his one chance to know the connection between the spiritual and the physical would be completed. Or maybe Erin was right and the pen would destroy his humanity and he'd come back mean and hard and the rest of his life would be ruinous for others. *Don't let anyone come between you and the Creator and don't ever come between someone else and the Creator.* Is that what he was doing — coming between Philip and the Creator, changing his path?

He could easily go along with Erin in a joint submission to the judge on sentencing — two years less a day in the correctional centre. He'd still be interfering, still taking the role of the Creator, making a decision that determined how a life unfolded. And it wasn't his fault that modern society wanted to be super connected all the time and exposed to microwaves that saturated people's brains, that short-circuited or overloaded neural networks until reality and fantasy overlapped, and that everyone wanted to live in Smart Houses that were automated, lights on, door unlocked, supper started with the fridge thawing a synthetic steak. Sure, their houses were smart, but were they?

59

"YOU'RE CRAZY!" LENORE FELT AN UNWONTED anger rise. She didn't like the sound of her voice, the pitch, the screech of it. She didn't like the feeling in her centre, the way it vibrated like a wire drawn taught and strummed. She wanted to be rational, to speak calmly, but the irritation in her core — the discordant hum, the buzz of it — overrode and came out in her words. "You're putting *us* at risk." Her hand on her stomach.

She should have had an abortion and not told him that he was a father. She could have continued with her life — her peaceful existence, her survival — alone. Surviving is easy; life is hard. Now she had tied herself to this man. She was dependent upon him and he was behaving like an idiot.

She spat, "What's going to happen when Head Office finds out you made a deal like that?"

"Head Office will just have to live with it. There's such a thing as prosecutorial discretion, you know."

"No there isn't." She left no space between his words and hers. "They didn't hire you to be a nice guy. They didn't pay for your university because they thought you were some bastion of integrity or because you have a social conscience." The words poured from her core, spilled out in a cleansing rush. "They deliberately recruited us because we were veterans, because we were tough, because we experienced a war. Do you think we got into law school on our own merit? Hell no, strings were pulled. You'd have to be pretty damned egotistical to think you got to where you are on your own."

"Well, I have to agree, strings were pulled to get *you* into law school . . . "

"You're a fuckin' idiot. You know that. You're going to get yourself fired. And you can be fired, Mister Smart Guy. Then what? We have a child coming. You think they're going to take me back once the maternity leave is done? No way."

"Why not?"

She wanted to tell him about her own reprimand. But that would mean telling him about Richard. She wanted to tell him where her fear came from, the fear that she was going to be fired. But she didn't. He'd turned this into an attack on her, but the blame was his. "If they fire you, they'll put me out the door one step behind you. Then what?"

The irritation that had turned into anger became sadness. The anger had invigorated her, filled her with strength, straightened her spine and stood her straight. This newest stage drained her, left her feeling empty and alone. The hum and buzz that had set her core vibrating felt drowned and dulled. It no longer filled her, it sapped her energy. She felt herself slouch, weakened, unable to carry it forward anymore. She felt her throat tighten and a sting behind her eyes as tears threatened.

No way. She was not going to cry in front of him.

She turned to walk away and felt his hand on her shoulder, gently.

"I really don't know what you mean. Why would you be fired?"

She pushed his hand away. "Don't touch me."

60

RICHARD CAME HERE OFTEN TO THINK, to look down into the water and let his thoughts flow. Secession. That was what it had been about. When Austin filed a petition to secede from Texas all hell broke loose and his uncles had gone marching down. He stood on the bridge with his hands on the railing and looked down at the black tumbling water of Montreal River. There was a beauty in the flow as it swirled over and around the rocks, dark and clear. The sky was not overcast and the river reflected the blue.

Today his thoughts ran back to the beginning of the First Intra, the stories he'd heard about it and the petition that had started it all. Was it the petition? It really had started well before that defining moment. When Guatemalans, Hondurans and Nicaraguans pushed through Mexico and poured across the Rio Grande into Texas they were met by the militias, by the *Patriots for Freedom* and *Texas First.*

It started with beatings, clubs, whips, chains. The Militias called it County Defence, to send a message to those coming behind. *If you come into our county this is what you can expect.* But those who received the beatings were not in communication with those coming behind and hunger has a way of driving people forward despite the risk.

Cows were slaughtered and eaten out on the pastureland. Crops were crushed. If a man or a woman or a child sleeps in the wheat, some of it gets trampled. When hundreds sleep in the same field, there isn't much left for the combines to pick up. Things went missing, especially anything that could be eaten or quickly converted into money to purchase food and maybe occasionally alcohol, or guns, or drugs. Houses were broken into despite American citizenry's right to bear arms.

And every incident was repeated in the news a hundred times until the sound of it became a roar and, if you listened to it, you couldn't help feeling afraid.

It was an invasion, and it overran Homeland Security. That it wasn't an invasion by a foreign power — no one compelled them to rush the river, they wore no uniform — didn't matter to the militias. Every able-bodied American had a duty to heed the call to arms, to repel the attack of American soil or die.

The beatings didn't work. Then the massacres started, to send a message to those coming behind: *this is what you can expect.* But the people who slept in ditches and wheat fields had seen mass graves before. The fresh dirt reminded them of their relatives who hadn't managed to get away, and why they had to get farther north where there was at least a chance at survival.

Then Austin, embarrassed at Texan brutality, petitioned to secede from the Lone Star State and Washington heard the petition, and some speculated that the Supreme Court would ratify it. There was good political reason for the American administration to support Austin, it made them look rational and liberal and civilized in the face of the atrocities.

Support for Austin might have made the President look good in some of the other States, States where he needed votes, but it turned the rest of Texas firmly and forever against what they considered to be a Federal interventionist unconstitutional Government. The Austin Petition and especially support for it from outside, from the North, resulted in the rest of Texas demanding succession from the Union. Then Nevada, then Alabama, then Tennessee, then all up the centre of the country, the secessionist movement caught fire. It wasn't so much Red States and Blue States, Democrat or Republican. It was more a difference between dry states and wet states.

The American people had for so long blamed government for everything wrong in their worlds, that when the climate turned against them, when drought withered crops and evaporated municipal reservoirs, they blamed Washington, they blamed the unconstitutional exercise of emergency powers, and even though no one rationally connected succession with the climate, there was a sense that government was the cause for this as well, and to break away, to make change, to do something, anything, might bring the rains.

While no one ever said that a super storm was the government's fault, the management of the state of emergency during and following these climatic events was always criticized. They weren't doing enough, or doing it fast enough.

Richard watched the water, looked into the depths of it. There was a chance to see a fish this time of year, coming up the river to spawn, Lake Trout and Whitefish, the salmonids ran in the autumn once the water cooled. They left their eggs in the gravel beds to over-winter, an exercise in patience.

He'd seen her today uptown. She hadn't seen him, had been looking down at her platform as she walked. He'd thought of going over to her, of saying, "Hello," "Nice day," "How have you been?" But he didn't.

She looked good. Much younger and healthier, her face smooth, and with that very becoming expectant glow. Pregnant women had more blood in their bodies, combined with hormone activity that increased oil gland output; the combination caused them to appear radiant.

She hadn't seen him. They hadn't spoken. It was better that way, better for them both to go in their own directions. He wondered about the man. Who was the father? It didn't matter. It wasn't him, obviously.

He did think about her, about the four days they had spent together, their conversations. She had really wanted to talk about the Second Intra, its place in history, its rightfulness or not. Even though she had lots to say about it in the abstract, she never quite got to her place in it, the part she had played. He wondered what her experience had been. She hadn't said anything except that she had been in the Fifth regiment. The Fifth had marched all the way down to Honduras.

He'd never got past San Diego. He'd lost his pack and spent four days wandering in the California desert.

The Second Intra had been a repeat of the First, just a little more intense, a little larger and more technologically advanced, the way the Second World War was a continuation of the First World War, and the Second Gulf War built on the First Gulf War, the Korean War repeated the Korean War.

No guns were fired, no missiles, no drones, no bombs were dropped, between the First and the Second Intra, but the hate continued to glow red as an ember. No one forgot and certainly no one forgave. There had been a video, famous now, of a young man from Maine, Shamus O'Hanlon. Everyone had seen it, memorized it, on both sides.

At the beginning of the First Intra, when Texas seized the huge military bases, Fort Hood, Fort Bliss, Fort Worth, Fort Sam Houston, it was expected that the soldiers there would fight for the side of the secessionists. Some did. But in those first days and weeks soldiers scurried away from their bases in confusion. Pilots stole planes and flew them to the side they thought they owed a duty of loyalty to. Both sides shot traitors, but it was the video taken at Fort Bliss that fuelled the inferno that followed.

Whoever made the video intended it as a propaganda tool to show that the North did not have the heart to fight, that this was going to be a short war, the enemy simply lacked the courage to stand up and fight.

Shamus was caught sneaking out of Fort Bliss at night, alone, crawling in the sand. The video was of him being led to a wall. "I jus' wanna go home. I jus' wanna go home. Please God Please, I jus' wanna go home." He was barely nineteen and, baby-faced, with freckles and red hair, looked even younger. The cameraman had captured something that he probably forever regretted. It went so much against his cause. The video has a close up of Shamus' face, his clear blue eyes, snot running from his nose. He's asked by the soldier who has him by the shoulder, "Where's your home?"

«Eustis Maine, Sir, Eustis Maine. Could you please just let me go home?"

"You're going home all right. Two more minutes and you're going to be in Eustis fuckin' Maine."

Some historians have likened that portrait to the Mona Lisa for its mystical quality, the pure beauty of it. It was one of those rare images sought by photographers and only very rarely ever captured. Shamus in his youthful beauty, in his last minutes. It captured the hearts and imagination of everyone who viewed it.

Eustis Maine became famous. It became a battle cry for the North, for Shamus, for decency, for God, for all that is good in America, and it justified all the atrocities committed by them; tit for tat, an eye for an eye.

But why did they bomb Mexico and Guatemala? Richard wasn't sure. That part of the story never made sense to him. It was reminiscent of the bombing of Laos during the Vietnam War, of the drone attacks on Pakistan during the Afghanistan War. He could not imagine that Texans had gone to hide in Mexico when things began to turn against them. Why would a secessionist, loyal to the extreme, leave the territory he claimed his birthright and hide in a foreign country? No, there was something else behind it, and he never did hear an answer that was satisfactory. Maybe it was just because they could. Maybe it was an attempt to kill Mexicans and Guatemalans before they got here. Maybe.

Then it was over. The fighting subsided and America was made whole again, and Canada was her friend. We had helped to hold North Dakota and Montana and Utah. We'd picked the winning side.

Then the Second Intra. Richard's war.

Riley Souter, his buddy since preschool, said: "I'm signing up. This isn't going to last long and I want in on it while it's there."

And Richard signed up too, not because he cared to be in on it or whether it was right or wrong, but just because Riley was going and wherever Riley went, Richard wanted to go too.

Riley, dumb fuckin' Riley, he was somewhere in San Diego, the Chollas Lake Little League Park, somewhere on that ball field, all over that ball field. There is no monument there, nothing to say that Riley and Wyatt and the others are splattered there. Why would they? Who wants to remember that? Why would anyone even admit to that?

Richard didn't want to remember, didn't want to go down that road again. He looked out across Kitsaki Bay, at the waves caused by the flow of the river as it dumped into the placid waters of Lac La Ronge, at the smooth mirror-flat water of the bay. There was a boat out there, someone fishing, maybe — it wasn't moving.

Why would they ever admit to firing on their own? The Chollas Lake Little League Park sucked Richard back, took him down the long march along the coast, through the liberation of California by the Seventh Infantry, all the way to San Diego, the bivouac in the park and the missiles. The drones came. Surely the drone operators saw them, knew they were Canadians, knew they were on the same side.

Then he was running east, away from the burning city behind him, and his pack, not that it had much in it, socks and a toothbrush, a bottle of water, was gone. He'd left it hanging on a post just in front of their tent. Four days in the Anza-Borrego State Park — desert, sand, rocks and creosote bush — and all he can think about in all that time is the pack.

The pack. He'd left it. He could see it hanging on the post, the woven straps that he didn't like, that gouged into his shoulders; he remembered the exact contents of it and where each item lay in relation to everything else: the bottle of water in the side pocket, the folding knife in the bottom right corner, a fire steel that his mother had given him for his seventeenth birthday wrapped in plastic with a bit of lint, a half bag of almonds, he liked almonds, always had liked almonds.

He'd thought about the pack, obsessed on the pack to the exclusion of everything else. Orders had been a one-in-two watch, a seven-and-five; seven on, five off, five on, seven off. He'd been on watch when it came. He'd been standing out near the gate, a rifle slung over his shoulder, when the drone came.

They were all his buddies, not just Riley, even Lieutenant Morrison who was an asshole even on a good day, Wyatt and Ringo and all of them, good guys. Good guys that were gone and all he could think about was the pack. Maybe because the pack was the only thing that was his, that was of him, that went away with them. Maybe he thought about the pack exclusively because he could not bring himself to think about them, and thinking about the pack kept his brain busy, kept him sane.

Everyone has a moment or moments in their lives, the memory of which never diminishes. For Richard, his moment was daybreak in the desert. He remembers how cold it was and that he woke up shivering and the only reason he was out of the coyote den he'd spent the night in was to walk around and warm up. He remembers the colours, the reds and the yellows, and the softness of the light; he remembers the sky, the sun climbing up behind a big pile of rocks, and it's April and the desert is in bloom and the pink and white flowers are on the cactus. He remembers the tiny oasis that he found, not much larger than the average back yard of an average suburban home: a bit of water, a pool between the rocks, small enough that he could step across. He remembers looking into the water when the sun cleared the horizon and struck its surface, suddenness of it — one moment black, the next sparkly and blue — as though something had exploded in the gravel bed beneath it, as though the light came up from the water and poured through him. A baptism of light, it filled his spirit violently, overfilled him, and his spirit was forced to grow, to expand to contain it all. With the light, he heard music, soft and clear, music you might imagine made by light shone through a perfect crystal. He tried to rationalize the music, the rhythm of it, in his own heartbeat; perhaps it was from the wind, but there was no wind on his face.

It was a moment of connection between him and God, between him and creation, between him and the universe. It was his moment of becoming: of becoming whole, of becoming real — a moment of healing, a moment of transformation. He stopped being a soldier and became human again.

He understood compassion, it flowed through him with the light. He understood forgiveness, the universe forgave him, blessed him, and filled him. The moment stretched out, became unbelievably long, the music reached a crescendo and faded and he was left alone in the desert looking at his reflection in the pool of water. He had brown hair then, without his present streaks of white. The face that looked back at him was tanned and healthy, brown-eyed, clear-eyed, the face of a man awoken and aware.

Richard hadn't returned to that moment in a long while. It felt good to remember it, to re-experience it, to bathe again in the light. In the magic moment there had been only him and the universe. He turned away from the river and the dark water, returned to the bridge and the traffic and the noise and the people.

He remembered Virgil's words. "*Never belong to an ideology, by belonging you become owned. Even an ideology of liberation will ultimately ensnare its adherents.*" There was truth to that. He remembered the battles, first of words, then of arms; battles between the democrats and republicans, between liberals and conservatives, between the Greens and the Capitalists, between labour and management; and each side believed firmly in the rightfulness of their ideas — if everyone were to agree with them the problems would be solved. Each side had its share of fundamentalists, people who believed in absolutes, in supremacy and rightfulness.

But what about the Ashram? His thoughts turned back to Walter and the threat of expulsion. Wasn't this just fundamentalism again — this idea that the Ashram was non-political, neutral in all things worldly? What about his place in the Ashram? Was he becoming caught up in their ideology? Probably. He tried to think his way out of it. What were the basics of the idea that Hayden applied when he'd started the Ashram? That people would live together, live like a family, share and take care of each other and be self-sufficient. So where did all the rules come from? From the members who couldn't completely grasp the idea of freedom, who applied the idea to create an *us and them* scenario. That's how wars start. When you decide that certain human beings are the *other.* And you can blame them because they are other and you imagine the differences and exaggerate the differences until in your mind you become the only sane, rational human and those, those others, are insane because they are not like you; they are less human, and when they are less human they are easier to kill.

He wasn't going to become trapped in that again. The memory of his moment was strong. He felt the power of it, the purity of it. It wasn't an idea. It was an absolute truth. It was the difference between knowledge and understanding. Knowledge is available to everyone. It is comprised of the facts and artefacts of reality. Knowledge is mechanical, physical, you can be hit over the head with knowledge. But understanding, now that is something different. Understanding can exist without words. It's like love.

Yeah. He worked it through. Understanding is like love; neither are necessarily logical, perhaps not even rational. Love doesn't always make sense, but it is true, it is absolute truth when you are in the midst of it; when you are caught in the whirlwind of it, you understand the true connection between humans and the beauty of the connection with the universe.

"Kraw!!"

A raven spoke. It's voice urgent. Not more than a meter away, it stood on the bridge rail, at eye level to him. Black eyes, shiny, clear — he read intelligence in them. A knowing and an understanding glimmered beneath the blackness and the blackness that overlaid it all was mystery, mystery — that which is unknowable to us, that only animals in the purity of their innocence possess.

It spoke again, in its coarse voice, a rasp in its throat, a single loud "Kraw!" There was no mistaking that it spoke directly to him, straight into his face from just an arm-length away. And because he was freshly returned from his moment of awakening in the desert, with his mind still clear from re-experiencing that moment, the bird made sense.

61

THE CHILL OF THE AIR AGAINST his skin, on the back of his hands and on his face, felt fresh and comfortable. The tingle of it awakened and invigorated him, such a beautiful feeling after a summer of heat and humidity.

He readied the ORV for an afternoon flight. It was Sunday, a day without thinking, a day to rest his mind, a day to soar and enjoy the sky, to be free — not just from work, from the office and the files, from the constant, never-ending line of humanity caught in the criminal justice system, but free too from Lenore and her moods.

Half an hour later he landed the ORV in a large aspen tree atop the Thunder Hills south of La Ronge for no other reason than he had never landed in a tree before. There was something about ravens and trees that seemed to him to go together. The landing had not been as difficult as he had imagined it would be. He didn't get tangled in the branches, the ORV did not crash and fall, the giant limb he chose did not break under their combined weight. They'd come in from the east, into the bit of wind that stirred the few remaining crisp leaves, pulled up at the last moment, brought both wings down and back and reached out with the talons. It was as though the ORV knew the manoeuvre, the memory of it somewhere in its DNA; instinct.

This aspen was the tallest and largest in the forest that crowned these hills. He looked westward toward Weyakwin Lake, toward the settled area. Wherever there was water, a lake, a river, you could be certain that its shores would be jammed with human habitations. What was it about people? Was it the memory of drought that drew them to water? Or was it something deeper, more fundamental? Did they collectively remember the time life crawled out of the oceans? Was this desire, or perhaps it was need, to see water, to look out across its expanse, something instinctual, something within the program of their original instructions?

What was it about people? George's mind continued to work. What was it about people that made them do all the horrible things they did to each other; the assaults, the threats, the violence that filled his files, that filled the courtrooms?

His mind spun.

Back again to Lenore; always back to Lenore.

Was he a coward?

She'd hinted that he was.

Suggested that he couldn't do his job. The job of a tough prosecutor, the job that he was hired for, that he was selected for, that he was trained for.

Was he a coward? He'd never fought, never been in combat. He'd rode along protecting the water trucks. When the bombs came he laid on the ground with his hands over his ears and waited. He remembered the smell of the dirt, strong in his nostrils as he waited to become nothing, certain that one of the bombs was his, that it would find him there in the ditch, convinced that he would not hear it, would not see the flash. He would be there one moment and then it would find him and he would become nothing, and all he could do was wait, and wait, and wait...

He'd gone through an entire war without ever firing a shot at anyone, not once, not even close. He never fought back. He just rode along.

Was that what he was doing now — just riding along?

He looked out across the forest. It was mostly deciduous now. He knew that not too long ago this boreal forest had been primarily coniferous, that with the warming, the forest had changed; that with the increase in nitrogen fallout, along with acid rain, the forest of today did not look anything like the forest at the turn of the century. Some plants can take a lot of nitrogen, others can't. The mosses withered, grasses proliferated, and the animals that preferred moss, like the caribou, had disappeared. The balance shifted, the land became something else. This new forest, this twenty-first century forest, though it appeared lush and rich, lacked history, lacked continuity. This tree, this giant aspen that stood above all the other trees in the Thunder Hills, had benefited from the abundance of nitrogen that had spewed out of the refineries toward the west. There were a few trees, but not many, that had grown immense enough to bear the weight of an ORV.

This is a new age. We've never been here before. There are no history books to tell us how to get through this. How was he going to get through this — this thing with Lenore? How should he respond to her moods, to her anger and the venom in her words?

"Stop it. Just Stop." George spoke aloud, gave himself a shake that set the ORV aflutter.

"Be calm. This is your day, your life, you chose what you are going to do with it."

He deliberately emptied his mind, forced it to be still, to be silent. A thought tried to stir, he banished it, closed his eyes and drew in a long slow breath, held it, then let it escape, let his lungs deflate, to emptiness, to nothing. No work, no Lenore, just a mind empty and at peace. He felt his heartbeat slow, become steady, felt the tenseness drain, not just from his mind, but also from his body and maybe from his spirit. He drew another breath, his mind still blank, his eyes closed, in a black nothingness. Slowly the black became grey, then more and more light entered, until the grey began to become white.

The ORV cawed, a sudden loud croak. It jumped and skipped along the branch, jolting and shattering his calm. He opened his eyes to the brilliance of an afternoon sun still high in the western sky, to the last of the late autumn colours still on the trees.

"What the hell?"

The ORV stopped immediately upon George's resurgence of thought. It took a moment, *what the hell was that about*? before he understood. When he'd emptied his mind, a mind connected through computers to that part of the ORV circuitry that was mind control, he had freed the Raven.

What does a Raven do when it is free?

It dances and sings.

Instinct. Every living thing knows three things: eat, don't be eaten, and procreate.

Because the ORV began with the original DNA of a raven, it too had those original instructions.

What about George Taylor? Was that all that he was about as well? Just another living organism? Was he coded the same way?

Of course he was.

Humans developed the ability to imagine, and imagined that they were somehow separate from the rest of the Earth's biota. But it was only an imagined separation. It had no basis in reality. We were given the gift of a mind, a gift to expand the experience of existence, something truly beautiful, and we have used it to separate ourselves from the world that we came here to experience. But just because we imagine ourselves outside of nature doesn't make it so.

Who was he then? Who was George really? At a very basic level?

He didn't have an answer. Nothing came to him. He closed his eyes and tried to let himself go again, back to the white place, the empty place. He didn't reach it, his mind wouldn't go there. Maybe, he thought, because if he did, the ORV would act up again. But he did get an answer, during the calm quiet attempt. A single word response to the question, Who is George? The word *human* opened itself from within some part of his brain.

And of course, like every good answer to every good question, it created two more good questions. What does it mean to be human? And, what is my role as a human? He didn't bother searching for the answers, instead he stepped the ORV off the limb, spread his wings, caught air, gave three hard thrusting flaps for lift and banked hard to the left. Then, as hard as he could drive the ORV, he powered upward, the light west wind at his back.

Once he had some altitude he let the ORV soar, flapping only occasionally to keep himself up there.

But again his mind came back to Lenore. She was human too. She was in their apartment, in that nook she called her study. That's all she did, it seemed, was study, obsessively, anything to keep herself occupied, as though she didn't want to experience life, except at the most abstract level, the level of an academic.

He didn't want to think about her. It would take him back to the argument. This was his day, his day to fly. He took the ORV into a long easy swoop, a gentle ride through the atmosphere.

What was he? A human. One of a species that had crawled out of the ocean, evolved into apes, then cave men, then . . .

Yeah, then us, consumers, arrangers. We arranged the planet, the entirety of it, for our convenience. What do we need: to eat, to not be eaten, to procreate? Eating isn't any problem. Food can be synthesized from nearly anything. To not be eaten? Well, we haven't worried about that since we killed the big cats and bears that used to come crawling around our caves. No, humans don't worry anymore about being eaten, not by anything larger than us anyway. But what about microbes? Didn't they eat us, one tiny bit at a time? And every time we think we cure a disease, a new one pops up.

What about procreate?

And again he thought of Lenore, of her growing belly.

The black widow spider eats the male when she is done with him.

Maybe, maybe the need to procreate is the most powerful of the three commands. Many species quit eating when the time comes to reproduce. Don't salmon swim up the river, lay their eggs, then die?

But why? Why procreate if the whole point is to experience life as physical and spiritual at the same time? Why a need to go on beyond the experience? He let the ORV spiral. There was still a bit of an updraft from the lake, as its water gave off warmth to the cooler air. He let it carry him up, rode it, wings outspread, soaring.

Because we are more than human. The species is greater than the individual. Everything is made up of something smaller. Wasn't he made up of cells? He wondered if any of the cells he came with, when he was born, were still within him. Didn't cells die, to be replaced by new ones? Just like the human species, one giant organism, made up of George and all the others.

And there it was, the need to procreate, to perpetuate the infliction of humanity upon the planet.

And he and Lenore were merely a small part in it all.

And Philip Charles.

No. Not today. He wouldn't think about Philip today. Tomorrow back in the office he'd figure out what to do about low-functioning, schizophrenic Philip, who listened to the wrong advice from his brain, a brain connected to the base instinct to eat, not be eaten and procreate.

What was he to do? What was George, the prosecutor, to do? His job? Recommend to the judge that Philip should go to the penitentiary for his transgressions, possibly destroying a life that had really only just begun its journey of experience? Or go along with Erin Lawson's joint submission for a deuce less a day and send Philip to a correctional centre?

If he did that, head office would really be pissed. He'd be accused of being soft, of not taking his responsibilities seriously. And Lenore was right, do that enough times and they would fire him. The courts might say that a prosecutor has discretion, and it was true to an extent. And head office usually didn't interfere. But on something like this they would.

Even though he didn't want to, George reviewed the file, ticked through one aspect at a time with each flap of the ORV's wings.

Susan McLeod's evidence.

Kevin Starr came along and laid a beating on Philip.

Constable Harten only saw two guys fighting on the street.

Maybe they should have interviewed the bartender at the pub where Susan had celebrated her birthday. Who bought her the drink, the bartender or Philip? How much did she really have to drink?

And then — a few wing beats, then soar, a few more beats and soar again — the solution came. It was simple. Cover your ass, George. Document the file. He could see it, the annotation, merely a few words. "After review of the evidence presented at the preliminary enquiry, I conclude that a reasonable likelihood of conviction is minimal."

If there wasn't any hope of getting a conviction, they couldn't blame him for accepting a deal that would appear to be something where nothing was possible. He let the ORV glide.

Raven pointed his beak at the sky, at the pale misty blue. He remembered a time when the sky had been brighter, when the blue had been deeper, a time when sky blue meant a richer colour. He turned his head eastward toward the low morning sun. There was a ring around it and it was flanked by bright sundogs on either side that flared nearly to mid-sky. It would have been beautiful if it hadn't been so ominous.

He remembered when sundogs meant three more days of cold weather. Not anymore. Now sundogs came out even in the summer. What did humans say? Red sky in morning sailor take warning, red sky at night, sailor's delight? Didn't mean a thing anymore. Red sky, blue sky, grey sky, indigo sky, were all the same, morning, noon and night.

He remembered when a ring around the moon was a guarantee; what you have now you will have for three more days. Those days were gone.

Even the animals couldn't predict the weather anymore. He'd once heard coyotes yipping and howling all evening, a sure predictor of change, and the weather stayed the same. Maybe if coyote forecast from a hilltop instead of from downtown . . . He let the thought drift away.

Not even the insects could say what tomorrow would bring. Where were the bees? Raven missed the bees. They'd been pretty, all yellow and black, and smart. If you were lucky enough to find a beehive these days, it might be on the ground or high above, because the few remaining bees didn't know anymore how much snow, if any at all, was going to come next winter.

Raven wondered if even the sky herself knew what she was going to do in the next hour. He unfolded his wings and tested the air with a tiny flutter before he put power to them, lifted from the rooftop and flew up to see . . .

To see?

Well, too see what the day might bring.

62

"On the road to Damascus, Mister Prosecutor. On the road to Damascus, don't you forget that."

The man was crazy, making nonsense noises. George would like to have ignored him, but the man was directly in front of them, blocking their passage. On a normal day, in a normal situation, when he was alone, perhaps on the street, he might have reacted differently, walked around the scrawny, unshaven man. But here in the courthouse, with Lenore beside him carrying their daughter, it was different. The man wasn't threatening him, he was threatening his family.

George stepped forward, chest to chest with the angry man, not because he needed to confront him, but to put himself in front of Lenore and Anna, to be the protector, to face into the aggressor.

The man's shabby clothing hung loose from his skinny shoulders, draped like sackcloth around his emaciated body. The bristling beard, hard eyes and hawk nose, turned up without any fear. The man had God on his side, God and the Word of God.

"Remember Saul, Saul the prosecutor." His breath stank of rotted teeth. "Remember when the Lord knocked him off his horse with a blast of light. Do you remember that, Mister Prosecutor? Do you remember that?

"Saul was on the road to Damascus to prosecute those who followed the way. A man of the law just like you, Mister Prosecutor. But he was no match for the Lord. Yeah, the Lord knocked him right off his horse." The little man's anger wrapped itself around each word spat up into George's face.

"And in the end the Lord changed Saul, made him a vessel of the truth, renamed him Saint Paul and sent him out into the world to spread the word. You remember that, Mister Prosecutor. You remember that. You too are on the road to Damascus and the Lord is waiting for you. Any moment now and you are going to be knocked on your ass. You just wait and see."

The man turned, flailing his arms as he left and shouted back over his shoulder, "You are on the road to Damascus, Mister Prosecutor, Ohhh, I wouldn't want to be you."

People were staring. His wife and daughter behind him, George suddenly felt unsure, a *Now What* moment. Ignore it and walk on, walk out of the building and go for lunch like they had intended, enjoy this space during the day that was for family, let it slide, let it pass, this was just a crazy man, a fundamentalist wrapped too tightly in his faith. He should have just let it go, let the little man walk away. But he didn't. He couldn't, the words had hit too hard, they'd shaken him.

He shouldn't have. He followed him, tapped him on the shoulder, and with a very gentle voice asked, "Why me?" What he meant was why, in a courthouse full of prosecutors, had he been selected for the rant.

The little man stopped, turned and looked straight into his face. Perhaps it was the mild tone that changed the man's anger into softness. He replied calmly, "Why did the Lord choose Saul to be remade in the light?"

The man in the shabby loose clothing turned and walked away making loud "Kraw, Kraw" sounds as he went.

63

You don't have to be crazy to live here but it helps.

George read the sign again. It was scrawled on a single board spiked to a gatepost.

"Hey, Mister Prosecutor."

He turned to the woman who'd spoke. "You know me?"

"No, can't say I know you. But I did see you at the courthouse."

"Oh."

"Name's Jasonia." She stepped forward with her hand extended.

He took it in his, shook it. Her grip was firm, but gentle.

"What brings you to Regis?"

"I'm not sure. I guess I had to see it for myself."

"That's the only way it can be seen. For yourself."

George looked away. Jasonia's eyes, that mix of blue and green and something else, were a little too powerful to look into for long. He looked back at the sign.

"It's not just graffiti," she offered.

"I was wondering about that." Why had he come to Regis, what brought him here? It was more than curiosity, more than a need to fill a Saturday morning, a need to get out. The apartment, and the city, and his thoughts had become too small, too tight, too confined and he needed to know. Truth? Yeah, it was truth he came looking for — the truth on the edge of the city. Who were these people who made up the bulk of prosecutions and also the bulk of the victims? Why were the victims reluctant to testify? What was the reality of their existence, so obviously different than the reality of his?

"What were you doing at court?"

She ignored him. "You looking for Ryan?"

"Who?"

"Most of the people you are going to meet — aren't outright crazy. But their brains work different. They say in Regis, if you don't hear voices, you're not listening. Come on." Jasonia tugged his sleeve, just once, just a little nudge, and he was moving down the packed sand path that led into the heart of Regis.

Some of the structures were more substantial than others. He hadn't expected to see a building of brick and stone amid the squalor of plastic and sticks and cardboard and rusted metal roofs.

Jasonia caught him staring. "The school."

"Really?"

"Yeah, really."

"But how?" He couldn't imagine these people building their own school. They didn't have the resources. Not just the bricks and mortar and stone. "Who are the teachers?"

"Volunteers, do-gooders, missionaries. It's a school. They teach you to read and write. But you have to read the Christian Bible. They'll feed you — wine and crackers. Food for the soul. Your mind and body can go to hell, just as long as they get to claim your spirit."

"Some good must come of it. They provide an education of sorts, don't they?"

"True enough. But it's not us they're helping. It's not our salvation they're worried about. It's their own. The more good deeds they do, the more people they save, fulfil their quota, the better their chance of getting into heaven." She started walking again.

The wind gusted sporadically out of the west, stirred dust and flapped plastic sheeting. It helped. The unfamiliar smells of human feces and stale urine and wood smoke were hard to adjust to. It would have been worse, he imagined, if not for the sand to soak it all up. If the ground had been rock or clay they wouldn't be able to scrape a shallow hole with their foot, squat until their business was done, then kick sand on top of the business. Perhaps if the holes they scraped were a little deeper, things wouldn't work back to the surface, to find oxygen, and like everything else that touches oxygen, go through a chemical reaction.

The pathways between the shanties weren't as crowded as he had expected. There were a few people about, no one in a rush, no one going anywhere. He did however note that they all stared, outright, blatantly. But nothing was said, and the stares seemed more out of curiosity than malevolence.

"How do you feed yourselves?".

"Any way we can. Those that have jobs go into the city everyday and do the work that city people feel is beneath them . . . "

"If they have work, why do they live here?" George interrupted.

"You don't get it, do you? Because there's a big gap between here and there. You can walk it in ten minutes, but to live in the city the first thing you need is a platform. That's your passport, your key. To get a platform you have to be registered. To be registered you need an address, you need a bank account, you need a credit rating, you have to prove citizenship. If you fall out of the paradigm you end up here. Getting back in is something else."

"Paradigm?"

"You live in that other world. In your world everything makes sense. You have a platform, you have a job, and you have a home. You've never known it to be any other way. The things you believe — well, they must be true. Everyone you know believes the same things you do."

Jasonia sat down on a rough bench in a bit of shade.

"Did you know that half of what you see isn't really there? Your brain just makes it up for you. If you measure the light coming into the front of your eye and the information your brain receives, you'll find that somewhere in the circuit the energy has doubled. Your brain receives twice as much information than the eye sees. What do you think that other information is?"

George shrugged.

"Shit you made up." She answered, a little quirk of a smile. "There's a story . . . " She patted the bench beside her. George ignored the offer. Remained standing. It didn't matter. She was going to tell him anyway. "When the Spanish first came to America in their sailing ships, the Indians on the shore couldn't see the ships. They were invisible because they'd never seen one before. Because they'd never seen one, their brains couldn't get what was coming from their eyes. There were these strange-dressed humans in front of them: two legs, two arms, a body, a head. That made sense. They could see the sailors. But where did they come from? How did they get there?

"It wasn't until one of them — a medicine man — figured it out. The other Indians couldn't see anything at all until he pointed it out to them. It was only after they were shown that they were able to see."

George countered, "But if we all see the same thing, what does it matter?"

"We don't all see the same thing. If all the people agree something is real and someone comes along who sees it differently, you say that person must be insane, and you segregate them until they agree. That's what Ryan says."

The wind began to gust stronger. Nearby, a loose sheet of corrugated metal roofing rattled loudly. George took the seat that had been offered earlier, close to Jasonia so that he could hear. The whipped up sand had a sting to it where it struck his face.

Jasonia laughed. "The way I see it, the only thing that's important is that we recognize that most of the paradigm is just shit we made up: class, social position, fashion . . . " she paused. "Law. We treat it like it's important, like the world would end if we didn't have it."

George interrupted quickly. "Don't you think law is necessary?"

"No." Her tone definite.

"Come on. Imagine what it would be like. Chaos, murder, gangs, looting . . . "

"Your paradigm. We live outside it. The police only come here when they're doing a drug bust. The people figure out how to live together. You don't have a policeman beside you every minute. You behave according to the rules of your paradigm because that's how you're programmed . . . "

"Programmed?"

"Half of what you see is just stuff you made up, and you've been making it up all of your life. You ever watch little kids when they play? Ever wonder what that's about, why everything they do is pretend? You take half a dozen four-year-olds and put them together and within a few minutes they'll be playing and most of their play is pretend. They're making stuff up. And we never stop. We keep living in our imagination until we normalize it and then we call it reality, and all we've done is taught ourselves that this world we imagined is something real." Jasonia stretched out her legs, leaned back against the wall and began gesturing with her hands.

"We live in this make-believe world where we believe in stuff like the economy. Now that's a big one — the economy. We used to believe in things like dragons and unicorns, now we believe in the market. Corporations are just something we made up. That's what your law did for you. Without law, without the Corporations Act, they wouldn't exist. You have high priests of the economy, you have universities dedicated to it, you worship it, you fight wars to defend it, you make human sacrifices to it."

George looked around at the squalor, imagined the hopelessness of living in Regis. Yeah, these people were human sacrifices.

Jasonia continued, "I seen you at court. You have a job. You make money. You spend money. You save money. And you stress about it, you obsess about it. It's something you made up, it's part of your pretend world. But it has real affects on your health. You worry about having the right clothes, the right shoes, the right job, the right education and you worry and stress until you give yourself a heart attack and all of that stuff is just shit you made up. A paradigm you give your life for."

She paused for a second, caught her breath.

"You believe your pretend world is real, that your politics and your religions are the only right politics, the only right religions, and you insist that the rest of the world imagines the same things that you imagine. And if they don't. If another group of people split off and begin imagining something different, then you use your laws and your armies to force them to imagine your pretend world."

"So, then what's real?"

Jasonia paused, looked directly into his eyes. "I am." She paused again, a full two seconds. "How about you, are you real?"

He thought about it. "Yeah, I'm pretty sure I'm real."

"You probably are."

She started listing things that were real: "Giving birth, nature, trees, ecosystems, animals, all this, this earth; war; the shit we make up about why we go to war might not be real, but war is real."

"Bombs," George remembered. "Bombs are real."

"Yeah, bombs are real," Jasonia agreed. "But Canada's not real. Countries are just shit we made up."

"No, I think Canada's pretty real." George stamped his foot on the packed sand to emphasise its solidity.

She began again. "It all started after Columbus. They just killed the Indians here. Then the Pope declared that the Indians were humans. So if they were humans, they couldn't just kill them and take their stuff. Then this Vitoria guy makes up this thing called sovereignty. He looked at European kingdoms, and said if you are organized the way they were, then you were a nation. If not, then you didn't have sovereignty and they could take anything they wanted. That's where it all starts, as a justification for ripping off the Indians. Then it grows. Pretty soon everyone believes in it. The king of Sweden round about sixteen hundred. He hears this thing about if you don't occupy a territory you can't claim it as part of your country. So he invites Finnish people to come into northern Sweden and occupy it for him. He promises them free land and no taxes for six years. So they came and settled it for him. They become known as the Forest Finns. Then in about nineteen hundred, the government of Canada invites these same people to come to the prairies and occupy it for Canada. See, Canada was worried that if they didn't occupy all the land they claimed, the Americans could come and take it from them. So they gave away free land to the immigrants, homesteads. They weren't being kind to the people they invited. They weren't being hospitable. They needed those poor buggers to hold the land for them so that they could claim to be a nation. So because of this idea of sovereignty that this Catholic guy named Vitoria made up, we get these huge population shifts all across the planet."

She waved a hand to indicate the expanse of shacks and shelters. "Ryan Talbot says that we have sovereignty in Regis."

George didn't say anything. His understanding of international law wouldn't give state status to a slum.

She must have read the look on his face. "Sure," she continued. "We meet the test. We occupy a defined territory to the exclusion of others and we have a government."

"Government?"

"Yeah, of course. Not like your government. Ours is more democratic. It's so democratic it's benevolent anarchy."

Her voice sounded dry, beginning to crack. "Do you have any water?"

"No, sorry, didn't bring any with me."

She stood up. "Water is real. Come on." She started to walk away.

George followed. "My daughter is real."

"What's her name?"

"Anna."

"Nice name, how old is she?

"Two."

Jasonia was saying something but he wasn't listening. He was thinking *Was Lenore real?* On days like today she didn't seem to be. She seemed made up. There had been a connection between them, then it began to fade. When Anna was born it strengthened again for a while before it dimmed to where they were now, two separate beings sharing space, sharing time, and little else.

Maybe she wasn't real, maybe she wouldn't be real, maybe today she would crash her car, drive it off the bridge into the river and float away. It wasn't the first time he'd had thoughts like these, of his freedom from her, from her moods and the sharpness of her tongue. He'd never come right out and wished that she would die, but once in a while his mind ran him through a scene where a police officer or someone from Victim's Services came to his door, hat in hand, and serious eyes.

"Chiclets are real." Jasonia's voice drew him back. She drank water from a plastic bottle, replaced the cap and tilted it toward him.

He declined with a slight shake of his head. "What do you mean chiclets are real? Do you think buzzed out, stoned people are more in touch with reality than straight people?"

"Who knows? Maybe there's more to their hallucinations than chemical-induced brain short circuits. It's possible. Honestly . . . I don't know what's real or isn't. And it doesn't matter. I'm not even sure if you're real or not. There's a chance that you are, and that's good enough. But Chiclets or alcohol. Same thing. In your world alcohol is accepted absolutely, it's completely ingrained into your paradigm, you use it socially, ceremonially, medicinally. You actually believe that drinking a poison is good for your health. Maybe a little poison *is* good for the heart. But so is strychnine. In small doses, it might even be better for the heart than alcohol. It thins the blood."

George wasn't convinced. "There's a big difference between drinking alcohol and taking strychnine."

"Not really. They both taste horrible. The only way you can drink alcohol is to mix it with something that kills the taste or else you convince yourself that something that actually tastes incredibly bad is a taste you prefer. Remember the first beer you drank and how horrible it was? The only reason you kept drinking it was because of your friends. It's really pretty disgusting to drink rotted grain. But you convinced yourself that it was good, and you convinced yourself that rotten grape juice was exceptionally tasty. You could just as easily have convinced yourself that strychnine was a good thing."

"I think the affects of alcohol play a big part in it."

"Not really," Jasonia countered. "Strychnine has affects. There used to be LSD. People loved it. Problem was, it was really hard to make. You needed a real laboratory. So . . . " She shrugged, turned her palms upward. "Some unscrupulous people, and there's always those, sold strychnine. The affects are similar in really small doses. Hallucinations, flashes of light, bright colours. And maybe a feeling of disorientation. If you wanted to, you could convince yourself that a tiny bit of strychnine was actually good for the heart. Strychnine is in Chiclets. That's what gives it its kick."

"Strychnine, really; I didn't know that."

She cocked her head, looked at him quizzically, "What do you mean you didn't know? You're supposed to be the prosecutor. You of all people should know. They make it uptown out of whatever they can put together . . . "

She suddenly stopped talking, head up, alert, She looked quickly around.

"Storms are real." She turned and began running back toward the school.

He looked over his shoulder once, at the dark grey cloud, tinged with green, as he raced behind her toward shelter.

64

I GET UP IN THE MORNING and put my right foot out the door, the left one gets jealous and follows, the next thing I know, I'm ten kilometres down the road. Katherine allowed herself a tight smile at the memory of Richard's explanation of how he'd become a walker.

He was gone again — off somewhere, walking.

That's okay, summer was coming. Summer and she would know where he was, he'd be in his boat from daylight until dark, harvesting algae, drying it, and taking it to the depot for sale.

But where was he now?

It was still good, she reminded herself. Life was good.

They had all they needed. Richard had work in the summer, honest work that paid honest money. They had a home at the Ashram, a good home; they were surrounded by friends in a safe clean place.

They had each other, and there was love there still. When she was in his arms, she could feel his love pour into her. When they were in bed and she was about to fall asleep and he put an arm across her back, she felt his compassion like a warm blanket that wrapped around her.

Their relationship was strong. It was safe. She just wished she knew what it was that made him bitter sometimes. What was it that sent him on his long walks, what was it that drove him? Something he never spoke of.

65

"How?"

The girls, Tammy and Idoya, out with Lenore for an afternoon glass, a splash of wine and a bit of gossip, understood the complete question. *How was it possible with cameras everywhere for Juan and Nicole to have an affair and keep it secret?*

Idoya answered, her Spanish accent adding enchantment to her words, "¿Cómo . . . Oh, you are so sweet, Lenore, so innocent and sweet. What would we do without you? My dear, there are places where there are no cameras. If you're connected."

Another one word question: "Where?"

Tammy, eager to show that she was in the know: "The gymnasium, only the better ones of course, and they cost."

"Really?"

"Really." Idoya's accent didn't hide the smugness of her answer, perhaps enhanced it. "The King James at Wadin Bay, Rosario's, The Place, there's a few of them."

"Well, how did Nicole's husband find out?"

"Nicole likes to brag."

"Oh, I see."

Tammy showed her distaste for it all. "Of course Nicole is free to ruin her marriage. But she also ruined Juan and Esmeralda's."

"Yes, Esmeralda. Poor thing. How's she handling it all?" Lenore asked Idoya, assuming that the details would be known within the Spanish community.

Idoya shrugged, pulled her shoulders up high, made a mock smile, her mouth closed and comical.

Tammy knew. "She took it very well. She was very dignified. No tantrums, no screaming. She sent the movers to the apartment to collect her property. I expect she'll cut his balls off in court though."

"I am so glad they didn't have children."

Lenore went silent. Anna was with the Nanny for three hours this afternoon to give her some time to just be and not think, some trivial time.

And it was good for Anna to spend time with the Nanny, time away from her. She was completely aware of the affect she had on her daughter; the stress and the tension that she couldn't shed transferred itself into the little girl when they were together. When the mood came upon her suddenly, out of nowhere, and she felt like she was going to panic and run, when she started looking around for a snug safe place, Anna either shut down completely, refused to eat or participate in any play, or else she began to scream — shrieks that sounded like screams of fear.

Then Lenore would call for the Nanny, abdicate motherhood, go for a walk, and a glass and a splash. Sometimes several splashes. Then when things were mellow and she was all good, she'd go home again, and the nanny — why did she always have trouble remembering her name? — would have Anna all settled down for a nap, or they would be playing together on the floor.

She'd almost struck Anna once. She had been leaning over the crib and the little girl had raised a fist toward her, a little pudgy baby fist. The anger had rushed through her with a suddenness that almost knocked her off her feet. The only reason she didn't strike was because, in that moment, she needed both hands to hold on to the crib rail or she would have fallen over.

"How's George?"

Tammy's question brought Lenore back to the table, back to the bright cheery décor of the uptown restaurant with its all-glass front and the afternoon light streaming in. They were three well-dressed women at a table near the front where they could see the people passing on the sidewalk, and where those people would see them.

"George . . . " Lenore didn't know. How was George really? The question wasn't exactly about him, about her husband. It was actually about their relationship — how were she and George? "Well, you know . . . " She faltered, chose to answer safely. "He's the same."

Tammy twirled her glass.

Idoya was looking around for the waiter. The young one, the one with the dark complexion, the one that looked like he might be a runner or a cyclist. She'd already commented on his lean muscles. "Different than men who go to the gymnasium to keep in shape. Maybe he's a soccer player."

Lenore needed something, anything, to fill the widening gap in the conversation. Take too long and they would think she had something to hide.

But how was George?

Quieter.

Not the same. Definitely not the same as before.

"The other day . . . " she didn't think through what she was going to say, just launched into something random. "At the courthouse, there was this strange man. He compared

George to someone out of the Bible. Paul — Saint Paul I think. Anyway . . . it really upset him. I told him it shouldn't, just a crazy man. You know how they are, people with mental health problems who get caught up in religion. I think they turn to religion for help with their problems and then . . . Well, they get carried away."

"They hear voices and think it's God talking to them." The disdain was clear in Tammy's voice. "I know about people like that."

"Yeah, something like that. Anyway, it really got to George. Now he's researching this Saint."

"Really."

"He's obsessed, he's taken it to heart. I think the guy was from Regis, an activist . . . "

Tammy interrupted, "You mean anarchist."

"I believe they call themselves ultra-democratic," Idoya added.

Lenore knew she had gone too far, had said more than she should have. Tammy and Idoya were friends, but they were dangerous friends, friends who were connected, friends who could put a word in a wrong place and end a career. She needed to rectify her story, excuse George.

"It's just George is stressed. The man was crazy."

That didn't help. She should just shut up right about now. She was making it worse.

"You know how George is. He gets something in his head and he won't quit until he completely understands it. That's what makes him such a good prosecutor. He's always well researched."

"But what's he researching, Christianity or dangerous ideas?" Tammy had found the loose thread in the narrative and wasn't going to let it go.

Idoya came to the rescue. "He's a prosecutor, Tam. Research goes with the territory."

The conversation lulled. Tammy had something to think about. Idoya caught the waiter's attention, though not the waiter she was hoping for.

Lenore looked out the glass front of the restaurant. She could see Bel Arial hanging in the sky to the south, the wine was warm and dry in her mouth, and she wondered if there were cameras up there. She didn't remember seeing any. But then most cameras were so small they wouldn't be seen unless there was a reason to make them obvious, to let people know they were being watched.

No, there probably weren't cameras on Bel Arial. Security was about watching the others, the dangerous ones, the ones from Regis who could put a knife into you, and the cameras were there for evidence when it came to court. The connected didn't need to be observed constantly. They did the watching. Security was designed to protect them, designed by them, for their benefit. Why watch yourself?

She left the restaurant earlier than usual, made an excuse about needing to take care of Anna. But she didn't go directly home. Instead she went out to Wadin Bay and bought a membership at the King James Gymnasium.

Why?

Well, she'd just had a baby and needed to get her body back into shape. At least that is what she would tell George, if he asked.

66

Ryan Talbot was famous for saying, "I am just a man." There were many who didn't believe him, who thought he must be something more. If Ryan showed up at your protest, you could be sure something would happen, usually something incredible, like the time at the Air Weapons Range. Twenty protesters sat on the ground and meditated. They didn't chant and swear and yell, there were no Stop War signs, there was no anger. Talbot said, "You can't stop anger with anger. Only love and compassion will save you." They sat for three days, didn't stop any traffic, didn't block the gate. They just sat and thought about peace. They neither ate nor drank, merely prayed and fasted, and on the third day the stone wall in front of them toppled over. No one had hit it, no one beat on it. There was no storm, no wind. The wall sagged, buckled and gently, slowly, lay over on its side.

Engineers were quick to point out that there had been extremely heavy rains the week prior and the ground under the wall was saturated, the wall had been constructed without proper footings, the wall was too high to stand freely, the stones inlaid on the south side of the wall were all larger than the stones inlaid on the north side.

But the wall had stood for over sixty years and there had been heavy rains before.

And the engineers answered, sixty years is a long time for a wall. It should have fallen over long before this, especially a wall as poorly constructed as the one in question.

Talbot became famous. He was modest, humble, soft spoken, peaceful and now famous. He attracted people in the hundreds whenever he protested, whenever he sat down and meditated in opposition to humanity's destructiveness. And miracles continued to happen. Most notably, security cameras seemed routinely to malfunction at any event where Ryan Talbot was present.

Richard wanted to be part of this movement, to meet Talbot, sit with him. This might well be the defining moment of this age. This might be the crack in the wall, when all of the illusions of humanity crumble and a new age emerges, an age of peace and rationality.

But he couldn't protest.

He'd given up protest to stay on the Ashram. This was his sacrifice for Katherine. Did she appreciate it? Did any of them? Did Walter and those other small-minded Ashram people who insisted upon exclusivity have any inkling of what was happening outside of their tiny world? Didn't they realize that silence was complicity, that by shutting themselves away, they condoned what happened outside the gate of their tiny Ashram?

Richard waved a hand over his platform, shut out the video of a circle of protesters sitting cross-legged on the ground. The video hadn't brought him peace, not the peace experienced by the participants together on the earth that they prayed to, that they prayed for. This was a peace that they envisioned for the whole world. He felt a tinge of anger, or maybe sorrow; because of a commitment, he was excluded from the beauty of their experience.

He pushed those thoughts away. They didn't get him anywhere. He lived on an Ashram with Katherine. There were rules — no protest, do not draw attention. That's the way it was. That's where he was. But such rationality didn't get him anywhere. It didn't stop the hurt. It was pain, of a sort, like an ache in his soul. It felt like he'd been cheated.

67

Never count the dead of the enemy. Soldier's rules, the rules of war. And there were soldiers like that, who could put it from their minds, who could look upon the bodies and not feel anything. Those were not people laying there, merely corpses. George remembered them, the men he'd once envied, tough men, doing a tough job.

He didn't envy them anymore. He simply wondered how they could do that. He knew the answer: because if they gave a moment, a single moment of thought, the bodies and the moments would pile up in their minds and crush them.

He was becoming like that — doing his job. There weren't bodies piling up. But there was beginning to be a long line of people being led away shackled and cuffed. And they weren't people to him anymore, they were files: assault cause bodily harm, assault with a weapon to wit a stick, uttering death threats, assault police officer, sexual assault . . .

Read the file, read the police reports, ascertain whether there was a reasonable likelihood of conviction, either negotiate a plea bargain with defence counsel, or run a trial — if a trial, then prepare witnesses, get a conviction, sometimes, rarely, an acquittal, but that didn't happen often. Then after conviction or a guilty plea, speak to sentence; for assault with a weapon, two years jail; for assault police, three to five — mechanical, mathematical. Don't count the bodies.

It was the responsibility of defence counsel to place the personal circumstances of the offender before the court: how many children he had, what grade he accomplished in school, whether he was employed, that he had been abused as a child, that he lived in Regis, that he was addicted to alcohol, to solvents, to chiclets, that he was suffering from a mental deficit that rendered him incapable of knowing that what he had done was necessarily wrong. It was defence counsel's job to present him or her to the judge as a human being before sentence was passed down.

Prosecution's duty was to the populace, to the victims. The system wasn't designed for George to care about what happened to the accused after sentencing. He had a job to do, a tough job.

The job was becoming harder. There was in his head a new mathematical formula that complicated things. If the average life expectancy of the average person in northern Saskatchewan was eighty-seven-point-four years and that person went to prison for five years, then they spent . . .

What was five into eighty-five roughly? Five into forty was eight, eight times two was sixteen. They would spend a sixteenth of their life locked away.

If a five-year sentence was a sixteenth — then a ten-year sentence was an eighth. An eighth of anything was a big chunk. Imagine an eighth of a life, an eighth of a person's journey.

And that person had come here to experience the physical in combination with the spiritual.

Eighty-seven-point-four years — that wasn't very long. Not to him, not now, now that he was well past the halfway point, and that first half, it had gone so fast.

Just a dot of blue light traveling across the universe.

He could recommend to the judge, "This man must give an eighth, or a quarter, or a half, or all that remained. He must give it and go experience only concrete and steel."

Because he spat on a policeman or ran when he was going to be arrested, he must be denied the experience of green, of nature; he must not walk on grass, not sit under a tree. He must be denied the sight of the stars, to look back where he came from. He must not know sunlight, or wind, or the softness of moonlight.

The bodies were beginning to pile up. Not so high that he was going to do anything about them, not yet. But the weight of them was growing, beginning to bear down on him. He wasn't sure if he could take any more.

68

"Hey Kat, why don't you give that a break."

Yeah, she could use a break. Katherine stretched out her hunched back, stood straight, felt the tightness in the muscle between her shoulder blades. How long had she been standing here at the workbench? She wasn't sure; hours — two, maybe three.

"Give me another couple of minutes. I just want to finish this up." She began sorting bits of soil into jars, putting them back on their respective shelves; a few more labels, dates, results, a few more notes.

"Come on, that's enough. Those will be here when you get back." Tasha took her by the arm and led her away from the back area of the greenhouse. "You're coming for tea with the girls."

Katherine hadn't been in the Earthship in . . . she tried to remember. Had it really been months? Since last autumn? She'd have to be careful of things like that. Friends were too important to ignore. Tasha, Emily, Vivienne and Geneva. The women lived in a series of domes made of recycled tires packed with sand, a safe secure place with walls a metre thick;

these women remembered that she had once been one of them and were intent upon keeping the bond between them strong.

The tea, rose hips and a bit of bergamot orange, did what it was intended to do — soothed her, relaxed her, settled her deep into the padded wooden chair.

"This is nice." She held her cup in both hands, felt the warmth of it on her palms.

"Well, we didn't think Richard would be making a nice cup for our Kat," said Vivienne, pouring for the others.

"No," Emily agreed. "There's something about tea between women that can't be found with a man."

The conversation, simple, easy, just talk between the girls, soothed and relaxed just like the tea. It brought a warmth to her core. She always found it easy to smile; the tea and the talk and the friends simply made the smile broader.

The Earthship had always been a safe place, a place where women looked after one another. It was the first place where she discovered that she belonged. It was where she had traversed the distance from being a solitary wandering girl, to being a woman, a woman connected to place and time and, importantly, to other women, to community. She had in a very real sense grown up here.

Something about it being made of earth, dug into the earth, gave it a spiritual quality, a connectivity that satisfied a deep need. Nothing can hurt you when you are in the womb of Mother Earth.

"How's Richard?" Vivienne asked. "We don't see him around much anymore."

"Oh, you know, Richard is Richard." Katherine would have perferred to talk about anything else, maybe those new curtains. They looked like Emily's work. Emily liked bright colours.

"I was up to see my sister Jenny the other day and saw him downtown." Vivienne started the conversation down a path.

Geneva, her tea in one hand and her walking stick in the other, went out into the sunlight.

Katherine was about to make excuses for him; *he doesn't have a lot to do here, he likes to walk*, but sat silent and waited instead.

"In the Blackwater Café," Vivienne continued.

Katherine didn't know the place. Had never been. She shrugged. A weak shrug. Her shoulders felt tired.

"He was with that woman who was here that time the Net went down. Lenore, I think her name is."

"And?" One word was all that Katherine had the strength to speak.

"Oh, nothing. They were just having coffee and talking." Vivienne looked away. Tasha and Emily were both examining the bottom of their cups, looking through the rose-coloured tea.

Katherine could not find her space again. The soil samples did not hold any meaning. They had become nothing more than bits of dirt. The greenhouse felt too warm, too humid, she felt her blouse stick to her back, she felt an unease and a tiredness that at once stirred her core and drained her of energy; she was angry and too weak to do anything about it.

Gossip, dirty life-destroying gossip. That's all it was, and friends shouldn't do that to one another. But maybe she was just killing the messengers and not hearing the message.

She stood in the doorway of the greenhouse and looked at the pine tree, its rough reddish-hued bark, the stub of the lowest branch sawn off sometime before her time. It had survived the invasion of the pine beetle at the turn of the century, an invasion that had swept in from the West Coast across the Rocky Mountains turning a green forest red with dead needles, the first visible casualties of global warming. When winter temperatures across the boreal forest failed to fall to the degree needed to kill the beetle, it burst out to occupy the new niche. Minus forty degrees Celsius, the old normal, which could be expected in January of each year, was what was required to kill the beetle. Foresters prayed for it, but they were outnumbered by those who were at the same time praying for warmer weather, for golfing weather.

The Cree Indians, the Nehithaw — how did she remember that word? Of the few words left to her by her father, how did that one remain in her brain while all the others were mute? — had once called December *the moon when the trees are covered in hoar frost,* and January was *the moon when trees cracked in the cold.* Those descriptions, along with the Cree, had long since disappeared.

"I know you." She spoke aloud to Raven who had swooped in to occupy that stub of a branch on the pine tree. "I know all the stories about you, and some that even you might have forgot."

Raven didn't answer, merely shuffled across the branch in a single hop.

She found a bit of peace in talking to the bird. Maybe it was just distraction, a refusal to think about the emotions that stirred, but maybe it was something more, something from beyond, something that needed to be spoken, brought to life with words. "They say that once long ago, on an ancient battlefield, a king was slain and laid among the dead. A real king, and because he was the last real king the magic that makes kings was still in him. There were many that had been killed, on both sides, and the valley was filled with bodies. The clang of sword and shield was silent and the autumn evening air was still.

"A raven, one of your ancestors maybe, or maybe it was you . . . "

Raven didn't answer.

"Maybe it was you . . . " now she was sure it was this same bird. "You came and ate the dead and you ate from the heart of the King. And when you did, you were cursed by the magic of kings and you became a wereraven, half man-half raven, a shape-shifter trapped between the two worlds, the world of man and the world of birds.

"They say you are to stay that way until you eat the heart of an innocent. Well, it won't be mine, my fine feathered friend, not this heart. It's not innocent anymore."

69

HE WANTED THE DISCUSSION TO BE about principles, but it turned into an argument about money. It seemed all of their discussions turned into arguments. It was getting to the point where George was becoming reluctant to start a conversation with her; better to just not say anything. And there was no winning an argument. She couldn't be convinced. Once she took a position, any position, whether it was rational or not, there was no dissuading her.

He used to love her tenacity, her strength. It had been part of Lenore's beauty, now he saw it as her ugly side.

He tried, patiently, calmly, "Maybe not in the first couple of years, but give it some time and it should work out pretty close to the same."

"There's no way in hell," Lenore snapped back, "that you are ever going to make as much money in private practice that you do as a prosecutor. What are you trying to do, ruin us?" She was on a roll, spitting anger. "What about this apartment, how are you going to afford this? And you're still making payments on that stupid bird of yours. Are you going to give that up?"

The words did as they were intended, struck George where they would hurt the most. Could he give up the ORV? The payments were steep. But that wasn't what hurt. Whether or not a changed financial situation could accommodate his passion. No, what hurt was that she called the Raven stupid.

Her words tore him. He loved her, he really did, even now, even with her eyes hard and her face in a grimace, he loved her. The rip, the tear, was between his love for her and for the ORV. It had become part of him. It gave him definition. George was an ORV pilot. He was a Raven man. He began to feel as though his heart was slowly being torn out. He felt very human in that moment, human and vulnerable.

He needed the argument to stop; needed to back it up somehow, take it back to where the discussion should be, about principles, about how he couldn't be a prosecutor any more, couldn't participate in a system that did that to human beings. That's where it had started. She hadn't listened. Instead she focused on the money, on the position.

"You have a daughter," Lenore continued, "and a responsibility to make sure she's taken care of."

George felt his own anger begin to rise. The hurt of a half second before shape-shifted into something else. He tasted anger, a hint of bile at the back of his mouth, his fingers began to curl into fists, his stance straightened.

How could she?

How could she throw Anna into it?

When she was first home from the division on maternity leave, she'd hardly touched the child. Wasn't mat leave there so that a mother could breast feed? Then in the year since she'd returned to work, the nanny had spent more time with the child than she had.

He spent more time with Anna than she did.

What the hell was she doing throwing Anna into the mix? She didn't even like her. And it was obvious. When Anna climbed onto her lap, she immediately set her down again; when Anna cried, Lenore looked at him first to see if he was going to respond; little things that grew until he knew the child wasn't liked, and Anna knew she wasn't welcome in her mother's presence.

But he didn't confront Lenore with it. Each time she ignored Anna it opened up a vulnerability that he could strike at. Instead he responded, "Enough now, I'm going to go for a little flight."

"No, you're not. You can damn well stay here and look after the daughter that you're thinking about neglecting. I'm going to the gym."

It didn't matter much. Either solution worked well. He could find silence in the apartment, or in the sky, though part of him would always prefer the sky.

But even after she left, the anger continued to boil, to control his thoughts. There was no peace in her leaving, only a replay of their conversation, over and over again, each word, each gesture, each facial expression, repeating itself. His anger turned inward, against himself. There were so many places where he could have said something, where he should have said something.

He blamed himself. He hadn't handled it well. He should have started the conversation differently. He knew how she was, how she felt about private lawyers, about her role in the division. She saw herself as a champion of justice, the one who did the hard work. Being a prosecutor was who Lenore was. It gave her definition. The idea that it somehow wasn't right, that ethically there was a problem, struck her in her personhood. When George had said that *he* was having trouble continuing to be a prosecutor, it signalled to Lenore that *she* was ethically compromised.

The anger simmered, turned back into hurt. Instead of having a rational conversation with his partner, he'd caused an argument. It hurt that she hadn't listened, hadn't heard when he pathetically tried to explain how it felt. It was his fault, his fault that she felt insulted, his fault that she became angry. And he knew better. He always knew how she would react. Why the hell did he start it?

Because he couldn't be a prosecutor. He couldn't participate in the *Put Crime In It's Place Programme*, which meant put everyone in jail, subtract a portion of their lives when they messed up. He just couldn't do it anymore.

70

SUCH A WIMP. WHY HAD SHE ever thought he was the man for her? Why had she pursued him? He used to be tough, tough enough to do the job. He looked like he was going somewhere once, like he might make head office, or even regional director.

Lenore pushed herself through her routine, forced her body to respond, felt the force in her legs as she squatted with her fists up, each holding a five-kilo weight. She didn't count the repetitions. It didn't matter if she did thirty or fifty or even a hundred. Numbers were a distraction. Instead she paid attention to her body. It said when the pain was right, and when she reached the pain, she pushed herself a few more, pushed through it.

But she wasn't enjoying it today. Today her thoughts kept spinning, drawing her attention away from her purpose. George could be something if he wanted. He was intelligent enough. She had to give him that. And he was a good father to Anna. He really was amazing with her; patient, far more patient than she could ever be.

But then George had never experienced what she had. He'd never looked in the pot. Lenore saw the hand in the bubbling water again, the image of it as clear as when she had first seen it. The smell was in her memory. Boiling meat. Her uniform had chaffed against her shoulders and the sweat had coursed down the centre of her back.

She stopped at the bottom of a squat, the weights in her fists at her shoulders. The music in the King James Gymnasium beat loudly and rhythmically, a thump, thump that usually matched her heartbeat in the middle of a workout. Now her heart rate exceeded the music, pounded harder, out of sync. She forced herself to stand; her hands and the weights dropped to her sides. She put the weights back on their rack and headed to the steam room.

She really should talk to someone about this, a counsellor, a psychiatrist, a priest, someone. But she hadn't, she'd carried it by herself, and now the pot was such a long time ago that she felt a bit foolish to try to talk to anyone about it. It really was something that she should have gotten over by now.

She knew the affect it had on her, how it infected her relationship with her daughter, though not so much now that she was getting older, beyond that pudgy baby stage. She turned up the heat in the steam shower to the scalding point, felt the sting of it against her skin, until all she could think about was the pain and standing in it, and how she was strong enough that she could stand the torture of the steam against her flesh.

71

RICHARD PACKED CANNABIS INTO THE PIPE, so rich that it was sticky with resin. It wasn't *green* as people commonly referred to it, as in, "Got a bit of green there, buddy?" It had many shades of colour: greys and browns and even a bit of black mixed with the leaf. He'd snipped at a large bud with a little scissors, carefully, almost ceremoniously, until he had enough to fill the bowl. And this time it was going to be a full bowl, not a half, or a quarter, not this time. He wasn't intending on just a quick buzz, a little high to get him by. No, this was going to be a complete pipe-full, a complete high.

His fingers worked without hurry, ensuring that every speck made it into the pipe. Then he tamped it with his little finger; not too tight or he wouldn't be able to draw on it; too tight and it didn't burn, and if it was too loose, it flamed up and burned too hot, too fast and didn't produce enough smoke.

He didn't concern himself with *why*. Why he wanted to get high and stay there, why he smoked so much more than usual lately.

He filled the wooden pipe, carved in the shape of a dragon, to just below the brim. This was his finest crop, his select seeds. It didn't have the THC levels of some that was out there. This wasn't *Master Blaster* stuff. But the high it produced was solid, respectable; and it had taste, a well-rounded taste that he liked to describe as *smooth* or *mellow*. He liked it because it didn't make him cough, not like some that had been shared with him, stuff that someone else grew — you never really knew if they used chemicals to enhance it.

Richard's weed was 100% pure organic, the only fertilizer was a bit of rabbit manure, and he never manipulated the genetics of the plant, not artificially anyway. He had encouraged cross-pollination of a few plants until he obtained a strain that he liked.

He was looking for a place, for a space that he couldn't find, somewhere other, somewhere not here, not of this time, somewhere good. He put a flame to the bowl, drew that first deep draw, that first hit, the pure hit, the perfect one, drew it to the bottom of his lungs, and held it there.

The world changed. He slipped into the other dimension. His shoulders slumped, free of tension. The stress left his face; his cheek and jaw muscles eased and his mouth fell open slightly.

He leaned back into the embankment until his head rested against the earth and he was looking up at the sky. He was here again, at the river, his place, with water and bridge and all the memories of all the times that he had stopped here to think, to sort through thoughts, to sift memories; where he re-found his rhythm and matched it to the rhythm of the flowing river.

He drew again on the pipe, unsure whether it was still lit. He exhaled and his breath was white. Still unsure whether what came out of his mouth was smoke or just his breath in the cold air, he tamped the bowl with his little finger, pushed down ash and char and relit it. This second hit had a stronger taste, more carbon. He smoked it all, from top to bottom, letting it go out between hits. The last hit was vastly different than the first. It tasted more of tar and resin.

He felt the chill of the air. *Where is global warming when you need it.* It was not something he would ever say out loud to anyone. The changed atmosphere was never spoken of in jest. The ramifications were too severe. It was far too disrespectful. Too many people had died, too much of the earth was uninhabitable. Everyone knew someone, a relative, a friend, who had died because of the storms, or of thirst, or in a flood.

Climate change never made it into a conversation, but it informed all discussions about the weather, it was the background knowledge that didn't need to be discussed. That discussion had worn itself out decades earlier when the blaming and finger pointing had stopped and the people dusted off the last drought or wrung out the last flood, or picked themselves off the ground from the last wind, or crawled out from the debris of the last tornado or hurricane. They were silent at the graveside as they lowered those that the droughts and floods and storms had taken.

His thoughts swirled, not unlike the smoke from the pipe, lazy and listless. His body was in one world, his mind in another. The universe was like that. It could accommodate something being in two places at the same time. He could be a particle or a wave at the same time, and all particles and all waves were connected in the great harmony. *There's a flow to the universe*, Virgil said. *Create a disturbance in one place and the flow will try to correct it. Minimize the disturbances that you create and try to follow the flow of the universe and your life will flow effortlessly. Listen and walk within the harmonics and you will experience good health and happiness.*

When you experience a disturbance in the harmony caused by others, be careful how you go about fixing it. Far too often humans attempt to repair the disturbance by creating even greater disturbances. You can never stop anger with more anger, violence can't stop violence, war can't stop war.

Richard sat up. He knew that. He knew about war. It never stopped. He'd seen how it affected those who went there, those who carried the germs of war with them, were infected by it, who needed to heal themselves, people like Lenore.

He could see her, in the Blackwater Café, her hand reaching across the table to touch his, her eyes, her green eyes, searching his face, searching his eyes, trying to look into his soul through his eyes, looking for answers to questions that only she knew.

"All my love, all I have and all I am, and only you, forever and ever, my wife." His vow sounded suddenly and loudly in his head and he thought again of Katherine. Kat at the Ashram. She walked within the harmonics of the universe, minimized the disturbances that she created and didn't accommodate the disturbances created by others. And when they were together, when Katherine and Richard were really together, they were part of the music, it flowed around them and through them, and their heartbeats and their laughter contributed to the song.

A woman approached, followed the shoreline, ducked under the low bridge, her head down as though searching the muddy bank for something. For what? Crayfish maybe, obviously something to eat. In another time, in another experience, she might have been pretty. Dark hair, dark skin and blue eyes. There was that about her, that blended heritage, perhaps Scandinavian and African, maybe East European and Mexican, or even Oriental, Mediterranean and Aboriginal. Blue eyes and dark skin didn't surprise anyone anymore. Just another example of the melting pot that some referred to as the mongrelization of humanity.

It was difficult for Richard to guess how old she might be, anywhere between her late teens and early thirties. Some soap and a hairbrush could possibly take ten years off her appearance.

He knew her. Well, not *her* personally, but he did know many in her situation. There had been a time when Canada took care of the poor, gave welfare, supported foodbanks. The change had been slow at first, a cut-back here, a program terminated there, a general turning and looking away. Or maybe the people didn't really look away, maybe it was that they became too busy looking after themselves. As the ability to earn a living and the idea of a decent living began to fade, and those who were still able to earn were forced to work harder and harder for a pay cheque that seemed to become smaller and smaller, the idea that everyone had to pull their own weight became more and more pronounced, until the puddle at the bottom of the socio-economic ladder turned into a pool that began to climb, one rung at a time.

When the planet's ecology shifted — gave a little shudder and adapted itself to the new climate — more people fell off the ladder.

When people don't have a home, don't have a fixed address, spend all of their time looking for food, they don't vote. People who don't vote don't get government's attention and, anyway, government was just too busy; there were too many wars to fight, too much was happening in the world, too many borders shifting, too many uprisings, too much immigration, the economy refused to remain stable, there were shortages.

There was a popular myth at first, that those in the pool weren't real Canadians anyway, that they were just illegal immigrants that Canada tolerated out of kindness, but really didn't have an obligation to assist. "We're doing them a favour by not sending them back." But the myth didn't — couldn't — persist. Truth swallowed it. Too many tenth generation Canadians were treading water.

"What'cha gots in nuh bag?"

Richard put his hand on his pack, perhaps protectively, maybe just to make sure it was still there. He didn't want this. Why couldn't she just keep walking? Why did she have to stop and talk to him? Why now? This was his high, his alone. He'd planned it, prepared for it, this was his piece of riverbank, his place, his peace. He didn't want people in it; just him, the earth, the water, the sky and the high.

Maybe if he didn't answer, she'd keep walking.

"What'ch yer name, honey?" She ran her fingers through her hair and smiled. Her jacket made that screechy nylon sound. He noticed that her teeth were good, mostly white.

He looked away, searched for something interesting on the ground.

"Aw, come-on, I ain't gonna bite'cha."

She was standing directly in front of him now, she wasn't going anywhere. He felt forced to acknowledge her presence. "What do you need?"

"Need?" She considered the word, her eyes to the right and upward slightly as though looking to that quadrant of the sky for an answer. "Right this minute, I guess, all I need is to keep breathin'. Ya, jus keep suckin' it in an' pushin' it out."

Her smile warmed him, disarmed him. "Don't we both, sister." He returned the smile. She was easy to be with.

"You got's a home?" Her question didn't set off any alarm bells. She was just another human on the journey who stopped to chat him up. She didn't want anything from him, she wasn't trying to manipulate or manoeuvre him.

"Yeah, I got's a home," he mimicked.

"Where's it at?"

"I live at Hayden's Ashram. Do you know it?"

"Noooo . . . " she let out a breath. "Ya, maybe . . . maybe I knowed some other time. You know, from before."

Richard wasn't sure what she meant by *before*. Before what?

"It's a good place?" Her stress on the last consonant turned the statement into a question.

"Yeah, it's a good place." He nodded. He agreed. Hayden Ashram was a good place.

"So, what'cha doin here den?"

Richard felt as though he had to scramble for the answer. He'd never considered the question before. If Hayden Ashram was a good place, what *was* he doing here?

He tried a dodge. "Just hangin out." He could tell by her face that she wasn't buying it, the way she looked at him, with that *Aw, come on now* expression. "What's your name, sister?" He tried to move the conversation along.

It didn't seem as though she was going to let him. Her eyes looked through him, or at least into him, slightly squinting, questioning, or not believing. Slowly she let him go, her face softened, turned back to smiling. "My name's Francis. You know, Saint Francis of Regis?"

Richard didn't know. He shrugged.

"Ya, you know. Da one who preaches to duh birds?"

Richard shook his head.

"Ya, Saint Frances. I go to duh birds and preach like dis . . . " she stood a bit straighter and began walking in a little circle with her head bowed. Her voice changed. Now she spoke clearly, and perfectly enunciated. "My little sisters the birds, ye owe much to God, your Creator, and ye ought to sing his praise at all times and in all places, because he has given you liberty to fly about into all places; and though ye neither spin nor sew, he has given you a twofold and a threefold clothing for yourselves and for your offspring. Two of all your species he sent into the Ark with Noah that you might not be lost to the world; besides which, he feeds you, though ye neither sow nor reap. He has given you fountains and rivers to quench your thirst, mountains and valleys in which to take refuge, and trees in which to build your nests; so that your Creator loves you much, having thus favoured you with such bounties. Beware, my little sisters, of the sin of ingratitude, and study always to give praise to God." She stopped, looked up and pointed at a raven looking down at them from the bridge rail. "You were dere. You remember don'cha. You was one of dem dat flew to duh nort. Remember when all duh birds went into four groups and one group went to each direction, remember, you went wit duh ones dat went to duh nort?"

Raven vocalized his displeasure at being pointed at. He gave a loud series of *Kaws* and hopped into the air, swooped low over the quickly flowing river before he banked off toward the south.

"Now what'cha gonno do?"

Richard was getting to his feet. "I think I'm going to go home."

"You do dat." She patted him on the shoulder, her fingers as thin as sticks. "You do dat, and you takes care of yourself now."

It started to snow as he walked back to the Ashram. Just a few flakes coming out of the northeast. With the sky overcast, the evening light became dim and grey.

72

"I WAS WORRIED ABOUT YOU."

"Why's that." Richard brushed the snow from his hat, gave it a little shake before tossing it up on the rack.

"Blizzard's coming, big one they say."

"Don't ever worry about me, my love." He reached out to Katherine.

"But I do." She snuggled into him, not minding the wet snow on his coat. "You're home now, it's all better."

It felt right. It felt good. He wasn't so high anymore — that mostly wore off on the long walk. He was here with Katherine, in his house; she'd made a fire and it was cosy and even a little too warm.

Her head pressed against his shoulder, her hair against his cheek; he spoke his commitment, to reassure, to comfort her. "All I have, and all I am, and only you, forever and ever, my wife."

"Only me?" she pulled back to look into his face.

"Only you."

"You sure?"

"I'm sure."

"There's nobody else?" her eyes were searching his. Questioning.

"There's nobody else." His tone matter of fact.

A different collision occurred outside, a much larger one. The jet stream — that current of air that circles the globe, meandering in a flow mostly west to east — had dipped south and with the dip brought down colder Arctic air. At the same time warm wet Pacific weather moved in from the west. If it had been just the Pacific pattern the result would have been a heavy spring rain, with perhaps some localized flooding.

If it had been just the Arctic air, the result would have been nothing more than the last visit of winter.

The Pacific met the Arctic and began a dance, a swirl, a competition or a copulation that birthed a heavy snowfall. The vigour of their meeting, of their joining, their energies, their joy, their exuberance, resulted in a hard driving wind that picked up in intensity as the night deepened.

She asked again, "Only me? Are you sure?"

Richard was sure. There was no one else; there hadn't been anyone else. Well not in a strict legal sense anyway. He could say honestly that he had not had sex with anyone other than his wife since they married. He had not committed adultery, if that was still a legal requirement of fidelity. But just because his answer met strict legal or objective parameters of truth, it wasn't completely true. There was still the recent thing with Lenore.

He felt the nag of the incompleteness of his truth, a little tug at his core. But he kept silent, perhaps because he didn't know how to tell it, how to put it into words, words that wouldn't hurt her, wouldn't sting — words that would give him absolution.

They stood, holding each other at arm's length, looking, each searching the face of the other — she for the reassurance she needed — he for the promise that if he told it completely, no one would be hurt.

A gust of wind drove snow hard against the window, hard enough that he heard the vibration from the glass.

Katherine looked up toward the roof. In other blizzards at other times, when the snow piled and piled and bore down, they sometimes found in the aftermath crushed houses, buried and collapsed.

He answered her question, even though she had not spoken a word of it. "It's okay, I built it to take the weight in the walls. The more the snow piles on the roof, the more it presses the wall timbers tighter together. It actually makes the building stronger."

He didn't realize what he had done. But then he did. He caught it. There was still a connection between them that didn't need to be spoken. He could hear her thoughts, he knew her heart and that was all the truth he needed.

"Tell me."

It was the way she said it, the way the words came out; she wasn't begging, not demanding; it was as though she was saying, *you can trust me, I trust you*, that moved him beyond his denial. Something in the way she spoke those two words assured him that no one was going to be hurt by this.

He took a breath, leaned back, needed the room to speak. "I met an old friend."

"Lenore."

"Yeah."

"So, what happened?"

"Nothing. Well, ultimately nothing, but almost."

"Almost what?"

"I almost went with her to the King James Gym. She invited me, asked me to join her there."

"I can imagine the workout she expected from you." The smile on Katherine's face was tiny but obvious.

"Well, you get the picture. I didn't go. Couldn't. But, to be perfectly honest, I wanted to, I was really tempted."

"Why?"

"I don't know." But he did know, He knew why he was tempted, he just didn't know how to put it into words.

"Sure you do." Katherine took his hand, gently led him to the couch, then sat beside him, hip to hip, shoulder to shoulder and held his hand in both of hers.

Richard felt his body stiffen, felt the resistance begin to grow, the urge to pull his hand back, to stand up and walk away, perhaps to turn and speak from a distance. But she wasn't holding him there, wasn't clutching at him. Her hands were easy on his, stroking, gentle, assuring. She was beside him, but not crowding.

"We've met a few times recently . . . " the words began on their own, as though they wanted to come out. "Just visiting, just talking, going for coffee. She was interested in my ideas, you know, the things Virgil wrote about. She wanted to know about the demonstrations, about Ryan Talbot and how it all fit together. I guess I must have became interested in her because she seemed interested in me."

"Did you tell her you were married?"

"Of course, so is she."

"Ohhh."

"Yeah, they have a kid."

"Ohhh."

"I guess it's not going so good for them. She's with another lawyer, a prosecutor."

"Well if they're both prosecutors, then they sure don't have to worry about money."

"We both know there's more to it than money."

"That's true." Katherine leaned back into the couch, stretched out her legs, pointed her toes, tilted her head until it touched the wall behind her. It was more than just a stretch of muscle that had stayed too long in one position. He looked at the length of her body, shoulders, abdomen, pelvis, thighs, noticed the leanness and the muscle and the curves and the roundness all properly in the places where curves and roundness are supposed to be in a well-proportioned woman.

"So, why were you tempted? It had to be something more than just that she was interested in you."

"Well, I guess, I was feeling a little rejected."

"By me?" Katherine sat up straighter.

"No." He was quick to answer. "Not you. The Ashram. I was pissed at the Ashram."

With those words, *I was pissed at the Ashram,* a realization occurred to him, a simple, straight-forward explanation for why he had been suffering. Why hadn't he seen it before? He'd read it so many times, he almost had it memorized. Virgil's discussion of choice:

Everything in your life is your choice, and every choice that you make has an impact on the universe. Every moment of your life you are making choices, even when you choose not to choose. Every choice will either follow the flow of the universe or it will create a disturbance. Once you've made a choice, you live with the consequences.

You cannot be forced to make a choice. Someone points a gun at your head and says, "do this," it's still your choice; you could choose to be shot. So, you can never blame others for your choices. Don't ever be a martyr. Don't make choices that your heart opposes. It's irrational to say, "I make this choice because I have no choice."

Never compromise. Once you've made a choice, accept it, embrace it, do it with love.

And that was exactly what he had done, wasn't it? He'd compromised. He

had chosen to stop attending protests, but he'd told himself that he had no choice: if he didn't stop protesting, he'd lose Katherine. Then, because he'd chosen to become a victim, to become the suffering martyr, his journey through the universe had become distorted and dark. Worst of all, as he trudged in the mire of resentment, his path had turned away from Katherine. At some point, he'd started to blame *her* for his choice.

The wind howled, its voice loud through the walls and roof of the cabin. He raised his voice to be heard. "The reason I didn't meet her at the King James Gym, is because I chose to come home."

Katherine leaned away. "You were supposed to go with her to the King James Gym today?"

"Yeah."

She snuggled back against him. "So . . . why'd you choose to come home?"

"Lots of reasons, good reasons, I thought about it on the way. When we first met, I offered her *Virgil's Little Book on Virginity* and she never took it. It's like she wants to find answers. She's always looking. She studies all the time, takes all sorts of university courses, but when she's offered obvious solutions, she turns away. I get the feeling that she doesn't want to face something."

"You never offered me *Virgil's Little Book on Virginity.*"

"You never needed it."

73

He wasn't going to show. Why would he?

Lenore sat in the steam room alone wrapped only in a towel.

The giddiness she had felt on her drive to the King James Gym, the rush of excitement and anticipation, had slowly diminished all afternoon with the growing realization that Richard was not coming. She tore away the towel and looked at herself, down the front of her body, beyond her breasts at her stomach, still pudgy from childbirth, past her pelvis and down the length of her legs, to her painted toe nails. It was all she had to offer, her body, and he had rejected it. He rejected her.

She felt the beginning of a sting behind her eyes, blinked to avoid the tears that came anyway. One tear from the outside corner of her right eye — perhaps its moisture would smooth the tiny wrinkles that had begun to form there — continued its slide down past her cheekbone toward her jaw line.

Her throat tight with a familiar ache and her sinuses loosened, she sat in the steam and let the tears flow, let the snot flow, let the sobs rise up from somewhere in the centre of her being where the pressure was building. She was letting out all of her worthlessness.

There was nowhere left to hide. She had run as far as she was able. She could not turn her mind from it, could not distract herself. She was forced to lift the lid and look into the pot, to reach in and take out the baby and hold it to her breast. Now she not only cried for Lenore, but also for the hot tiny body that she could feel as she clutched it to her chest, her arms wrapped around it and herself.

74

"I SAW THE THUNDER BIRD AGAIN. I dreamt about it the night before it happened."

"Hmmm . . . "

"Now I'm a single parent." It wasn't a complaint, just a truth put out there, out to the wind and the sky and the mountains.

"That's one way of looking at it."

"What's the other way?"

"Your daughter is motherless."

George thought about that for a while, the truth of it. Not having a partner probably wasn't nearly as difficult as not having a parent. Why was Isadore the only man on earth that he could talk to, not only about mystical things, but about those things that were important to him? Maybe it was because Isadore was patient, waiting for the end of the story, waiting for him to exhaust himself, waiting for him to tell how it happened.

The wind rose and fell several times before either spoke again.

Isadore spoke softly. "You blamed yourself."

George didn't answer. Of course he had. Days and weeks and months of *what if, if only, maybe if I had.*

"Suicide does that," Isadore continued. "The real victims of suicide are the people that are left behind, the ones that blame themselves. At the funeral of someone who has taken their own life it's always the same; people thinking *what could I have done to prevent this.*"

"We're not really sure it was suicide, though. It might have been an accident."

"Don't do that to yourself. You have to quit doubting. You came to me for advice. Well here it is. Accept that your partner committed suicide."

George accepted. In his mind he saw Lenore tie her towel through the door handle so that no one could get in. He saw her disable the sensor so there was no high-temperature shut off. He accepted that she deliberately cooked herself to death.

He opened his mouth wide and tilted his head back so that he was looking at the sky. He drew in air deeply to quell the fire that was beginning to burn somewhere near his core. As he exhaled, he let go his sadness and his guilt.

Isadore kept talking, softly, gently, but firmly, "Pick yourself up, dust yourself off, stand up and continue on. Your life has changed. Death does that to us. You are a different person now than you were before. Find out who this new person is. He's wiser than he was, stronger too." Isadore reached over and patted his shoulder.

75

"You have to tell him."

"No, that'll just create more hurt. He has had enough."

Katherine insisted, "He should know."

"Why?" Richard felt uncomfortable at the thought of going to the courthouse, finding George Taylor there among all the lawyers, asking him for a few moments of his time, taking him aside, perhaps down the street to the very Blackwater Café where he and Lenore had met so often recently and telling him about his dead wife's plans for infidelity.

"Because he should know the truth. He shouldn't have to go through his life believing something that's not right."

"What difference could it make now? Why interfere? Come on, Kat, what good can come of that?"

Katherine took a breath, deep, filled herself with it. "You believe that you should cause no hurt. I get that. That's one of the things that I love about you."

"Well, I think it's a little more complex than that, but yeah, cause no hurt is definitely part of it," he agreed.

"Do you want to know what my philosophy is?"

"Sure."

"It's not much different than yours. Walk in the world in a good way. Have a good life and, if I'm really lucky I might get the chance to help others."

"Okay," he answered. "Simple enough. But how would it help George Taylor for me to tell him about Lenore?"

"Imagine that he goes through his life believing something that isn't true. Say for instance, that he decides to build a shrine in her honour, any sort of shrine, maybe it's a building, or he has a street named after her, or just keeps a collection of photographs in a special place in his home, or maybe the shrine is just a place in his mind. He's going to go through his life and base his decisions on what he believes to be true. He's going to try to live the best life that he can. We all do. Everyone on the planet . . . " she quickly added, "or in the universe. We all make decisions based upon the best information available. Right?"

He nodded in agreement. So far there was nothing to argue against.

"Well, what if the information is wrong?"

He didn't answer, stood mute while he thought about it.

"You think telling him will cause him more hurt. I think you'd be saving him from further hurt, you'd help him in his healing. We all deserve to know the truth. We all deserve to live a good life. But really, it's not him that I'm thinking about. It's you."

"Me?"

"Yeah you. You too deserve to have a good life. You shouldn't have to carry that lie with you. If you tell him, the same way that you told me, in that gentle caring way of yours, not only will you save him hurt down the road, you'll absolve yourself."

Richard thought about that, about the implications of it, about absolution. He looked again at Katherine, her face, devoid of any makeup, clean. All she ever put on her face was fresh water and a gentle soap. Her hair, long and straight, hung to below her shoulders. The way she stood — simply there, occupying a space, nothing more, and definitely nothing less. She stood, sure of her right to exist, to be — to be here, to be Katherine. There was nothing posed in the way she stood. She wasn't playing a role. She wasn't pretending to be Katherine. She simply was.

He was beginning to understand her philosophy, *live a good life and help others.* It wasn't so simple. *Live a good life* required that you live a pure life, without untruths, and not just the untruths that others tell you, but without any untruths on your own part. Living a good life required that you always speak only the truth, and good and truth become the same thing.

Everything that he knew and understood, the enormity of his ideas, suddenly collapsed into the simplicity of *live a good life.* All of the words written on all of the pages, all of the debates, the long discussions, the words, upon words, upon words, became an unnecessary and futile enormity.

At the same time, the idea of a good life grew in intensity and in size, until it swallowed all of the philosophers of all time, and all of their words and all of their books and stood alone in its simple naked truth.

Raven stood on the back of the discarded kind of like leather couch. It had weathered nicely in the rain . . . he smelled it, no mold. This was a good couch. It would last a long time. He wondered why nobody wanted it. Why was it out here in the alley?

Stuff.

Humans had too much stuff.

How was he supposed to clean this up?

Even if humans stopped making more stuff, they would have enough to last them another hundred years.

But no.

No, they kept making more.

And they didn't even know what to do with what they had already.

It was starting to make him angry. He dug his talons into the kind of like leather fabric. It didn't tear. He couldn't rip it.

That angered him more.

He drove his beak into it, made a hole, a small hole.

It was going to take him forever to rip this thing apart and then he still had to spread it around. Why couldn't humans clean up after themselves? Why was all the work left up to him?

76

"BUT, I DIDN'T PRAY THAT THE wall would fall down."

Richard felt a bit giddy. Here was Ryan Talbot, in his house, having a cup of tea, visiting with him and Katherine. The man had walked up to the gate of the Ashram and asked for sanctuary. The admissions committee, if it could really be called that any more, had met for less than five minutes before accepting the application.

And the sanctuary he sought wasn't from the powers that be, not from the government, or the military, or the police, or corporate security. No, he wanted to escape from his followers, wanted a bit of peace; in the end, especially now that Regis was gone, he wanted a place where he could pray, nothing more.

"I was praying for the soldiers inside, for their good health and happiness."

"So what happened to the wall?" Richard picked up his son Mike and sat him on his lap. He was only five, but he should hear this.

"I honestly don't know. Like I said, that wasn't what I was praying for."

"And the cameras that malfunctioned?"

Ryan shrugged, his long brown hair brushed against his shoulders. He sipped his tea. "Who knows? Probably just poorly made. Cameras quit every day. People put two and two together and get a miracle." He shrugged again. This time, Richard could see the tiredness in it.

"Well, you can stay here as long as you like." Katherine leaned against the door, their daughter Harmony on her hip, hungry child, pulling against her mother's blouse, little hands searching.

"Thank you. I really do appreciate being allowed to stay here."

Richard looked away for a moment, out the window toward the big pine tree bathed in evening light, that rich light that made the tree look as though it had been dipped in bronze. He took a deep breath, slowly exhaled.

"I don't know how long I'm going to stay. I can't make any promises."

"None of us can." Katherine hoisted their daughter. The child was beginning to be a handful, one moment trying for a breast, the next trying to get down.

Richard agreed with a nod, but it surprised him that Katherine, the woman who was so much part of the Ashram that in his mind they were the same thing, would say that no one could promise how long they were going to stay there. He assumed she meant it in a larger sense, that no one could promise how long they were going to be on the planet.

Harmony managed to free herself from Katherine's grasp, wriggled herself away from the hip, shimmied down her mother's leg with a determination that bent Katherine's will to her own, until her little feet were firmly on the floor and she was loose from her mother's hands that reached out to stabilize even after she took the first few toddling steps away. Both parents watched with that blend of pride and fear that all parents experience when a child first begins to walk. Pride in the ability, and fear that they are going to fall and hurt themselves.

Seven steps across the floor, then the little hands clutched at the fabric of Ryan Talbot's pant leg. He set his cup down on the table next to him and picked up the girl that was trying to climb onto his lap. "Hey little one, is this where you want to be?" He set her diapered bottom on his knee.

"You know, I often said that I was just a man. Most people took it as meaning that I wasn't God. What I meant was that I was just a man, not a woman." Harmony was quite obviously content simply to sit on this man's lap. She held on to his sleeve with one hand to steady herself and looked up into his face. "You see, women are born with special knowledge, understanding, intuition, something . . . Not really sure what it is. A man — well, a man can learn that, but it takes some effort. We have to pray and fast and study to get to the same place that women are at naturally. The problem is that we men are jealous of women." He winked at Kat. "That's why we tend to deprogram little girls. We teach them that what they know is wrong. We tell them that they are lesser human beings, that the things that they know intuitively, things that they know with their spirit, cannot be trusted. So they grow up and lose that gift that they were born with."

Richard assured him, "We believe in equality here."

"Equality. Really . . . You think men and women are equal. Can you give birth?" Ryan didn't wait for an answer. "Women have the gift of life. And that's something no man is ever going to understand. We're incapable of knowing it." He tilted his head and looked closely at the little girl. "There's things this girl knows that you and I will never understand." He looked back up at Richard. "Oh, there's things that you and I know, things written in our original instructions that we are capable of grasping . . . but carrying life within ourselves, never."

"DNA."

"DNA." Ryan swallowed the last of his tea. "Something I've been thinking about. The Abrahamic religions of Judeaism, Christianity and Islam all believe in the written word of God and have for centuries fought wars over the correct interpretation. I too believe in the written word of God. I just don't believe that it is exclusive to the Torah, the Bible or the Quran. Why would God write something in simple orthography, on papyrus or sheepskin or paper or something else that was just going to fall apart, when he could write it in DNA, put it inside of us so it would last forever?"

He put his cup back on the table. "We all have our original instructions written inside of us. If we pay attention, pray and study and listen, we can figure it out; we know right from wrong, and once we start to understand our own original instructions, then we can start to learn about the original instructions of all the other life on the planet, and our connection to that life."

77

"R. VERSUS PRICE, EIGHTEEN-EIGHTY-FOUR, TWELVE QUEEN'S Bench Division, United Kingdom, Queen's Bench." George quoted the citation then looked up at Garth Bendig leaning against the doorway, smiling, listening to that thing between lawyers, the deciding case. Bendig Taylor Law Office didn't have an open-door policy. No one ever thought about making anything into a policy. That was just how it was. No one shut the door to their office unless they wanted to give a client that sense of confidentiality that clients sometimes thought they needed. But between Garth and George, client's cases were discussed, shared; ideas were bounced back and forth. They'd been partners now for ten years, and while they weren't making a killing at the enterprise, they were making a living.

"Tell me." Garth came in and took a seat, stretched out his legs and leaned back into the chair.

"Interesting one. This woman came in a couple days ago, had two kids with her, cute, a boy, and a girl a bit younger. At first I thought it was just a matter of writing a will for her. But it turns out, it's about what she wants done with her body after she's gone."

"What's that?"

"She wants to be cut up and spread around on the ground to decompose." George leaned forward. "It's about soil. About giving her body back to the soil."

"Religious reasons?"

"Well, not exactly. She did say she was part Native Canadian — Cree, she said. But, no. Not entirely religion. She's spent the last couple of decades or more doing soil research and is convinced that the soil needs protein."

"Scientific reasons, then."

"Partly, yes."

"Isn't there a Cemeteries Act or something that covers that?" Garth offered.

"It's the . . . " George looked over at his notes. "The Funeral Services and Cremation Act of Saskatchewan, Twenty Sixty-One. Already checked. There's nothing in there to prohibit it, as far as I can see, as long as it's on private property."

"Health Regulations?"

"As long as it's not in a public place."

"So what's this R versus Price thing you got then?"

"Yeah, it's an old case, but it's still good law."

"I'd say eighteen-eighty-four was an old case," Garth agreed.

"Well, it seems this guy Price thought he was a Druid. He dug up his son's body and cremated it. Most of the case is property law. Is there property in a dead body? The court ruled there wasn't. But Mr. Justice Stephens in that case makes an interesting comment." George looked at his notes again. "'It matters not whether a body decays or is cremated. One is fast and one is slow.'"

"Maybe, but I sure as hell wouldn't hang an opinion on something that weak."

"Oh, I agree, I agree completely, but in combination with there not being anything in the Funeral Services and Cremation Act or in the Health Regulations directly on point . . . "

Garth grinned. "If there's no law specifically against it, then it ain't illegal. So, this client, she a bit of a nut job?"

"No. No, not at all, quite rational actually. She was talking about how the Cree used to put their dead up on platforms wrapped in a buffalo robe. The body decayed and the birds spread it around, then the insects carried it in little pieces underground and then the ancestor would come back to life through the grass and the trees and such, then the bigger animals ate that grass. The Indians killed those animals and ate them, and so on. So, to an Indian, ancestors were part of the soil, part of that life cycle. I guess there's the connection between Indians and Mother Earth and all that stuff."

"So, she does have religious reasons."

"She doesn't want to go that route. I mean, she said she doesn't want to rely on religion over much. But I agree, that would be the best way to frame it. She did say she lives on an

Ashram. She wasn't here for long. Her kids started acting up. You know the way kids are. The boy was a year or so younger than my Anna." George looked out the window for a second, at the sky, the lake, and the fringe of forest to the south.

78

George didn't tell Garth that he knew who the woman was, that he knew her husband was Richard Warner.

But when he was alone again in his office and the search engines had spun to stillness and the research that had occupied his mind was satisfied, his thoughts turned back over the last decade since Richard and Lenore and the steam room at the King James Gym.

Most people believed that he had left Prosecutions because of Lenore's death. He saw no reason to tell them otherwise. Let them believe that he had quit being a prosecutor out of sorrow, or even out of fear. It didn't matter.

Garth had come to the funeral and put a sympathetic hand on his shoulder. George remembered the look on Garth's face when he'd turned to him and asked, "Could you use a guy with a lot of criminal law experience in your office?"

But that was a long time ago; now he rarely practised any criminal law — couldn't. Couldn't bring himself to do it, to participate in the system. As a prosecutor he'd had trouble with sending people to jail, as defence counsel he had trouble telling the court that his clients weren't responsible. It felt like he was turning them into the victims. "It's not his fault, Your Honour. He had a horrible upbringing." "It's not his fault, Your Honour, he was extremely intoxicated at the time of the offence."

The worst was when he'd successfully defended the same man twice for assaulting his wife. The third time, it was clear that the man had decided he could beat her whenever he wanted and George would keep him out of jail. It felt as though George's own fists were pounding her into submission.

George understood that by participating in the system he perpetuated it. The adversarial system had no winners, only losers — people who were so unhealthy that they were a danger to themselves and to others — and the system, the damn system, had no answers, no curative powers; it responded to homelessness and mental illness with incarceration because it didn't know any better.

Disillusioned.

George stood up, walked over to the window and looked out. *Disillusioned.* The word reverberated in his mind. How many times over a lifetime? The war: he was going to be a hero and save civilization. Yeah, right! How do you save civilization by behaving like a barbarian? He understood full well why he liked to fly a Raven. It was because no one can drop bombs on you when you're up there, and you carry no bombs. He became the Raven and everyone else was beneath him.

Jasonia, he remembered. She wasn't an illusion. She'd helped to open his eyes; but not as wide as the day he'd helped the remaining inhabitants of Regis pull the bodies from the collapsed shacks after the crack-down. The survivors came out of the crammed schoolhouse when the dust from the drone attacks subsided to find a flat Regis. That was real. The funeral pyre was real. He could still smell the smoke. It had gotten through his skin. Sometimes reality just slams you in the face and the illusion that had been your life simply crumbles away.

But Lenore. George had at first blamed himself, believed that his thoughts had killed her. It was Isadore who had set him thinking that way. "*Now that you've seen a Thunder Bird, you have to be careful. You have a powerful helper. Everything you do or say is a prayer. Even your thoughts are prayers. Watch what you think.*"

And he hadn't. He'd imagined an end to Lenore; that something would happen to her and he'd be free. And then it did. And when it was done, and they'd lowered the coffin into the earth and the grief dragged against him so that even his flesh, his muscle and his bones, felt the weight of his sorrow, it did not feel like freedom.

His grieving and guilt had ended abruptly when Richard showed up, hat in hand, calm, apologetic, not wanting anything other than to redeem himself, to set right a wrong. *Disillusioned.* His image of Lenore had shifted, become something else and he had forgiven himself.

Disillusioned. Jasonia had probably died in Regis. "Half of everything you see is an illusion. So . . . then . . . " This view from the window — the street, the people, the city, humanity, ecology . . . He looked upwards. The sky today was an unthreatening pale blue . . . How much of it was real? How much of it was an illusion? And to be disillusioned, to shatter the illusion . . . maybe to be disillusioned meant to be able to see clearly, if only for a moment before the illusion reasserted itself.

Ravens are real.

Why not, why the hell not? Take the rest of the afternoon off and go for a little ride.

79

"Why?"

"Why what?" Ryan Talbot leaned back against the bare wood wall.

"Why did you give up on protest?" Richard sat beside him. There was no urgency to their work. The roof was on the cabin they were building together, all that was left was to cut a hole to fit the window and a few finishing touches here and there. Autumn afternoon became autumn evening and two men who had experienced the satisfaction of physical work sat together and relaxed. Soon Ryan could move his few belongings from Richard and Katherine's into his new home, this sturdy timber-frame cabin. The next day or the day after that. No hurry.

Ryan took his time to answer, thought about it, looked toward the sun on its approach to the western horizon, then summed up: "It's pointless to protest against real insanity."

He took a deep breath. "This might take some time."

Richard looked around. "It's all right, we have time, there's nothing urgent that needs doing at the moment."

"In the 1850s humanity succeeded in legislating an end to slavery. Most people thought that it was impossible. Slave labour was such a huge part of our experience that we could not imagine our world without it. There were even religious explanations for it. It was part of the Bible. It was God's will. Some humans were simply born to be slaves; some people were less than us, they were *the other.* Some believe that we can put an end to war." Ryan's voice lost its edge; a sadness crept into it. "The majority of people to this day believe that war is natural and necessary. Again, it's written in the Bible. God takes sides in war. He helps the Jews kill their enemies. He helped David kill Goliath. War is such a part of our experience as humans that we cannot imagine not having it.

"We honour the soldiers and say that they go away to fight for our freedom, even though after every war we lose more freedom. We have to increase security because we just fought a war that proves that there is a threat. So the soldier who agrees to participate in the insanity actually helps take away freedom. That he goes to fight proves that security is necessary."

The hurt in Ryan's voice tightened his words. "We say that there are others who are going to come here and hurt us unless we go over there and kill them first. And those others say we have to kill these people who come here before they kill us. And so, we kill one another and we kill wives and children, and in the end it is mostly the wives and children that are killed and not the soldiers because the soldiers have guns and can protect themselves. The wives and the children and the grandmothers and the grandfathers are the ones that pay with their lives for our security. Then the children that survive remember that we killed their mothers and their brothers and their grandmothers and they hate us for the rest of their lives and it's that hatred that we put in their hearts that is the threat. So, the soldier that goes to war doesn't win our freedom, he takes away our freedom because he makes more enemies that we have to have more security to protect ourselves from."

Richard squirmed with the memory of his time in uniform. He felt again the weight of the gun-strap on his shoulder.

"It's insanity because we know that killing is wrong. We know it with every sense of our being. If I were to kill you now, I would be a murderer and everyone would agree that I should be severely punished. The law would agree. But if it happened in war and you were my enemy, then I would be a hero. They would pin a medal on my chest and have a parade. But you would be just as dead either way.

"Some days I believe that there is hope for our species, when I see acts of kindness and generosity. But then the same person who will pet a puppy will say something completely insane."

Ryan's words seeped through Richard's skin like acid and awakened old wounds that began to sting. He didn't want to hear about war, but he couldn't stop listening. "Tell me," his voice not much louder than a whisper.

"I've heard it said that war is good for the economy, or we need war to keep the population in check. And that's bullshit. There's no such thing as an economy. That's something we made up. We used to believe in dragons and unicorns, now we believe in a mystical thing called an economy. We have to fight a war and go kill people so the economy stays strong?" He tapped the wall behind him with a knuckle in emphasis. "You and I just built this house. If we build a city and then destroy it, of course it's good for the economy because we have to build that city again, but we're no further ahead. If we spend our resources building ships and planes and tanks and guns and bombs and then have a war and use them up, of course the economy looks good, and we can all work at building more guns and bombs and get ready for the next war. But if you stand back and look at it, you'll see that it's absolute insanity.

"Protesting against war is like standing in front of a mental hospital with a sign that says, *Stop Being Insane.*"

The two men sat in silence, waiting for the anger to cool. The senselessness of war. Neither of them wanted it. Anger didn't get them anywhere. All anger did was confuse their thought processes and lead them down paths they did not want to tread.

Richard felt a gladness for the silence, for a moment to reflect and pull his thoughts back from San Diego. In the analogues and war records, San Diego would only earn one short paragraph — thirty-seven killed by friendly fire — but his entire history was written there.

Off to the west of the two men, beyond their sight, a buffalo pawed the ground and snorted, a young bull coming of age, feeling his testosterone, his need to mate, to challenge and show his strength.

Richard didn't want to think about war anymore. He had spent decades trying to forget, to get past it, to put it away, to leave it at an oasis in the desert. "What about the environment? Don't you think that's something worth protesting for?"

Ryan was slow to answer; the sadness was again in his voice. "If we cannot raise our level of sanity to the point that we care about other humans, about our own species, we will never learn to care about all the other species we share the planet with."

Said Raven

I tried, I really did. I tried to tell them. Spoke for hours, as clearly and calmly as I could. They just wouldn't listen.

I know — I know — I know. You can't tell anyone what to do.

But, I thought, maybe, maybe, maybe they might hear me and change their ways, see what they're doing.

But they don't remember. They don't remember that I fed Elijah in the wilderness. They don't remember that I showed Cain what to do with the body.

There's hope. There's this one human I know, he's learning, he's starting to get it. Saw him just the other day, out playing in that thing of his that looks just like me. It's not one of us, but it looks like us. It's almost alive. Not quite, but almost, almost, almost. Anyway, saw him do a loop. I felt proud to see it. He did good. He took that cousin of ours, that almost-alive Raven and he did a loop, a real honest-to-goodness ass-over-tail-feathers roll, belly to the sky. You see something like that and you can't help but feel the joy. It's like he shares it with you, oh the joy, the joy, the joy.

And there's this woman I know, she knows us. Talks to us. Once in a while I hear her pray for the earth. She really, really,

really loves the earth. You can just tell that she's going to teach her kids to love the earth too.

You know there was a time when it all worked the way it was supposed to. Yeah, I remember, I remember, I remember those times. Used to be when the wolves ate a buffalo, we'd come and clean up after them. Those were good times. We picked those buffalo bones clean, and then we spread them around on the prairie, made designs with them, raven art. And the sun would shine and bleach those bones so white, so white, so white in the tall green grass.

Then the buffalo left, I don't know where they went. And the wolves too. I miss the wolves. They were fun. But it ended up I made art out of their bones, all their bones.

I've made designs from cormorant bones too. Yeah, for a while there, Eagle was doing pretty good, that old grandmother survived a long time. In the fall, when the cormorants were nice and fat, she used to go where they nest, you know, on those islands. And she'd eat and eat and eat. Sit in a tree right above the nests and fill herself until sometimes she was too fat to fly. Then I'd come along and clean up those cormorant bones, pick them down until there was just a little skull attached to a string of back-bones. I made those cormorants look like the fish that they ate, then I carefully arranged them on the beach, white bones on the brown sand and close to the water, because cormorants were fishers.

But these humans. Try cleaning up after them. It's impossible. I remember this sack from the back of a human's house one time, a plastic sack, and in the short grass behind his house I arranged all those Styrofoam plates and cups real nice. I used that star pattern, made his backyard look like the Milky Way, I did. Help him remember where he came from. Well, he didn't like that I guess, came out of his house with a gun. I tell you, I got the hell out of there.

They don't like our art. I swear they don't even see it. No appreciation. And when you try to tell them, try to explain it to them, they just swear at you.

That's why I'm going back to the forest, what little bit of it there still is, before it's all gone. Even if I have only mice bones, It'll be better than here.

I give up, I give up, I give up. Enough now. There's just too much to clean up.

Humans are not like us. See, we're mostly spirit in a physical body. Humans, well they forget they're spirits, go around thinking they're only flesh and penises and bellies and lungs. Don't get me wrong. I got nothing against experiencing life to the fullest. I've mated many times, sex in the sky, the two of us and the blue, making babies on the fly.

Maybe that's it. I betcha it is. The reason we remember we're spirits is because we fly. We remember that long flight across the universe. Humans are stuck walking on the ground, that's why they forgot. I betcha that's it.

Hey, it's a good day, I figured something out. It's a good day, it's a good day, it's a good day, hey.

The reason that guy flies in that pretend Raven? It's because he's trying to remember his spirit. I betcha, I betcha, I betcha. Well, I wish him the best, but I'm gonna go anyway. Back to where the humans don't go. Just for a while.

Oh, I forgot to tell you.

I've made art out of human bones too.

And I'm pretty sure I'll do it again, and again, and again.

Photo by William Hamilton

HAROLD JOHNSON is the author of four novels and one work of non-fiction. After a stint in the Canadian Navy, Johnson became a packsack miner and logger across northern and western Canada. In 1991 he quit the mines to pursue a bachelor's degree in law from the University of Saskatchewan and a Master of Law degree from Harvard University. He now works as a Crown Prosecutor in La Ronge, Saskatchewan and lives with his wife Joan at the north end of Montreal Lake where they continue the traditions of trapping and commercial fishing common to Johnson's Cree background.